Praise for Cory Doctorow and *The Bezzle*

"Righteously satisfying . . . A fascinating tale of financial skull-duggery, long cons, and the delivery of ice-cold revenge."

—*Booklist*

"Robert Heinlein was always known—and always came across in his writings—as The Man Who Knew How the World Worked. Doctorow delivers the same sense of putting yourself in the hands of a fellow who has peered behind Oz's curtain. When he fills you in lucidly about some arcane bit of economics or computer tech or social media scam, you feel, first, that you understand it completely and, second, that you can trust Doctorow's analysis and insights. That makes for a great reading experience."

—*Locus*

"It's a novel of issues, presented as they should be, detail by devastating detail. The issues and ideas are this novel's warp, the specificity and sometimes surprising emotional truths its weft."

—Maria Farrell

"Cory Doctorow is one of our most important science fiction authors."

—Kim Stanley Robinson

"Cory Doctorow doesn't just write about the future—I think he lives there!"

—Kelly Link

also by cory doctorow

cory
doctorow
the
bezzle

tor publishing group
new york

This is a work of fiction. All of the characters, organizations, and events portrayed in this novel are either products of the author's imagination or are used fictitiously.

THE BEZZLE

A Tor Book
Published by Tom Doherty Associates / Tor Publishing Group
120 Broadway
New York, NY 10271

www.torpublishinggroup.com

Tor® is a registered trademark of Macmillan Publishing Group, LLC.

The Library of Congress Cataloging-in-Publication Data is available upon request.

ISBN 978-1-250-86588-5 (trade paperback)
ISBN 978-1-250-86589-2 (ebook)

Our books may be purchased in bulk for promotional, educational, or business use. Please contact your local bookseller or the Macmillan Corporate and Premium Sales Department at 1-800-221-7945, extension 5442, or by email at MacmillanSpecialMarkets@macmillan.com.

First Tor Paperback Edition: 2025

Printed in the United States of America

0 9 8 7 6 5 4 3 2 1

For the comrades. We fight on.

part one
there's no crime in avalon

How do I know so much about prisons? No, I wasn't ever locked up—I mean, jail, sure, if you manage to live as long as I do without pissing off some small-town Deputy Dawg so much that he sticks you in the pokey overnight, you're not living. But I was never incarcerated in a state or federal facility.

But yes, I know a lot about prisons.

It's a long story.

I mean long.

Look, it's a beautiful night. We could just listen to the owls hunt the furry critters. Or we could push our sleeping pads together. It's a warm night.

Okay, I'll tell the story. But remember, you asked to hear it.

Yes, it's a fraud story. They're all fraud stories. But at least this one doesn't have anything to do with cryptocurrency. This one's from decades before that business. This is from the Mesozoic era, the second great era of high-tech scams.

Yes, I mean the dot-com bubble. Yes, I know you were there, too. But you were working for a big, serious company. You didn't see the churn and the froth. Why, I bet you've never even heard of CabCandi.

Yeah, "CabCandi." Like "taxi" and "junk food." It's exactly what it sounds like.

They raised seven million bucks.

1

Avalon is a chocolate-box town on an enchanted island, twenty-two miles from the Port of Los Angeles. Catalina Island: the redoubt of the Wrigley chewing-gum fortune, acquired by William Wrigley Jr. in 1919, and developed as *the* chic spot for Hollywood's smart set.

For years, starlets, leading men, producers, and directors plied the channel on wooden ships out of Long Beach, drinking cocktails on the three-hour crossing, vomiting discreetly over the railings.

They caroused at Old Man Wrigley's "Casino": the largest building on the island, a twelve-story art deco roundhouse with a ground-floor cinema with its own pipe organ, and, above it, the largest ballroom in the USA, known to a glamour-hungry nation as the source of a weekly broadcast live from "high atop the Casino on beautiful Catalina Island."

The one thing the Casino didn't have? Gambling. Wrigley fancied himself a sophisticate, and his casino took its name from the Italian word for "gathering place." The fact that this confused everyone who visited, for the rest of time, only reinforced Wrigley's superiority.

There was no gambling at the Catalina Casino, because gambling leads to crime, and there's no crime in Avalon. That's what the tourist brochures tell you. It's what the four thousand year-round locals tell you. It's what the two-thousand-odd beautiful people who own summer homes on the island tell you. If you're one of the members of the thirty-five-thousand-strong

July Fourth weekend crowd, you'll come home and tell it to your friends.

There's no crime in Avalon.

Scott Warms brought me to Avalon in 2006, one year after he sold InterPoly to Yahoo! and became a millionaire at twenty-three. Scott had been forced into the sale by his investors, and I'd helped him, a little, untangling their creative accounting so he didn't get crammed at the sale time and lose the equity he'd bargained hard for at twenty-one, when he founded the company.

Scott didn't want to work at Yahoo!, and truth be told, Yahoo! didn't want Scott working there. But Scott's Yahoo! shares wouldn't fully vest for three more years. He was already a millionaire, but if he hung in—or got fired—he'd be a decimillionaire. Corollary: if he quit, he'd *lose* tens of millions of dollars. At twenty-three years of age, three years felt like an eternity to Scott, but he had plans for those remaining millions—$20 mil if Yahoo!'s share price held, maybe more if it went up.

So Scott and Yahoo! were playing chicken. He wanted them to fire him, but not for cause, and so he became an expert on California employment law—Scott could become an expert on any subject in six months. California employment law only took him two. He made sure that he engaged in precisely as much fuckery as the law allowed and not one nanogram more.

Which is how he ended up on Avalon. Scott was formally a vice president, as was typical for the CEOs of the dozens of companies Yahoo! bought with billions pumped into it by Soft-Bank's Masayoshi Son. That meant that he was entitled to five weeks of paid vacation every year, which no Yahoo! exec came close to taking. Not even the French ones.

Scott took every single day he was entitled to. Twenty-five days of paid leave translated into 12.5 four-day weekends per year. Add in federal and state holidays and sick days, and that number went up to twenty-four four-day weekends per year. Then there were the conferences, off-sites, and team-building retreats, at least one of those every month, and then the time off in lieu of the travel days and overnights, and Scott was taking thirty-two short weeks per year, plus two weeks at Christmas.

He was entitled to a plush office, which he generously allowed other teams to book as a meeting room or getaway space, because it was so often empty. Scott liked microbrewed beer, and his grateful coworkers often brought by a bottle of something they'd taken home from a brewpub or made in their garage, and they'd put it in his grocery-store-style glass-door refrigerator with a post-it of thanks and tasting notes.

Scott was part of an executive committee that was supposed to evaluate possible acquisition targets, companies like Inter-Poly. The only times Scott came close to quitting Yahoo! and forfeiting his $20 mil were when a really promising start-up came through the door. The combination of a smart founder and a great product made Scott pine for all the time he was wasting. Even worse was his dreadful knowledge that if he gave an honest assessment of the start-up he'd just heard pitched, he'd trap some other naïf like him in the Yahoo! quicksand.

He had a good nose for this stuff, and he'd use the preliminary documents to schedule his long weekends, making sure he was in town and present only for meetings where they were hearing from stupid companies making stupid products. He found it physically painful to sit through their pitches without tongue-flaying their founders. But at least he could honestly sit down with the rest of the committee afterward and recommend that the company stay the hell away from the wretched start-ups they'd heard from that day. Generally, the committee would all agree with him.

The sole exception was CabCandi, a start-up that wanted to fill taxi drivers' trunks with candy and use a web-based dispatch to turn major metros' cabdrivers into a circulating snack-delivery service for hungry stoners. Scott correctly pointed out that this was a profoundly stupid idea. The other committee members pointed out that CabCandi had much better fundamentals than its rivals, the successors to Kozmo.com. Scott replied that Kozmo had collapsed and the post-Kozmo stoner-snack dot-coms would do no better. The committee overrode his objections and offered a term sheet to CabCandi, $7 million on $12 million, pre-money. But they were outbid by Battery Ventures, who offered $9 on $14.

After CabCandi, Scott decided to use one of his sick days and go to Avalon, and he invited me down for the long weekend.

"Fly into Long Beach, Marty, and we'll chopper over." He was deliberately breezy, clearly wanting to impress me. I'd been in helicopters. They're noisy. But Scott was as eager as a puppy and he just wanted me to have a good time.

"It's a date," I said. "Let me check Expedia for flights from Oakland."

"Southwest is your best bet. They're not on Expedia, and they've got a website that doesn't suck."

It didn't suck, which was quite an accomplishment for an airline, to be frank. I caught the 5:15 and we touched down in Long Beach at 6:07, four minutes ahead of schedule. Scott met me at the baggage carousel, bouncing on his toes with excitement.

"Marty Fuckin' Hench!" He grabbed me in a big hug. He was still ninety-eight pounds soaking wet, tall and bony. He'd gotten rid of his ponytail and gotten a millionaire's haircut, something that transformed his cheekbones and prominent teeth from skull-like to aquiline, and he'd replaced his crooked wire-rim glasses with a pair of aviators with clear lenses, which was a statement, though I couldn't tell you what it was trying to say.

He released me from the hug. "Scott Fucking Warms," I replied. "You're looking good." Sky-blue Hugo Boss blazer with turned-up cuffs, striped shiny lining, and orange satin accents at the slash pockets; obligatory Japanese denim as stiff as cardboard; some kind of designer sandals that looked like something Salvador Dalí would put on Jesus' feet.

"I'm so, so, *so* glad you came, buddy. Catalina is crazy, like nowhere I've been before. They've got *bison*. Oh, here are the bags!" There'd only been eight people on my flight, and only four bags spilled onto the belt. I grabbed for mine, but Scott got it before me and shot the handle. "Come on!" He took off for the private airfield.

I followed him out the door and into the cool, sea-scented Long Beach night, across a couple of crosswalks and then up to a gate where a private security guard checked his ID and mine against a list on his screen.

I was just a forty-something forensic accountant back then, with a good line in unwinding high-tech scams, and I was far from a rich man, but I'd flown private a few times—sometimes clients claim they can only fit in a meeting on their bizjet—but I didn't see the attraction, not then, when it just convinced me that I was working for someone with more dollars than sense, and not much later in life, when a big score set me up with enough money to fly private any time I want.

I keep waiting for the day when private fliers are subject to even one percent of the indignities of a TSA checkpoint, but every time I fly, it's the same. I could have brought a wheelie-bag full of C-4 and packing nails through that checkpoint and they wouldn't have known about it.

I sure hoped no one mentioned this to Osama bin Laden.

The helicopter was waiting for us, Scott's bag already aboard. We climbed in using the little running board, and the pilot—a grey-hair with the bearing of an ex-military pilot gone to fat—welcomed us aboard and showed us to our headphones, giant earmuffs with curly-cable umbilici that plugged into armrest one-eighth-inch jacks, reminding me of my old high-school hi-fi set. Once we snapped into our five-point harnesses and opened our complimentary mineral waters, Scott toggled some switches on an overhead panel and we were on a channel with the pilot.

"We're all ready, Captain," he said.

"Roger that," the pilot said in perfect air force monotone.

"Going private now, Captain," Scott said.

The pilot gave us a thumbs-up and kicked in the engines and my whole skeleton began to buzz with the chopper's roar. We lifted off and Scott let out a *whoop!* and drummed his thighs.

"Oh, buddy, I can't *tell* you how bad I needed this," he said. "And it's *so* good to see you."

"It's good to see you too, Scott. How's life in the punctuation factory?" That's what we called Yahoo!, in tribute to that asinine exclamation point.

"Don't ask. Let's talk about this weekend instead. Normally I stay at a friend's place; there's about a half dozen people I know with summer places there and they've all got guest rooms, but I thought it might be awkward for you to crash with a stranger, so I booked us rooms at the Zane Grey Hotel."

"As in the author?" Zane Grey pretty much invented the cowboy novel. My old man had dozens of his books and would always circle the *TV Guide* listings for the movie adaptations—there were more than a hundred of them, and he loved every one, but insisted that none of them came close to the books.

"Yeah! It's his old house! He built a summer place there, old Pueblo style, and just kept adding on to it every time he got a fat check. It's a hotel now. Gorgeous. I got us the penthouse. Four balconies, a patio, harbor views."

Maybe I made a face. My business did just fine. The dot-com bubble had sucked in billions for every harebrained scheme you could imagine, and some of that money disappeared into creative spreadsheets. Hardly a month went by without my being called upon to find a couple of million that had been made to disappear through a black hole in one of those spreadsheet cells. My take was 25 percent of whatever I recovered, and I recovered a *lot*. But even so, I didn't have punctuation factory money. This Zane Grey place sounded pricey.

"It's on me," he said. "My invitation, my tab. I insist. I've wanted to stay at this place since I first laid eyes on it. Man, I can't wait."

We were high over the channel now. The deepest channel off any coast, anywhere. It's a crime scene. There's no crime in Avalon, but just offshore?

That channel is the final resting place of tens of thousands of barrels of DDT, dumped there by Montrose Chemical in steel that was thoroughly, utterly incapable of maintaining its integrity at the bottom of a three-thousand-foot saltwater channel.

Down in those depths, there's crimes whose perps belong in front of the International Court of Justice for crimes against humanity.

The sun was just setting, right in our eyes, the Pacific-blue sky turning the color of fresh blood, then dried blood, and then— that flash of green, just as the sun dipped over the horizon.

"There it is!" Scott pointed and bounced a little in his seat. From the air, Catalina Island was a rugged Mediterranean hillscape with a picture-postcard seaside village nestled in its little harbor, where ranked yachts bobbed and a ferry backed and filled to turn around. The towering Casino anchored the town to the right: a cream-colored squat cylinder topped with a dark rice-paddy hat of a roof whose red-brick color flared in the last rays of the sun. To the left, the harbor turned into a beach road that girded a cliff. We banked that way and there was the helipad, lit up with spotlights.

The pilot angled us in, leveled off, and sank down, both skids kissing the ground at the same moment. A couple of ground crew in hi-viz ran out to tie us down, and then the pilot un-buckled, stepped into the passenger area, and opened the door, stretching out his arm in an "after you" gesture. We stepped out into the Catalina night.

2

Old Man Wrigley launched his chewing-gum fortune in 1891. Company lore says he was a door-to-door soap salesman who had the bright idea of putting a free piece of gum in with his soap and the gum was so popular he got out of the soap biz and jumped into gum.

Wrigley might have been good at gum, but he was better at business. Specifically, he was extremely good at convincing investors to back him as he acquired 95 percent of the world's chicle-tree forests. All the gum in the world was Wrigley gum: either Wrigley made it, or someone else made it and paid Wrigley for the privilege.

In 1890, a year before the Wrigley Company was founded, Congress passed the Sherman Antitrust Bill, named after its primary author, Senator John Sherman, William Tecumseh's baby brother and a man almost as grimly determined once he set his mind to something. In his impassioned speech to the Senate, Sherman said, "If we will not endure a King as a political power we should not endure a King over the production, transportation, and sale of the necessaries of life. If we would not submit to an emperor we should not submit to an autocrat of trade with power to prevent competition and to fix the price of any commodity."

The Sherman Act was law when Wrigley set out to corner the market on chicle, but it was a weak and struggling thing. Sherman's main target was a robber baron who cornered the market on something far more precious than chicle: John D.

Rockefeller, who owned the oil, the railroads, the banks, and the state lawmakers who oversaw them. Rockefeller's Standard Oil company fell to antitrust law in 1911—twenty-one years after the Sherman Act's passage, and eleven years after they put Sherman himself into the ground.

That buying 95 percent of the world's chicle violated the Sherman Act is beyond doubt, but is it truly a crime if no one prosecutes you? What if you spend your fortune in harmless and charming ways, say, by buying the Chicago Cubs (they call it Wrigley Field for a reason) and then bringing them to your celebrity weekender island for spring training every year?

Clearly this is not a crime, because there is no crime on Catalina Island.

The Zane Grey sent out a driver in a liveried golf cart to take us in. The island had strict limits on cars and the waiting list was more than a decade long, but the golf-cart policy was more generous. The driver was a kid named Antonio who told us he was a local, whose great-grandpa moved there before Wrigley bought the island. Graduated Avalon High, the local K–12, and married his high-school sweetheart. Antonio told us all this as he drove us away from the rotor wash that blew our hair and found its way up the cuffs of our pants.

Once we were on the long, quiet curve of the sea road, Scott leaned forward. "You an In-N-Out fan, Antonio?"

Antonio looked around at us so quickly that the golf cart actually swerved a little and he had to look forward again to get it back in the middle of the lane. "Sorry, sorry!" he called. "In-N-Out?"

Scott said, "I bought a sack of burgers in Long Beach before we took off. They might even still be warm. Fries, too."

"Really?" Antonio said. "Damn. I mean—Sorry, I mean—Sir, could I possibly buy one of those from you?"

Scott smiled and clapped him on the shoulder. "They're for you, Antonio. Six double-doubles, six orders of fries. No milkshakes, I'm afraid. I couldn't figure out how to pack them so they'd keep cold."

Antonio slowed the golf cart, pulled onto the shoulder by a chest-high railing. "Seriously, sir? I mean, that's very generous of you."

"It's not my first time on the island. I usually stay with friends out in Hamilton Cove. I know enough locals that I know what to bring."

Antonio's smile was wide enough to lift his scalp and send his chauffeur's hat askew. "Thank you, sir! Thanks very much!"

He got the golf cart back in gear and we sped down the road, past the ferry docks, through a tiny roundabout and onto a beachside tourist strip of souvenir shops and breakfast places and busy bars open to the night, then swung onto the town streets, lined with pretty little vacation homes and locals places. At a Ralph's Grocery, we turned left to parallel the beach road for a few blocks, then descended to the beach again, fronted now by a seawall. Another cute roundabout got us onto a steeply pitched driveway walled in with whitewashed rustic plaster.

The golf cart struggled up the hill and creaked into the hotel's entrance court, where another employee in matching livery hopped to and helped us out of the cart and unloaded our bags. Scott interrupted him, got his bag back, and unzipped it, producing a grease-spotted In-N-Out sack, which he solemnly presented to a wide-eyed and grinning Antonio. Antonio took the sack and pumped Scott's arm in energetic thanks, while the bellman took custody of Scott's bag again, looking jealously at the sack.

No need to stop at the check-in desk; we were expected. The bellman and one of his colleagues humped our bags up the stairs to the penthouse while we followed. They showed us around the three bedrooms, the four patios, the kitchen, the dining/living room, switched on lights, and accepted a twenty each from Scott. I got the distinct impression that either of them would have preferred a burger.

Once we were seated on the patio with beers from the ice bucket that had been waiting for us on the kitchen counter, Scott clinked with me and we both drank and watched the little shore boats run people around the moored yachts in the twinkling harbor below us.

"About those burgers," I said.

He laughed quietly. "No fast-food chains on the island. Local council's orders. Preserves the character of the place. I happen to think they're right, but a weird side effect is that the locals fetishize In-N-Out and McDonald's. Forbidden fruit. Did you see how that guy's face lit up? Absolutely worth having everything in my suitcase stink of hamburger for the weekend."

There's no In-N-Out in Avalon.

We stayed up late chatting and watching the moon paint a milky river on the ocean, and slept in the next morning. Scott woke me to let me know that room service had just arrived with breakfast, and I joined him on the patio for muesli, sourdough toast, unpasteurized honey, cold German breakfast sausage, and fresh-squeezed orange juice and a press-pot of Kona coffee. We ate it while the high sun baked the patio tiles and made our flesh sting, and then we put up the big shade umbrella.

"You brought a sun hat, right?"

I had, my uncle Ed's old air force mechanic's hat.

"You'll need it," he said. "Lots of open space on the bison tour."

Antonio was our tour guide. He had a permit from the island trust, which the Wrigley family had created and then donated 98 percent of Catalina Island to. That let him drive us—this time in a four-wheel-drive jeep, not a golf cart—up to high ground, past the country club and the zip lines, and through the gates into the wildlife reserve.

"The bison were brought over in the twenties, for a Zane Grey movie shoot," he said, as we climbed a winding country road. "The director wanted big suckers, so he brought males. Now, your male bison doesn't much like other males, won't stay in their company for long, so they busted out and took off.

"Old Man Wrigley liked how they looked, so he brought over thirteen females, so they could have Christian relations." He smiled to let us know he also thought this was foolishness. "But bisons are more pagan than Christian, they get together in harems, a bunch of lady bison and just one big old bull."

He downshifted the jeep as the road got steeper. "Now, this was once the stagecoach road," he said. "Visitors headed for Two Harbors would take a horse-drawn coach across the island, about a day's journey. Can you imagine how those horses had to work on this hill? You see those trees there?" He gestured at the evenly spaced, mature, straight trees running along the outside edge of the road. "Either of you gentlemen recognize them?"

Scott smiled. "I've had this tour, so I'm not going to answer. What about you, Marty?"

I've been a Californian ever since I dropped out of MIT, got my accounting certificate, and lit out for the West Coast, where all the computer companies were. I have a pretty good grasp of California plant life, though mostly focused on the Northern California varieties. These ones had strange, streaky bark, like they'd been partially peeled.

Unmistakable. Still, I could tell Antonio was busting to show off, so I said, "Sorry, I can't place them."

"That's because they're Australian," he said, looking over his shoulder to grin at me, then looking back in time to keep the car from crashing into one of those trees. "Eucalyptuses. They were Ada Wrigley's idea. We call 'em the guardrail trees. See, they're spaced close enough that a car can't squeeze between them. A few cars have crashed into them, but they never went over the edge." He downshifted and cranked the wheel around a hairpin, then put his foot down again. The engine revved. "Ada liked them because they're also called 'gum trees,' and she was a Wrigley. Beautiful, aren't they?"

They were. Australia has a lot of beautiful plants and animals and most of them are, frankly, monsters. The eucalypt is no exception. Its reproductive strategy is to drop those heavy, oily leaves around its base until the trapped heat and the highly flammable oil consummate their tragic love affair and burst into flame. The ensuing forest fires reduce the eucalypts to ashes, but the same goes for all the plants that might compete with them. The difference is that eucalypt seedpods *need* fire to open up and release their seeds, and the fires that coax them open also eliminate all the canopy cover that might compete with them for sunlight, while the ashes of the fallen competing trees enrich the soil with nutrients.

That life cycle played out in Australia for millennia, but it's been playing out in Southern California since the 1850s, when nitwit settlers imported them and planted them in an act of slow-motion arson that gives PG&E a run for its money in the competition to see who can burn down the state first.

We saw our first bison half an hour later, after driving past a few hikers with tents on their backs, heading to an inland campsite. It was a cow, a big one. She was standing on a distant hill, placidly contemplating the dry gulch that separated her from the dusty road Antonio had been traversing.

We came to a stop and watched her. Scott rolled down his window and got out his SLR and a long lens and snapped some pictures.

"The Tongva people lived here for eight thousand years," Antonio said, in his tour-guide voice. "They called the island

Pimu. They traded with people from all over the Americas, and anthropologists have found artifacts made with materials from thousands of miles away."

In 1924, the "amateur archaeologist" (that is, grave robber) Ralph Glidden opened his "Indian museum" in Avalon Harbor. It was a "museum built of bones," filled with the desecrated remains of Tongva people and their grave goods. It remained in operation until 1950. The looted remains—including thirty thousand teeth—sat in storage until they were given a Tongva burial in 2017.

The conquistadores enslaved the Tongva, used them to build the missions that every California schoolkid studies in the fourth grade. Their children were kidnapped to those missions and forcibly stripped of their language, culture, and faith. Later, the Americans enslaved them again—this time through indenture, after the act of being an "Indian" in California became a crime in a dozen petty ways. Tongva convicted of crimes were sold to white settlers under the 1850 "Act for the Government and Protection of Indians."

The Tongva were never put on a reservation. They learned Spanish and styled themselves as Mexicans, and in 1921, the *Los Angeles Times* declared they were extinct. Meanwhile, their children were still kidnapped by federal agents and sent to the Sherman Indian High School in Riverside, where they were tormented beyond all reason.

The Tongva of Pimu had a front-row seat for all of that. They were forced off the island in 1930 by the Spaniards, who renamed the island after Saint Catherine of Alexandria, whose fourth-century martyrdom took place sixteen hundred years *after* the Tongva settled Pimu.

There are fewer than four thousand Tongva left on this Earth today. None of them live on Catalina Island.

There is no crime on Catalina Island.

3

We spent the afternoon dozing in a cabana at the Descanso Beach Club, drinking Scotch-and-soda highballs and watching the pretty young people frolic. Then we strolled back to the penthouse and picked at the high tea the Zane Grey had laid out for us on the dining room table.

I took a nap while Scott plugged in his laptop and paid $0.25 per minute to dial up to his ISP's local number and answer his email. Then I rose, slugged back the last of the coffee in the pot Scott had brewed, took a shower, and got dressed for dinner.

We were going to a party.

Antonio was waiting with the golf cart when we wafted down the stairs, preceded by some fancy cologne Scott bought in an airport duty-free and insisted that I try. It was nice—a little too citrusy, a sort of musky Lemon Pledge, but nice.

Antonio drove us back out past the Casino—lit by floodlights that showed off the art deco murals of the naked mermaid over the doorway—to a slip where a shore boat was tied up. He locked the golf cart up and stepped aboard, then held the rope tight while we did the same.

"They don't like it when we approach by boat, but it's a pretty night. Life vests under your seat, gentlemen," he said. "Don't worry, you won't need them. I'll go slow."

He did, puttering out around the curve of the Casino. "There's heavy artillery down here," he said. "From World War II, back when this place was full of soldiers in case the Japanese tried to take it over. When the war was over, they just pushed it into the harbor."

"The army, huh?"

Scott smiled, his face lit up by the big white moon. "Not just the army. Spooks. This is where they created the OSS, who became the CIA."

There's no crime on Catalina Island.

The party was in Hamilton Cove, a private condominium development out past the Descanso Beach Club, all stepped white walls and orange tile roofs. Very exclusive. "I don't come out this way much," Antonio said. "They don't really mix with locals, and not many of our guests have friends here."

"They're nice places," Scott said absently, scanning the ziggurat of condos set into the cliff face for his friend's place. "Ah," he said, pointing. "Looks like they're in full swing. Good. I hate being the first ones at a party."

Lionel Coleman Jr. grew up in the hotel business. Lionel Sr. owned two of the nicest hotels on the Sunset Strip; a famous little exclusive boutique hotel in Malibu; and a big conference hotel in Palm Springs. Junior didn't like running hotels. He liked finance. He convinced Senior to let him throw a lot of money around at the end of the Clinton administration to help pass the 1999 REIT Modernization Act, and then he took the family business into high gear.

Real estate investment trusts were created in 1960 as a way for mom-and-pop investors to shelter the retirement income from a duplex or a granny flat. The 1999 act transformed this modest, working-class tax shelter into a vehicle for high finance. Junior realized that if he sold his family hotels to an REIT, the rent he paid to them would be tax-free. But of course, he'd still have to pay tax on the income the hotels brought in.

But Junior had an angle for that, too: this newfangled financial crime called a taxable REIT subsidiary. This was a separate company, owned by Junior's REIT, which provided all the day-to-day management of Junior's family hotels.

So let's sum up: Each hotel had three corporations that kept it running. First, there was the family business, which owned the hotel's IP. That's the company's husk: its brand, its trademarks, its phone numbers and URLs and goodwill in the form of positive reviews in a half century's worth of travel guides.

Then there was the REIT, which owned the actual hotel *building* and collected rent from the family business—rent that was tax-free, because a REIT was born to be a way for Gramma and Grampy to live out their dotage with dignity, collecting rent from a little duplex or a granny flat over the garage.

Finally, there was the TRS, the taxable REIT subsidiary. This company negotiated with the family business on behalf of the REIT, collecting a management fee in exchange for actually payrolling the desk clerks and chambermaids, paying the laundry service's invoices, keeping the pools clean and the kitchen's fridges stocked with food.

The three businesses were a shell game. Find the pea (the pea being the taxable income). The taxable income moves from one company to the next: you rent a room, the hotel remits enough of the room charge to the TRS so that it breaks even, owing no tax. Or, if Junior had some money from somewhere else he wanted to hide, the TRS could make a loss, and get a tax credit to offset those other profits. Remember: the consulting fees the TRS charged were based on fictional "hours of consulting time" that Junior's accountants generated each quarter by working backward: take the number of dollars that Junior wanted the TRS to absorb, divide by the hourly consulting fee, charge accordingly.

The remaining money—the actual profits—flowed through the REIT, and were tax-free. Junior plowed these into more hotels, and then a couple of strip malls; then he discovered middle-income apartment buildings, twenty to fifty units, and he bought up a dozen or more of those, mostly in the halfway-affluent suburbs of Detroit and Cleveland, the last pockets of money remaining in the collapsing rust belt.

Junior—Lionel, as he asked me to call him when he greeted us at the door and clapped Scott in a big, back-thumping hug and treated me to the equivalent handshake, hard squeeze and a flurry of pneumatic pumps—explained all of this to me as I drank his rum out of a bulbous piña colada glass, over ice and coconut milk. It was good rum, good enough that I'd have happily drunk it neat.

It was from a French distiller, a company that finished dark Caribbean rums by aging them in Cognac casks, as a means of mobilizing idle capital. Le Bureau National Interprofessionnel du Cognac only allowed its members to produce for a few months per year. Junior explained this to me as he drowned another two fingers of rum in coconut milk and ice for himself. He was about to say more, but a fit-and-fifty type with squash muscles and a Tommy Bahama shirt came over to trade backslaps and introduce the very, very young woman he was there with. I took advantage of the distraction to pluck a lowball glass off the bar and help myself to two fingers of dark, spicy rum.

Katya—the very, very young woman—caught my eye as I ditched the piña colada glass on an end table and smiled. She was pretty, and extremely well turned out. Blond, Slavic, very thin, snowplow cheekbones, and a little black dress with a YSL clutch that looked real.

Junior and Tommy Bahama were still trading stories of financial conquest. "It's my first time on Catalina," I said to Katya.

"Oh," she said—a big round Eastern European vowel sound. "I come here many times. JK likes it." JK was Tommy Bahama. "It's so beautiful," she said. "So many beautiful animals."

"I saw the bison today," I said. She had ice-blue eyes and a pageboy haircut that showed off her long neck and her diamond-studded earlobes. I got over any illusions about dating much younger women years ago—thankfully—but she gave off a vibe (parted lips, tilted head, sly eyes) that got me a little tongue-tied. "They were so great. So . . . big."

She smiled, not quite a smirk. "Excuse me," she said, and headed for the bathroom. I stood on my own at the bar, nursing my neat rum (it was even better than I'd imagined) and feeling like a fool. JK was deep into a story about a zoning-board fight in Palm Springs, where he also owned some very large hotels, and Junior was loving it.

I was about to move off in search of Scott when Katya returned, touching me on the elbow. Her eyes were no longer sly. Her pupils were dilated so wide they almost swallowed her irises and when she smiled, she bared her front teeth—as white and square and even as Chiclets.

"Sorry," she said. "Tell me more about buffaloes?"

"Bison," I said. "Buffaloes are in Asia. Learned that today." I tapped my left nostril. "You missed a spot," I whispered.

She bared her teeth even more and wiped away the white powder from her own left nostril, rubbed it on her gums and then wiped her hand off on her dress, looked down to make sure she hadn't left a streak, then back at me.

"I have some to share, if you'd like," she said. "JK gets lots of it."

I looked at JK and Scott, who were enumerating the many ways in which a certain Palm Springs city councilor was biddable. "He won't mind?"

She tilted her head the other way. "That's not our way," she said.

Why not? "Why not?"

I let her lead me to the powder room.

In the enclosed space, she smelled of expensive perfume, floral and fresh and outdoorsy. It was a good Catalina Island smell. As soon as she closed the door, I became uncomfortably, overpoweringly aware of her position relative to mine, the inches between her bare arm and mine feeling electrically charged. I was not the kind of guy who found himself in the bathroom with beautiful younger women who wanted to share their cocaine.

"Let's do this," she said. Her accent gave the *d* a plosive pop, made the *th* a softer *d*. She bared those perfect teeth again, then dug a little bottle out of her clutch and held it up so I could see that it was nearly full of white powder.

"JK gets good drugs." *Draaghs*. I loved that accent.

"Have you two been together for very long?"

She gave me a searching look, like she was trying to figure out if I was pulling her leg. "I see JK when he books me," she said. "He likes variety, so only every month or so. But yes, for a year, I think." She watched me absorb that and her smile got wider. "You're a nice man," she said.

She produced a small, silver coke spoon and held it so it caught the light. She mounded it high with coke and held it up to my face. She took my chin with long, cool fingers and tilted my head, brought the spoon up to one nostril and pinched the other, her fingers resting on my lips. "Cheers," she said, and I took a deep sniff.

She stared into my eyes as the coke came on. My skin felt all-over tight. My pulse thudded in my throat, where her thumb still had my jaw, and in my lips, where her fingers rested. She looked at me this way and that, chin tilting, staring into my eyes like a jeweler assessing a gemstone. Finally, she gave the tiniest nod and withdrew her hand. My skin tingled where her fingertips had been.

She held my gaze for another minute. "My turn," she said, and scooped out her own mound. She sniffed it daintily, wrinkled her nose, closed her eyes and turned her head to the ceiling, giving me a long look at her long neck, the vein in her throat, her collarbones and the top of her cleavage.

Then she shivered from top to toe and looked me back in the eyes. "I don't think you're rich, Marty," she said.

"No," I said. "Not like our host."

"Not like JK."

"No," I said.

"At first, I thought you might be. You're not one of these people, and sometimes that means you're from a higher level. But you're just someone's friend, aren't you?"

"I am," I said. I looked at her cocaine vial, now noticeably depleted. That was a business-development asset, and she'd wasted it on me. I wanted to apologize, but I didn't want to offend her.

She followed my gaze. "It's okay," she said. "I knew you weren't rich before I gave it to you. You seem interesting. Not boring, the way those rich ones are. It's nice to chat with someone who I'm not doing business with."

There it was. I'd passed by an uncountable number of sex workers who were soliciting on the street, and objectively, I must have passed an equally uncountable number of sex workers who were just out shopping or going to the movies or the doctor's office or the daycare center. I'd even learned to recognize the telltale signs of a man's sex-worker habit from his financials, after a couple of divorce jobs where I got hired to audit the family books (big cash withdrawals, obviously, but that could also be drugs; for sex workers you also needed to look for regular charges from certain anything-goes payment processors, the kinds of places that host reviews or make arrangements).

But I had never (knowingly) conversed with a sex worker up until that moment. I was worldly enough to suppose that questions about the job, or how she got into it, would not be welcome.

Clearly she was good at what she did: not only was she carrying a two-thousand-dollar handbag and accompanying a very rich—if very dull—man, but she'd smoothly flirted with me in a way that had left me tongue-tied and disoriented. If I'd had the same kind of money as Tommy Bahama—*JK*—and she'd named a price, I'd have been very, very tempted.

But I was just someone's friend. Thankfully.

"I've never been here before. What should I see?"

"At the party? Nothing. The view, maybe. It's a good view."

"No, I mean on the island."

She narrowed her eyes a little. "I knew. Just making a joke. On the island, you should see the gardens. Very lovely. I go to them when JK is scuba diving. Boat tours are good, you can see the seals and the pelicans and sometimes a whale. But the best are the beaches, on the other side of the island. Two Harbors."

"That's the place the inland road joins up with? We took a buffalo tour today."

"Bison," she said. A smile. "Two Harbors is beautiful. Two beaches, like this." She put her hands side by side. "This one, rough. This one, calm. Between them, a long rock, like the tail of a whale. The local people go to them. Very hard to get to if you don't know a local."

"But you go?"

"When JK is busy, I make friends." She shrugged. "I like people."

I almost cracked a joke about that being a good thing, considering her line of work, but I thought better of it. She must have seen what I was thinking, because she smiled again.

"That way too," she said. "But not just that way."

The cocaine rush had settled down to a kind of hyperalert state, thoughts chasing thoughts.

"One more?" she said. "A little bump?"

I should have said no, but I said yes, and she offered me the vial and the spoon this time, and I helped myself to a modest hillock. Sniff, sniff. Once again, she stared into my eyes as the rush hit. In the moment of drugged clarity, I realized that what I'd taken for sexual arousal was, instead, a clinical curiosity. She was trying to read something in me, find out who I was. It was a smart business strategy: screen potential clients in these unguarded moments. Speaking as someone who'd had a few bad clients—including one that tried to kill me—I appreciated the tactic.

No, not that time someone tried to kill me. No, not that time either. And no, not that time. How many times has someone tried to kill me? Jesus, what a question.

Look, the first time someone tries to kill you, it makes an impression. The second time, too. And the third. By the tenth, it's just bad. *Not memorable. Just* bad.

This isn't like those other stories, all right? Just let me tell it. You wanted to know why I was such an expert on prisons, and this is that story.

Don't sulk, it's unbecoming.

Look, I don't have to tell this story. We can just sit here and admire the Sierras and watch the stars.

You're bored of stars? Really? These are really good stars, you know. Okay, I'll tell you.

But try to appreciate the stars. Some people go their whole life without seeing this sky.

"What do you do, someone's friend?" she asked as she put away the drugs and checked herself in the mirror.

"I'm a forensic accountant," I said. When I don't want to make an impression, I just say *accountant*. I guess I wanted to make an impression.

"I know accountant, but forensic?"

"I find hidden money," I said. "Like when one business partner is stealing from another, or an ex-husband is hiding money from his ex-wife."

She digested this. "We could be a team," she said. "I know a lot of ex-husbands." She had a good poker face. Only the quirk at the corner of one perfectly styled lip revealed the joke.

"Tell you what, if you ever meet an ex-wife you like, you can get in touch with me. I'm a little picky about who I work for, but I bet you've got good radar."

"I'm also picky," she said. "The trick is to charge enough that you can afford to turn down the bad ones."

"That's my strategy, too," I said. "I charge twenty-five percent of whatever I recover. That means I only have to work a few months out of the year to cover my expenses."

She giggled. "We have the same business model, Marty. I also only work a few nights every week. But tell me, how much choice do you really have in your clients? If you charge twenty-five percent and you only work a few months a year, then you must be chasing big dollars, and most people don't have big dollars."

"That's true," I said. "There are some nice rich people, sure, but most of the people who need my services can't afford them. Like the guy at the In-N-Out whose paycheck is twenty-eight dollars and sixty-eight cents light because the franchise owner is listing fake deductions."

"Not worth your time for seven dollars and seventeen cents," she said.

"You're good at math," I said.

"Moldova gold medal for math when I was fifteen," she said.

"Very good at math."

"Arithmetic," she said. Dismissive. "I miss set theory. *That* is math."

"I'll take your word for it. Accountants mostly just do arithmetic and a little stats, and most of that is just spreadsheet formulas I paste in."

"Very simple." Dismissive again. "What about your burger men, then? How do they get help?"

"Sometimes I do a freebie," I said. "When I hear about someone in need."

She shook her head. "I don't do freebies," she said. "Everyone is in need." Then she giggled again. "Come on, even JK gets tired of hearing himself talk at last." She checked her nostrils in the mirror, patted my cheek, and led me out of the bathroom.

If anyone noticed me leaving the bathroom with this beautiful, younger woman who was in JK's entourage, they didn't mention it. It was that kind of party.

I found my way back to the bar, following Katya in my peripheral vision as she glided back to JK's side and insinuated herself in his conversational knot. Lionel Jr. was in conversation with another older man with another younger woman, whose cheekbones and Slavic eyes rivaled Katya's. She gave me a cool look, and my incipient cocaine paranoia insisted that she had somehow gotten a subliminal tip from Katya letting her know about my relative pauperhood.

Lionel gave me a distracted half smile when I asked him if he minded my fixing myself a drink, and I got another lowball glass and three more fingers of that fantastic rum and drifted off.

The sea breeze on the balcony smelled incredible and was just cool enough to take the edge off my buzz. Moonlight reflected on the sea, a rippling streak spilled along an endless, inky expanse. A few lights flickered among the yachts in the bay, and the sky was sprinkled with the stars that managed to outshine the lights from the other condos.

I took it all in, breathing that salt air deep into my lungs. A bat or a night bird rippled past, then another.

"Beautiful, isn't it?" Scott had one of Junior's piña colada glasses, with a pair of tall straws and a big pineapple slice for a garnish.

"It's amazing," I said.

"You're not enjoying the party," he said. It wasn't a question.

"It's fine," I said. "Not really my scene, but I'm not a snob. I'm sure that a lot of those people are interesting, fulfilled, thoughtful souls. I'm perfectly prepared to make small talk with as many as it takes to find some."

He sipped his drink. "You're a good guy, Marty. Yeah, some of these people are fine to chat with, but that's not why I like 'em. I like 'em because even though they're rich as hell, they take it easy. I work with so many millionaires who want to become decimillionaires, and every decimillionaire I've met dreams of being a centimillionaire, and *they* all want to be billionaires. Give any of them a three-day weekend and they'll spend it making a new pitch deck for the start-up they're cooking up.

"These guys, they're not dot-com types. They want to be rich as hell, sure, and they all want to get richer, but they're doing it so they can do this—go somewhere beautiful, get loaded, go sailing or lie on a beach."

I nodded. "I can see that. That's how I operate, I guess. Do a few jobs, make a few months' nut, then hit the road for a while or just get a stack of library books and work my way through them at the local cafés, or even audit a course at Stanford, then take another job when my reserve fund bottoms out."

"Exactly."

"Difference is, I'm not the kind of guy whose idea of a fun time is golfing or yachting or whatever these guys do."

He looked up at the stars. "Some of them aren't so bad," he said. "And being out on boats can be a damned good time. It's not just parties like this."

"Parties like this?"

He turned and looked at me. "Yeah, Marty, parties like this. I know it's not your scene, but you'd be surprised at some of the connections you can make here."

"I nearly made one of those connections myself," I said. "A very young woman from Moldova, very nice and smart as a

whip, but she was looking for a professional kind of arrangement and she's very far out of my league."

"Yeah, there's a lot of that here, too. But it's not like these
guys invented it or anything."

"Sure. They call it 'the oldest profession' for a reason. But
don't you think there's something, you know, *off* about a sixty-
year-old rich guy out there shopping for twenty-year-olds?
Nothing against the relationships or the sex I had at twenty, but
one of the good things about adulthood is learning and growing. Those kids haven't had a chance yet. They may be smart as
hell, but at twenty, what have they got to be smart *about*?"

"I hear you. I guess it's an island tradition. You know Mar-
ilyn Monroe got married at sixteen to a twenty-one-year-old
she'd met when she was just fifteen? They moved out here when
she was sixteen, while he was in the army. Back then, that was
legal."

"No crime on Catalina Island," I said.

"Well, yeah. No crime anyone cares to prosecute." He stared
at the stars again, moved closer, dropped his voice. "I've been
thinking of committing a crime," he said. "A little salvo in the
war on drugs. How do you feel about magic mushrooms?"

I had to laugh. Scott was definitely a mushrooms kind of
guy. What was he doing at this powdery little event? I dropped
my voice, too. "How do they mix with cocaine?"

He shook his head. "You *have* been making friends here,
haven't you? In my experience, the two make for a pretty good
combination. The shrooms take the edge off of the coke, that's
for sure. I don't know that I'd mix a *lot* of either—"

"I've only partaken very modestly," I said.

"Then, speaking as your physician, I advise in favor of it."

4

We did something stupid, but it turned out okay.

After thanking Junior for his hospitality and failing to catch Katya's eye to thank her, too, I telephoned Antonio and asked him to meet us in a real car—no golf cart.

We ate the mushrooms while we waited for him. He showed up with the Zane Grey's 4x4 just as they started coming on, and we were all giggles as we piled into the back seat.

"Take us to the reserve gates," Scott said. "We're going to see the foxes and the squirrels."

Antonio didn't start the car. "Sirs," he said, "I don't think that's a good idea. My pass to open the gate to the reserve is very important to me and if I take you in there, I could lose it. It would be really bad for me, and for the hotel."

Scott's face glowed in the dark car. "You raise an excellent point, Antonio. I wouldn't want to get you in trouble. Just take us to the gates and let us off."

Antonio's hands tightened on the wheel and he stared out the windshield for a long time. "I don't think that's a good idea," he said again. "I'm sorry, but you could get really hurt."

Scott nodded as though this was an excellent point he was seriously considering. "Thank you for that, Antonio. But you know, there are hikers out there in the reservation right now, sleeping in their tents. All we want to do is have a little stroll under the stars. An hour, maybe two, max. We'll stay on the road, and you know there won't be any cars, and we'll come back to you when we're done." Then, seemingly as an afterthought, he added, "Of course, we'll pay you for your time here." He named a price. "That's twice what the hotel charges for you to drive us around. I'll pay them the usual rate, too."

Antonio kept looking through the windshield.

I wanted to say something. This money-flinging negotiation was bringing me down. Antonio was a poor townie, the kind of kid whose idea of extreme wealth was a sack of In-N-Out burgers. Scott was a dot-com millionaire playing a game of high-stakes vesting chicken with Yahoo! It wasn't a fair fight.

I was about to say something when Antonio looked back at us. He stared into Scott's eyes and named a price. It was double Scott's price.

Scott's eyebrows went up. "You think you're worth that much?"

Suddenly, Antonio looked a lot older—and shrewder—than he had before. "No. Hell no. That's not what I'm worth. That's enough that I would feel like an idiot if I turned it down."

Scott applauded like a kid clapping for Tinker Bell. He was really high. Was I that high? Maybe I was, but if so, the coke and the shrooms were duking it out and producing something improbably even-keeled.

"That is a *gorgeous* way of putting it, my friend. You've got a deal." They shook, awkwardly, over the seat. "Let's roll!" Scott howled. Antonio put it in gear and we rolled down the windows and stuck our heads out as he wound his way up the mountain roads.

The steep vertical rise meant that we quickly escaped the light pollution from Avalon and Hamilton Cove. When Antonio pulled up to the gates of the reserve and doused the headlights, we were plunged into incredible, textured darkness. The starlight and moonlight were an eldritch glow, bathing the land. The mushrooms combined with the shadows to make them dance and sway, weaving faces and bodies and fanciful creatures out of our peripheral vision.

Antonio gave us each two disposable water bottles, admonishing us to pack out the trash, and made us set alarms on useless phones—we'd carried them out of habit, even though there was no reception on the island—to remind us when we'd been gone for an hour, 90 minutes, and 105 minutes.

"Back here in a hundred and twenty minutes, correct, sirs?" he said. He knew we were off in some giggly, distant place, and that there were lots of ways things could go wrong. It was written on his moonlit, shining face. I felt bad for him again, then got distracted by an interesting shadow and swung my head this way and that to see if it would move from my peripheral vision to my central vision.

We ducked under the boom bar that controlled access to the reserve and set off up the road. When we reached the first sharp turn, I looked back over my shoulder at Antonio, standing in front of the jeep, his worried face turned toward us. I waved and jogged to catch up with Scott, who was already around the corner.

Turning the corner was like stepping into another world. Now we were fully cut off from the lights of the town and the headlights of the Zane Grey's 4x4. From one instant to the next, the number of stars doubled. I stopped and gawked at them, thunderstruck. The psilocybin made them appear to be wheeling in the heavens, and I suddenly felt the movement of the Earth beneath my feet, all 1,000 m.p.h. of momentum, and I staggered backward and nearly lost my footing.

"Oh my God," I breathed.

Scott had gotten ahead of me, but he doubled back and joined me in gawping at the sky. "God *damn*," he added.

It was then that we saw our first fox. Who knew how long it

had been watching us from the roadside, but some small rustle in the perfect silence of the mountain night alerted us to its presence.

"Island fox," Scott whispered. "They're island dwarves. Miniatures. The Catalina fox. You'll only find them right here."

She was a puppyish little thing, more like a house cat than a canid—tilted eyes, curious little mouth, brushy, swishing tail. Her stare was bold, much more grown-up than her babyish proportions, big feet, and stubby legs. She looked at me like I was the most interesting thing in the world, her gaze a skewer that pinned me in place.

"Hello there," Scott cooed. "Hello, hello."

One of her ears flicked toward him, then recentered itself. I felt like she was about to tell me something—something vitally important, which she was taking a long time to work her way up to. I often talked with people who had something to say but didn't know how to say it. I knew how to wait. I knew how to listen.

I waited. The stars whirled overhead.

Finally, she lifted one front paw, then the other, a little two-step, and then she turned and sauntered into the brush and the night.

"Goodbye," Scott crooned. "Bye, bye."

"What a beautiful animal," I said.

"They're amazing," he said, bouncing on his toes a little. "Island dwarves! There's an island giant, too: the Catalina squirrel. It's the same size as the Catalina fox! Giant squirrel, miniature fox, they met in the middle. One diurnal, one nocturnal. They take turns! We'll have to keep our eyes peeled for a squirrel, collect the set!"

I couldn't tell if he was just high and making stuff up (he *was* high, but he wasn't making stuff up). I didn't care. We kept walking up the road. Our phones gave us the sixty-minute warning. It felt like only seconds had passed. "The walk back is downhill,"

Scott said. "It'll be shorter. Let's give it another fifteen minutes, then turn around."

It sounded good to me. Everything sounded good to me. I was pretty sure the fox was tracking us through the brush at the roadside—at least, I heard sounds off in the woods that I took to be the fox. The moon tracked across the sky and the shadows shifted. The stars dazzled. Scott's regular breathing at my side was like the deep breath of the universe.

Our phones beeped the seventy-five-minute mark, startling us both. We looked at each other and giggled.

"We should get back," I said. "Antonio needs his sleep."

"You're right," he said. "Poor Antonio. Let's go back."

"Let's go back," I said. We giggled.

We turned around.

We saw the bison.

I don't know how long she'd been following us. It was a she, not a he, because the bulls had enormous anvil-shaped heads while their dainty sisters' heads were merely gigantic.

She was *gigantic.*

She regarded us placidly with her gigantic moon-shining eyes, her moon-glinting horns, her moon-dappled, plate-sized hooves. She continued to regard us as we stood, frozen in place.

"Slowly," Scott said. I knew what he meant.

"Slowly," I agreed.

The bison snuffled. She shifted. She lowed.

Ever taste a bison burger? That *gamey* taste, like beef, but *wild,* somehow? Impolite? Maybe a little dangerous?

That's what a lowing bison sounded like. Wild. Dangerous. More than a little dangerous, in fact.

"I think she wants to get past us," I said.

"Why do you think that?"

"Because ninety-nine percent of the preserve is behind us, and that's where she lives."

"That's sound logic," Scott said.

"I think we should get out of her way."

"Yes," Scott said.

We shuffled—no, we *inched* to the edge of the road, stepping into the ditch. I found myself leaning up against a tree. It was one of those incendiary eucalyptuses. That meant that I was right on the edge of the cliff. *Nice going, Marty.*

She continued to stare at us. She snuffled again, lowed a little, then shifted her weight. She gave the impression of an old lady, settling in for a long wait. Like she wasn't going anywhere.

"Now what?" Scott said.

"We wait," I said.

We waited. When the ninety-minute alarms on our phones detonated in synchrony, we both jumped. My heel slipped a little on the scree covering the drop-off and for a minute I was sure I was going to fall to my death, but I caught that eucalypt and wrapped my arms around it and got my footing back.

"Marty," Scott said.

"It's okay," I said. "I'm okay."

"*Marty,*" Scott repeated. I looked up. The bison was headed toward us.

Large men can sometimes trick you into thinking that they are slow, because when something very large starts moving, it's hard to gauge its speed. Many's the little guy who's discovered the hard way just how fast someone big can move, once they get moving.

That bison was moving *fast*. It was *lumbering*.

"*Fuck!*" Scott opined. He had to do so over his shoulder, because he was already running downhill, skirting the cliff edge, bouncing off of eucalyptus trees, making scrabbling noises whenever the scree at the cliff edge gave way and he nearly died.

I was right behind him, though he was faster than me. I thought I heard the bison chasing us, but I couldn't be sure, because my breath was so loud that it drowned out every other sound. We rounded a bend, and then another, and then I crashed into Scott, who was doubled over, hands on thighs, panting. He went down and did an actual *somersault* in the middle of the road, and I went flying past him, and only just managed to roll as I hit the ground, saving me from sanding my face off on the asphalt.

I pulled myself to my feet and got ready to run, but when I looked back, the bison was no longer chasing us. I checked my dash and went back to Scott, who was making gasping noises. A cold finger of sobriety stole up my spine.

"Scott," I said, "Scott, are you okay?" He was facedown on the road, making strained hiccup noises. I reached for his shoulder, remembered my first-aid training (don't move someone if they might have a spinal injury), and stopped myself. Then I gently touched his shoulder. He groaned and tried to turn over. "Stay there, buddy," I said. "You could be hurt. I'll go get Antonio and—"

He heaved himself onto his back. He was laughing so hard he couldn't catch his breath. "Holy—" he managed. "Oh, oh, holy—" He broke up. "Holy *shit*!"

I started laughing, too. Partly because I was still a little high, but mostly because he was right: *Holy shit* indeed.

"Come on," I said, helping him to his feet. "Before she comes back. We're late for Antonio anyway."

"Yeah," he said, "can't keep Antonio waiting." He dissolved into more giggles.

We started off downhill again and I discovered that I'd bruised a knee and pulled a calf muscle. Scott limped, too, and periodically hissed something like *son of a bitch,* but for all that, we both still giggled from time to time.

The moon had dipped below the hillside when we rounded the final corner and saw Antonio. We waved at him and he waved back at us, conveying his frustration and worry even at a distance, even in the dark. I was marveling at the expressive power of body language when he froze and jumped back.

"Shit," I said. I looked over my shoulder, knowing what I'd find.

A bison can be surprisingly quiet, given that they weigh half a ton. I don't know how long she'd been following us, but she was pretty close by that point.

Scott didn't turn around. He didn't have to. "Do we run?" he whispered.

"It hasn't come for us so far," I said. "I think running might give it ideas."

"Fair," he said. Still, we picked up the pace.

Now that I knew she was there, I started to notice the sound of the scuff of her hooves on the pavement, the huff of her breath. Was she getting closer? "I think she's getting closer," I said.

"Don't run," Scott said. "Almost there."

I didn't look over my shoulder. Instead, I stared hard at the shadows over Antonio's face, trying to make out his expression. I was so fixated on his face that I didn't even notice what was in his hand until I reached the boom gate and rolled beneath it: a can of bear spray, held out at arm's length.

I noticed it as I scrambled to my feet. I couldn't miss it at that point, because it was inches from my face. I flinched away and hit the dirt again, just as Scott crashed into me from behind. I ended up half beneath the 4x4, panting, one leg trapped under Scott's body.

We untangled ourselves with much fumbling and banging of foreheads but eventually formed up behind Antonio, who was still aiming his bear spray. A few yards up the hill from us, the bison stood placidly on the other side of the boom gate, which came nearly to her shoulder.

"Can bison crawl?" I whispered.

"I don't know," Antonio said.

"Can they break those bars?" Scott whispered.

"I don't know," Antonio said.

"I think we should leave," I said.

"Please get in the car, sirs." Antonio continued to stand his arm's-length bear-spray vigil while we got in the car.

I got in the passenger seat and leaned over to open the driver's door. "Okay," I hissed. "We're in."

Antonio backed into the car and handed me the bear spray. "Please put the lid on that," he said, while he efficiently started the engine and put the car into reverse. He put one arm behind the passenger-seat headrest, craned his neck around, and reversed at a fast clip for a good five minutes, putting a couple of miles and several sharp bends between us and the bison. Only then did he pull over, relieve me of the bear spray, and execute a precise three-point turn.

"I'll take you gentlemen back to the hotel now," he said. Not a question.

"Thank you, Antonio," I said.

"Are bison even nocturnal?" Scott said.

"Not usually," Antonio said. "But there are stories about kids running into bison with insomnia. Normally they just keep their distance."

"I think that one liked us," I said.

"We're pretty likable guys," Scott said. Antonio didn't venture an opinion.

Scott paid Antonio the agreed-upon sum and then half again, at the foot of the Zane Grey's driveway. Once Antonio had the money tucked away, he drove smoothly up the driveway and put the 4x4 in park.

"Thank you, Antonio," I said. "We did something foolish tonight and you were extremely patient with us. Brave, too."

In the Zane Grey's driveway lights, Antonio's face was unreadable. "It's all right, sir. Honestly, by the standards of some of the tourists we get here, that wasn't all that foolish."

Scott snorted. "Good night, Antonio," he said.

The next day I soaked in the suite's big tub for an hour and then put antiseptic—wet-bar vodka—on my many scratches and abrasions, and iced my knee with minibar ice cream, and took a couple of Tylenols.

Scott wasn't as banged up as I was, but he still winced when he stood to join me.

"Brunch, I think," he said, peeking out the balcony door at the bobbing yachts in the harbor. "Oysters and *micheladas*?"

Until he uttered those words, I couldn't have imagined eating, but I found myself suddenly ravenous. What was the last thing I'd eaten? Some of Junior's canapés off a tray circulated by a townie waiter in a black vest and bow tie. Meat on a stick, but with a fancy name, "*gado-gado* sirloin."

"I am in your hands," I said. I winced, too.

"Let's go," he said.

We were ready to walk into town, but as we headed down the steps to the driveway, Antonio materialized. "You gentlemen need a ride?"

Seeing him after what we'd put him through the night before was embarrassing to me, but if Scott felt the same, he didn't show it. "Yes please," he said. "Down to the beach, where all the restaurants are, Mr. Antonio."

Antonio tugged the brim of his chauffeur's cap. "Aye, aye," he said.

I got in the back seat, but Scott slid into the front and the two of them chatted the whole way, their conversation drowned out by the little two-stroke engine. I took advantage of the short ride to soak up the scenery and nod at the locals and tourists we passed.

We feasted on oysters and *micheladas* and laughed about the bison. I was just polishing off my dozenth Hog Bay oyster when someone squeezed my shoulder from behind. I craned around and there was Katya in a bikini, a wrap around her waist, smiling warmly. I looked around for Tommy Bahama but he was nowhere to be seen.

"He's golfing," she said, reading my mind. It came out *golf-ink*. "I've been shopping." *Shoppink*. "Can I join you?"

"Of course," Scott said. "I'm Scott. I think I saw you at Lionel's last night?"

"Correct," she said. "Katya." The waiter was already at her elbow, an older guy who didn't or couldn't hide his fascination with her bare skin. "Martini," she said. "Dry, vodka, two olives." Then she spotted our drinks. "Actually, one of those." The waiter smiled at her, visibly wobbled when she returned the smile, then backed away, keeping her in view for as long as possible.

"You left early," she said.

"We had an adventure planned," I said. Scott chuckled, and she looked curious, so I told her about the bison and Scott mentioned the mushrooms, and she laughed in the right places, clucked over my war wounds, and dazzled our waiter with another smile when he brought her *michelada*. We ordered another round and more oysters, and then I had the extraordinary experience of watching her eat an oyster.

"You had a better time than me," she said. "Next time, I come with."

I couldn't tell if she was kidding, but Scott said, "We're going out this afternoon. First a glass-bottom boat, check out the wrecks and the seagrass, then back into the hills for sunset. We want to see a squirrel *and* a fox on the same trip this time."

"Oh," she said, and smiled. "What time will you be back?"

"What time do you need to be back?" Scott was smooth.

She chewed her lip. Wow. "Six," she said.

"That's exactly when we were shooting for," Scott said.

All of this was news to me—the glass-bottom boat, the squirrel-fox safari—but I was game. I liked Katya, and not merely because of her professional excellence. Here on the island of ubiquitous tourists, scraping townies, and reclusive plutocrats, I was neither fish nor fowl. So was she. We were fellow square pegs.

Or so I told myself.

She was good company, to be honest. She had funny stories about Moldova and about powerful people—not her clients, she was very discreet, but people who were adjacent to her clients. She'd been to Davos three times, and had wicked gossip about what Bill Clinton said to her when she met him. I'll leave it at that. No, I'm sorry. It's *her* story to tell.

Antonio had chartered a glass-bottom boat while we were at lunch. It clearly seated dozens of people at a time, but it was just the three of us. Antonio claimed that he got seasick and stayed on land. Before we left, Katya asked him for directions to the ladies' room and disappeared for a while.

"She's amazing," Scott said.

"I like her, too," I said.

"She's out of your league," he said. "Mine, too. That JK guy is seriously rich, as in, his 'fuck-you money' has its own 'fuck-you money.'"

"That's okay," I said. "I'm not in the market for her professional services."

He shook his head. "Sure thing, buddy."

I wanted to argue, but she came back and we set out for the kelp forest reserve. The fish were incredible and the captain was knowledgeable and personable, and struck exactly the right balance of giving us time to chat with one another and admire the fish and chiming in with interesting facts. Every now and again, he flung handfuls of stale bread crumbs into the water, attracting schools of well-trained fish, and even a little mako shark, whose dead stare and supple grace struck us wordless.

"Magnificent," Katya breathed.

"Incredible," I agreed.

"Wild," Scott said.

Words didn't do it justice. We eventually took our cue from the captain and fell mostly silent, letting the wildlife do the talking. Staring into the depths, I experienced what I can only call an out-of-body experience, the sensation of flying over an alien landscape, something out of the sci-fi novels my old man used to push on me. When I came back to my body, I felt supremely relaxed and calm, an echo of the feeling I'd had the night before when I'd finally crawled into bed and felt the last ebb of the magic mushrooms. A cosmic feeling.

We debarked at the green tourist dock in contemplative silence, and piled into Antonio's golf cart with distant smiles on our faces. I sat in the back with Scott, while Katya sat up front. After a few minutes, Scott started to look confused.

"Antonio—" he said, leaning forward, but it was Katya who looked back at him.

"Don't worry, this one is on me," she said. I gathered from this that we were headed somewhere other than the nature reserve. A moment later, we drove past the helipad we'd landed at, then turned right and past laden hikers, then got caught up in a stream of golf carts that were actually carrying golf bags, and then we passed a golf course itself. Finally, we turned off the road and pulled into a driveway.

Antonio parked the cart. "It's yours for thirty minutes," he said, checking his watch.

"Thank you, Antonio," Katya said, giving him one of her lovely smiles. She faced us in the back seat. "Come now," she said, putting on a sweet schoolmarm affect. "We only have half hour."

We got out and followed her up a sweeping stone staircase into what turned out to be the botanical gardens, which doubled as a Wrigley memorial. It was all Arab tile and desert succulents, flowering bushes and murmuring fountains.

"Gorgeous, yes?" she said, as she led us expertly through the ancient, massive cacti. She'd produced a filmy top from her handbag, and the afternoon sun turned it translucent. Somehow, that was even more striking than her bikini top had been when it was uncovered.

"It's gorgeous," I said. She knew what I meant and favored me with a little smile.

"It's magic when you're alone. The first time I came, no one else was here. It was a Thursday, because JK wanted to go on a dive with a friend who was leaving Friday morning. None of the weekend people were on the island yet. I had it all to myself. Now I have a deal with the head gardener, a price for a few minutes all on my own."

"It's amazing," Scott said. "It feels so ancient."

"The landscaper who designed it brought old plants from his nursery in Pasadena. They really are ancient, even if they've only been here since the 1930s. These tiles are from the island, too—there was a big pottery business here once."

Then, as on the boat, we fell companionably silent. The nature didn't need words to embellish it. It spoke just fine in silence. I wondered how much it cost Katya to get her thirty minutes of exclusive access, then I wondered how long she had to work to earn whatever it cost. Then I made myself stop thinking about that and let the plants speak to me.

A California condor screamed overhead and we looked up in time to see two big birds, a mated pair, circling high overhead, perhaps looking for a fox the size of a squirrel or a squirrel the size of a fox. I wondered if the female had laid eggs, and, if so, whether the eggs shattered when she sat on them, casualty of the DDT in the channel, bioaccumulating through plankton and fish.

But the condors were magnificent, especially from the gardens, and the moment stretched like taffy, a feeling that recalled the mushrooms from the previous night.

"Okay," Katya said. "It's time."

"Wow," I said.

"Wow," Scott agreed.

"I'm so glad you liked," she said. "It's my favorite thing here on the island." We started back toward Antonio. "You know, I told JK about this place and he made a joke. 'You can lead a horticulture,' he said."

"Ugh," Scott said. "That's terrible. And mean."

"He was so proud of this joke," she said. For a moment she looked genuinely sad, then she recovered and smiled another dazzler. "Let's find squirrel!"

"You heard the lady," Scott said. "Antonio, take us to the squirrels!"

We saw two squirrels, a fox, and a bison. We even stopped at the toy airport on a mountaintop and bought one of the legendary giant cookies from its bakery. Antonio bought two, for friends in town. It was fine. Cakey. Big, though.

We got Katya back to Hamilton Cove a few minutes before six, and then went back to the Zane Grey to clean up and drink bourbon on the balcony while the yacht lights switched on and the shore boats began to buzz around them, ferrying people to parties.

We had a party to go to, too. Scott knew a lot of people on Catalina, and they all had parties.

We had a good time. It was nice. We split Scott's last mushroom cap on the way in, just a taste that elevated the night for me. Coming down on the patio later that night, drinking bubbly water from the minibar, Scott and I talked about everything and nothing.

The next day, we did it all over again. The day after, we went home.

5

Scott brought me back to Avalon three more times that year. We had a little routine, where he'd meet me at the Long Beach terminal and hand me a giant sack of In-N-Out (he was tired of getting hamburger smell on his party clothes) and I'd cradle it on my lap in the chopper. We'd hand it over to Antonio at the helipad and he'd stop at a couple of houses in town on the way to the hotel to distribute the bounty before it got cold. We all appreciated the absurdity of it.

The third time, Antonio asked if we'd mind if he drove a little farther to hand off the burgers. Scott had a flask and a good story about the latest empire-building pettiness at Yahoo!, and we were happy for the delay.

Antonio drove us past familiar Avalon neighborhoods and up into the hills where the stately manor homes perched. We'd been to parties at houses like these, but the street was unfamiliar. Scott paused his story while we took it in.

We turned a corner and found ourselves in an unexpected traffic jam. Dozens of golf carts jockeyed to get in or out of a driveway in front of a once-grand, run-down place, two stories tall and squatting on a double lot, with a cracked fountain in the center of its circular drive. People—locals—dashed from their carts to the porch, where a few grinning guys presided over a stack of styrofoam clamshells and a folding card table with three landline phones, which rang constantly.

Antonio ran over to the porch / nerve center with the sack of burgers and handed them off to one of the grinners, who bent over a laptop and typed something, then disappeared into the house. Antonio shook hands with one of the other porch-minders and hustled back to the golf cart, sliding behind the driver's seat, turning the key, and cranking the wheel to plunge us into the traffic jam.

"I gotta ask," Scott said, grinning. "What the hell is all that?"

"It's a long story," Antonio said.

"We're not due at the Longines' until nine," Scott said. "We've got time. How about we stop for a drink and you can explain it?"

Antonio didn't want to drink in a bar wearing his Zane Grey chauffeur's livery, so we went to the Vons and bought a bottle of Maker's Mark and a pack of red party cups and he ensconced us in a remote alley off a narrow street, where he loosened his tie and accepted three fingers of brown liquor from Scott.

"Come on," Scott said. "What was that?"

"That was me getting right with my upline," Antonio said. Thus began the tale.

Wherever there is a prohibition, there is a black market. Ban dumping DDT in the city dump, and Montrose will sink thousands of barrels' worth of the stuff in the channel.

Old Man Wrigley wanted to run a classy island, no tacky burger chains or plastic-booth fried-chicken joints. The Colonel could take his eleven herbs and spices and stick 'em up his ass. He was not welcome in Avalon.

I don't even think Old Man Wrigley was wrong. On the scale of weird rich-guy delusions, "no fast-food chains" barely registers, especially not compared to "let's get thirteen bison cows to keep these thirteen bulls company so they can have Christian relations," or "let's plant arson trees along the roadway in our tinder-dry island."

But where there's a prohibition, there's a black market. Over the years, various entrepreneurial Avalonians have set up burger-legging enterprises of varying degrees of sophistication, mostly involving fishing boats. The private pilots landing at the toy airport and the weekenders at the heliport have also kept up a steady supply. The teachers at Avalon High were good eggs, and they always had the bus stop at a McD's or Burger King on the way back from away games and field trips so the class could stock up and treat their friends back home.

No one had ever systematized things. Not until now.

The burger racket—they called themselves the Fry Guys—had *organization*. If you needed a burger, you could call them and they'd dispatch one to you, from a variety of mainland franchises, either "fresh" (not more than a few hours old, anyway) or flash-frozen in the deepfreezes they kept in their base of operations—surplus from a fishing fleet that had gone bust.

The raw materials came in the usual way—boats, planes, and choppers—but rather than being distributed on an ad hoc basis, they all went through the Fry Guys' clearinghouse. The Guys kept meticulous records and made sure everyone got paid—far more than they ever had in the days of informal burger handoffs to friends.

The Guys knew—or discovered—that lurking beneath the placid surface of the island's dining options (Mexican places, steakhouses, a couple of pizza places, one beachside burger shack, a single hippie vegetarian place) there was an insatiable appetite for fast food, and not just fast food, but *brand-name* fast food, from the mainland chains that advertised heavily on satellite TV and spent fortunes to be featured as product placement in Hollywood blockbusters.

The Fry Guys had a soup-to-nuts way to service this demand, including paying local kids to circle the depot to speed orders off to hungry diners. But the key to it all was inventory: sourcing a steady supply of burgers and fries. For this, they set up—

"You see," Antonio said, "I've got four downlines and an upline, and he's got six downlines. I owe him a certain number of points every week—"

"Points?" Scott said.

"Yeah, there's different points for all the different burger places. The Fry Guys set them, and they change them up, based on the demand from the locals." A worried look passed over his face. "But In-N-Out is always tops, so that was a real solid you did me." He shoulder-checked us to make sure we were reassured. "So my upline recruited me and I owe him a hundred points a week, but my downlines owe *me* a hundred each, and—"

"And the points cash out for U.S. dollars, somewhere?" Scott asked.

"Yeah," he said. "Every month. Or you can roll them over, because it's a sliding scale—like, if you cash out a thousand points, that's a hundred bucks, but if you cash out five hundred points, that's only forty-five dollars, and . . ."

And on and on. By the time he was done, I literally had to bite my tongue to stop myself from giving Antonio an education he hadn't asked for and probably wouldn't appreciate.

A Ponzi scheme is an investment fraud where the early adopters get paid from the money that the latecomers brought in. A pyramid scheme is when there's a sales element, with sales reps having to bring in more sales reps. I'd seen plenty of both.

This was still a couple of years before Bernie Madoff got caught, but my whole career had been defined by this kind of scam. It was how I got my start. Get this: I got hired by the *scammers* to help ruin some of their wayward sales reps, and then, once I figured that out, I switched sides. That caper forever attuned me to the scent and shape of this con. I could spot it a mile away, and I could certainly hear it in Antonio's voice. His words quivered with the excitement of easy money and exponential growth.

I turned to look at Scott and found him grinning widely. He caught my eye and gave me a look, like, *Well, isn't this just hilarious?* I looked away.

Once we were in our usual penthouse suite, we cracked beers and sat on the patio and had an argument.

"We can't let Antonio get sucked into this" was my opening bid. "He's a nice kid, and he's gonna get ruined."

Scott's eyebrows climbed to his hairline. "Are you kidding me, Marty? How do you propose we get him out of this? In case you haven't noticed, every single person that kid knows is up to their chins in it. You think he can opt out?"

Right up to that minute, my only consideration had been how we would get Antonio out of this scam and then equip him with the talking points and other tools he'd need to get his friends and family out of it. I'd assumed that Scott would be in on this with me. We both liked Antonio, and besides, didn't Scott try in his own small way to keep other nerds from getting sucked into Yahoo!'s financial void?

It turned out I didn't have the faintest idea about that.

"The suckers can't be discouraged," Scott said. "I do everything I can to get the good ones away from Yahoo!, but they *want* to be scammed. They know it's a scam. They know better than anyone. These start-up guys are hard-core techies, they know everything that's wrong with every stupid Yahoo! acquisition. They watched the good ones get mismanaged into the dirt. They don't care. No one cares. You can't scam an honest man, and there are no honest men."

"Including you?" I shot back. He'd made me angry. This kind of talk made me furious. I'd heard so many scammers absolve themselves with it.

"I sold out to Yahoo!, didn't I?" He spread his hands out, taking in the harbor, the yachts, the chocolate-box town of Avalon sweeping off to the right. "It made me a rich man. I got what I wanted."

I shook my head and drank more beer. "Don't give me that, buddy," I said. "Your investors sold you out. You've done everything you can, ever since, to get out and to help other people.

You aren't a scam artist and you don't have to convince yourself that you—and everyone else—are on the make to explain how you ended up in your golden handcuffs."

We traded some more volleys, and opened more beers, and tried to recapture our normal, good-natured feeling of being a couple of debauchery-focused beach bums with a fat bankroll, but it eluded us. We had discussed going to a party that night—another one at Junior's—but the beer was sour in our guts and we decided we'd order dinner in.

The Zane Grey had menus for a dozen of the best local places and a special arrangement to get takeout from them even if they didn't normally offer it. The concierge sent up a binder full of menus and we perused it listlessly.

"I think we should order Big Macs," Scott said at last, glaring at me to let me know it was a challenge.

"Be serious," I said.

"I am serious. You say this is just a scam, but how can you know until you've tried it? I tried every one of those Yahoo! acquisitions I complain about. It's called eating your own dog food."

"I'd rather eat dog food than flash-frozen, microwave-reheated McDonald's."

"Maybe they've got fresh stock. Last ferry came in less than an hour ago. We should check it out."

I don't know how I lost that idiotic argument, but the next thing I knew, Antonio had been summoned to the room and he was grinning at us uneasily as we explained that we wanted him to facilitate an order of the Fry Guys' freshest, highest-quality merchandise, money no object.

Antonio looked like he thought we were pulling his leg, and also looked like that made him uncomfortable as hell, which prompted me to jump in and assure him that we were serious and definitely in the market for some bootleg fast food, at what-ever the going rate was.

I was ashamed to see how well that worked—how much Antonio trusted me. If I said this was on the level, he'd believe it.

"What kind of burgers?" he said.

"Oh," Scott said, airily, "I think we'd better try them all."

Once again, Antonio looked like he thought he was being made the butt of a joke, and once again, it fell to me to reassure him. "We just want to get a sense of the inventory," I said. "You know . . . the range on offer. Want to get a full picture, for future orders."

"But you sirs live on the mainland," he said. He wasn't stupid or credulous. Lots of smart people get sucked into scams. "You can get fast food whenever you want."

"We *like* fast food," Scott said. "Don't you?"

"Sometimes," Antonio said. "But only because it's a change, to be honest. I don't think I'd eat it on vacation."

Scott shrugged. "Maybe we won't, either. But who knows, maybe we'll discover a new favorite. But to do that, we'll need to try it all, see what's what." He smiled. "We'll pay, of course."

Antonio looked from Scott to me to Scott to me. I felt like a heel. Suddenly, he beamed at us. I felt like more of a heel. "Can do," he said. "I'll see about getting you a bulk discount, okay?"

"That'd be really great," Scott said. "Thanks, Antonio."

I felt like the biggest heel in the world.

It was disgusting.

I don't like fast-food burgers at the best of times, but the Fry Guys' product—old, cold, frozen and reheated—was *inedible*. Antonio brought up a microwave—normally supplied to guests with babies who needed to heat formula—and installed it with a flourish. We let him reheat the first course—Whoppers with all the trimmings, rimed with frost and mummified in thicknesses of plastic wrap—and put on a show of enjoying our first bites while he watched us nervously.

After he left, we enjoyed a guilty round of jokes about how foul it had been, then, after a brief intermission, nuked some McDonald's fries (soggy) and Big Macs (soggy, frozen in the middle, greasy and slimy). We left the Wendy's and the In-N-Out and the Arby's in the fridge, then carried the microwave out onto the balcony in an unsuccessful attempt to get the microwaved grease smell out of the $2,500-per-night suite.

Sitting on the balcony with our beers and our reeking microwave and our indigestion, we pondered the harbor and the stars and each other.

"I'm sorry," Scott said. "This was stupid."

"It's okay," I said. "I think we got a sense of the merchandise, at least. Food like that, maybe this Ponzi will fall apart before it can destroy the local economy."

So we went to the party. Antonio drove us to Hamilton Cove in his golf cart, in an oddly subdued mood. He waved goodbye to us and promised to come by in two hours if he didn't hear otherwise.

Lionel Coleman Jr.'s weekly parties were in a rut. I was barely through the door and in possession of three fingers of neat rum, hold the garnish, when I started to think about sneaking off with the mushrooms I was sure Scott had brought with him.

Scott and I might have been the only people in the room who weren't either in real estate, or the women the real-estate barons brought in tow. I spotted Tommy Bahama with a different woman. Katya was better-looking if you ask me (but no one asked me).

Everyone I met asked me what I did. It was that kind of party. I told them "accountant" even though "forensic accountant" would have doubtless spooked some of those guys. Forensic accounting is real-estate Kryptonite. It might have been fun to watch them go wide-eyed, but on the other hand, it also would have likely meant having to listen to their boring stories of how they hid their money. There's a certain kind of guy who likes to workshop his fraud schemes, subject them to red team analysis. I wasn't in the business of helping people perfect their schemes.

I wandered into the kitchen, hoping to find a glass of water and escape the company, and found myself underfoot as the servers shuffled around the tiny space loading up their hors d'oeuvres trays. I was about to show myself out when one of them opened the giant Sub-Zero fridge and I saw that it had been filled to bursting with fast-food bags.

The caterer—a high-school-aged girl with her hair in a long, loose braid—caught me looking and made a face. "I can't stand the stuff," she said.

"Me neither," I said, and helped myself to a shrimp skewer off her tray as she squeezed past me into the living room.

I went looking for Scott. Those mushrooms were growing more tempting by the second. Instead, I found Junior.

He was a good ten pounds heavier than the last time I'd seen him, and he had a whisky flush that crawled up his plump cheeks to the bags under his eyes. His hair and forehead gleamed with humidity. He looked like shit.

"Hey there, Lionel, looking good," I said.

His smile came out as a grimace. "Thanks, Marty. Been busy lately."

"Condos? Malls? Mausoleums?"

"Something better," he said. "You wanna get some fresh air with me?"

I couldn't say no. He was my host. Besides, maybe Scott would be out there.

It was getting hotter, so despite the night, the air on the balcony was sultry. Junior rooted around in a Rubbermaid storage box and came up with a bottle of tequila reposado, which he uncapped and slugged out of, then wiped the mouth off on a sleeve and handed it to me.

I swished a burning mouthful of smoky liquor past my teeth

a few times, then swallowed it, enjoying its heat. I passed it back to him and he hit it again, and offered it back to me. I waved him off and he took one more slug before capping it.

"How's business?" he asked. I thought about how Scott liked these guys better than nerds because they could unplug from work. Their version of unplugging was pretty different from mine. If they weren't asking you what you did for a living, they were asking you for your latest quarterly numbers.

"Uneventful," I said. He just stared at me. "I'm taking a break."

He cocked his head, a little drunk. "A break?"

"I work contract," I said. "When I get a little buffer built up in the bank, I knock off and bum around for a while, burn it off, then go back into harness. It suits me."

His mouth worked wetly for a moment. "You're, what, a bookkeeper or something?"

There are CPAs who'd bridle at being called a bookkeeper—it's a class-hierarchy thing. Not me. I preferred it when men like Junior were vague on what I did. Who knows, maybe someday I'd be called in to audit him. The more he underestimated me, the better.

"Something like that," I said.

"You want some work? I need a bookkeeper."

"No," I said, patiently and slowly, like I was speaking to a toddler—or a drunken second-generation real-estate tycoon. "I am taking a break right now." I remembered my manners. "Thank you, though."

"But you'll like this one," he said. He was still sweating, and I imagined that the beads on his forehead were at least 50 percent tequila by volume. "It's interesting. Fascinating, even. I just don't have the time to keep it going."

"Like I said," I said, "I'm not in the market—"

"Come with me," he said. "I'll show you." He grabbed for my wrist and I pretended I didn't notice, while stepping back discreetly so he missed. He was slow. "Come *on*," he said. "You'll like this."

There was no graceful way to turn him down, so I followed him back through the party into his office, a room that had been decorated to be a powerful man's den before being turned into a midden by a drunken slob. Dark wood paneling and framed Chamber of Commerce plaques presided over a litter of fast-food wrappers, dirty cups, spilled piles of paperwork, and, there on the corner of the desk, a brass-framed mirrored tray showing straight lines of powdery residue.

"Here," he said, shoving a pile of papers onto the ground to free up a rolling chair, "have a seat." He took over a giant, heavily instrumented executive desk chair that sighed out a musty fart as he settled into its cushion and hammered the space bar on his 110-key keyboard. His giant LCD monitor came to life and demanded a password, and he didn't even try to hide as he typed the corners of his keyboard, then the keys next to them, in a clockwise rotation: Q|?ZW}>X.

I found myself looking at a gigantic spreadsheet, one that spanned the whole width of the thirty-five-inch monitor, in type that couldn't have been more than 10 point. I automatically squinted to start reading it, but Junior was already tabbing away from the numbers to some bar charts.

"That's my growth." He wiggled the mouse over some impressively rising bars. "That's my projected growth." Much taller bars, shaded gray, reaching upward to the top of the window.

"That's a lot of growth," I said.

"I know, right?" He giggled. "And all from this garbage." He kicked out at a grease-stained McDonald's sack.

I'm slow, but I'm methodical. The fridge full of fast food. His bloat. Some of the words on the briefly glimpsed spreadsheet. I have unwound a lot of scams and I comfort myself in the knowledge that you don't have to be smarter than the scammer—just more thorough. They have to make no mistakes. I have to find one mistake. That's why I always win.

"Fast food," I said. "You can't get that on Avalon," I said.

"That *used* to be the case. But prohibition just creates arbitrage opportunities. Everyone who's studied the rumrunners knows that. Anyone who's studied the War on Drugs knows it. The only person who didn't know it was William Wrigley Jr." Another Junior. Maybe growing up in your dad's shadow stunts your emotional growth.

"I heard something about that," I said. "Some kind of—" I fished for the euphemism. "—affiliate marketing business?"

He nodded hard. "That's it exactly. Yeah. Bringing in a couple grand a day right now. Net."

I did some numbers in my head: population of Avalon, markup on the burgers, operational costs, wage bill. "That's a lot of burgers," I said.

"I know," he said, and grinned.

"No," I said, "it's a *lot* of burgers. Too many. There's no way people here are eating enough fast food to make that much money."

A cunning look swam up through his bleariness. "You're right," he said. "But it's not hamburgers that're bringing in the money. All that growth is from affiliate fees."

We held each other's gaze. He'd just told me that he was running a scam. There aren't many things that the FTC will prosecute as a pyramid scheme—the guy who cofounded Amway was also the head of the Chamber of Commerce and his congressman, Gerald Ford, ascended to the presidency while Amway was being broken on the rack by the FTC. Ford swooped in to rescue this prominent, respectable pillar of the business community, and they crafted anti-pyramid-scheme rules that were so loose that almost any scam could fit comfortably inside of it.

But there *was* a bright line. *There had to be a product.* If the bulk of the revenues were coming from affiliates paying other affiliates to recruit still more affiliates, well, that's the kind of thing that the FTC would actually raise an eyebrow at, and possibly bestir itself to prosecute.

Junior knew this. I knew it. He knew I knew it, and vice versa. Technically, this was now a criminal conspiracy.

I made a noncommittal grunt.

He pretended it was a sign of interest. "Thing is, this is a hell of a lot of fun. There's just so much *opportunity* here, so many different levers you can yank on to change the *dynamics.*" Somehow, he made "dynamics" sound like a sacred object of veneration. "Make a little change to the upline/downline split, or banked points, or option values, and the whole thing changes *completely.* It's like a model train set for money."

"Sounds like you're having fun." I worked hard to keep the judgment out of my voice. Either it worked or he was incapable of imagining that I would find any of this the least bit distasteful.

"Dude, it's *so fun.* But the problem is, it's eating my life. Thing is, all these fuckers"—he gestured at the list of names running down the leftmost column of his giant spreadsheet—"are always trying to figure out how to max out, you know, game the system. They're like ants, crawling all over my model, looking for the tiniest crack so they can get inside it and chew it up from the inside. I've got God-view on the system, so I can see things they can't, see around the corners, but it's still a full-time job keeping it running."

"Attackers just have to find one mistake, defenders have to be perfect."

He looked dazed. "Say that again?"

I did.

"That's fuckin' *amazing.* Wait—" He rummaged in a drawer and came up with a leather-bound notebook, the size of a paperback book. He produced a heavy nib pen from another drawer and turned to a blank page. "Say it one more time."

It took two tries before he had it transcribed to his satisfaction. He blew on the wet ink and then closed the book. "That's amazing," he kept saying, while I thought about all the ways Junior got to play attacker—against city planning councils, against the IRS—and how that had made him so monumentally unsuited to defending against his legion of "affiliate marketers."

"I need a bookkeeper," he said. "Someone to process all the data coming in from the field and run scenarios for me. I'll supply the strategy, you turn it into numbers, I'll get you a commission. Sound good?"

It sounded awful. For the millionth time, I was glad to have chosen a trade that made it possible for me to choose who I worked for and who I never, ever had to work for.

"Sorry, not my thing."

He acted like he hadn't heard, or maybe like he didn't believe me. "You'd take points off the gross, even before I get my cut." He clicked idly around his spreadsheet, flipping through the tabs. "Thing is, I just can't keep this up, but I love it so much. It's killing me, the time I put into it. I need a number two. What do you say?"

"Same as before, Lionel. Not available. Thanks for asking, though."

This time, it registered. His eyes narrowed, and color rose up his neck. "Jeez, I'm not asking for much. Just a few hours a week, easy money. Guy who wears a Casio digital watch and a pair of Old Navy jeans, you look like you could use the money. Don't tell me you don't need it." He sniffed and looked pointedly around at his office and its plaques and trophies. "*I* don't need it. The money from this isn't the point. I lose this business, it'll barely register on my bottom line. I'm in it for the thrill, you understand, and I'm offering to cut you in for a piece here. It's rewarding work. Stimulating."

"I get all the stimulation I need," I said, mildly as I could.

The flush rose to his cheeks and ears. "Fuck's sake, dude, I'm not asking you to take on a full-time job. Just some consulting work."

"I'm not in the market." Just as he was about to say something back, I added, "Thank you, though." Flat. Obviously insincere.

"I guess we don't have anything else to talk about," he said.

We never had anything to talk about, Junior.

"I'll be getting back to the party, then," I said, and watched him think through whether he wanted to throw me out. He very much seemed to be the kind of man who could decide on the spur of the moment that a relative stranger was the only person who could solve his problem, then swear eternal enmity on the basis of a polite refusal. But he was also the kind of guy who liked to throw jolly parties where he could show off to his frenemies and their expensive dates.

"We should get back," he managed, gargling the words through his rage-choked throat.

Scott figured out something was up within seconds of our return to the party, and he wasn't the only one. Junior had a face on like a bulldog chewing a wasp. He cut a line through the crowd to the kitchen, pausing only to snatch a bottle of Scotch from behind the bar.

Scott wasn't the only one who clocked this performance. A low buzz of conversation followed Junior out of the room. Scott sidled over to me. "What's the story?"

I shrugged. "He wanted me to work for him." I shrugged again. "I don't want to work for him."

Scott rolled his eyes. "Don't blame you."

The buzz was fading. Junior gave no sign of emerging from the kitchen. Scott wandered off to talk with a younger guy, clean-cut and dull-looking. I poured myself some more rum. There wasn't anyone I wanted to talk with, except maybe Scott. Maybe.

I wandered out of the condo, sipping from Junior's heavy-bottomed rocks glass, and down to the front entrance. There I found Antonio, sitting in his golf cart, smoking a cigarette and looking at the sliver of moon. I was halfway to the cart when he spotted me and discreetly ground out his cigarette.

"Evening, sir," he said, as I slid in next to him on the passenger side.

"You been waiting here all this time, Antonio?"

He shrugged. "I don't mind. I had some work to do, anyway."

"Work?"

He produced a pocket notebook, the cheap cardboard-bound version of Junior's leather-clad number, and riffled the pages, handing it to me open to neatly penned tables of numbers. "Projected earnings," he said. "I think I've got another downline about to come on, and between that and my regulars from the mainland who bring in product, and the sales channels I've got in town . . ." He trailed off as I looked the numbers over. This was the other side of Junior's giant spreadsheets, a kid who was getting into debt based on guesses about how a rigged casino would pay out for him.

"I see," I said. "Well, best of luck with it, Antonio." I handed him the notebook, waited a decent interval, and swilled the rest of the rum. It wasn't my job to save Antonio from his own greed. Like Katya said, *I don't do freebies. Everyone is in need.*

Antonio wasn't stupid. He knew I disapproved. In the pecking order of Catalina Island, I was allowed to tell him he was wasting his money, but he wasn't allowed to argue back—never mind that he was vibrating to argue with me about it.

It wasn't my job to save Antonio from himself, but we were beached outside of Hamilton Cove until Scott got bored of Junior's party and what the hell else were we gonna talk about?

I spoke with care, forcing sobriety into my cadence and words. "Antonio. If you would like to talk about this, I'm happy to discuss it. As you might remember, I'm an accountant, which may sound boring, but I'm a *forensic* accountant, which means that it's my job to untangle scams. I have seen a lot of scams, and it is my professional opinion, backed by experience *and* the evidence of my own eyes, that you are involved in a scam. The Fry Guys are a pyramid scheme with some Ponzi thrown in. It's a rigged casino and you're the mark. They're going to clean you out.

"I'm willing to bet that you disagree with me. I've met a lot of people who were where you are, halfway through the con, not yet at the part where it all goes blooey, and those people are *invested*. They've put their labor and money into the con. They've roped in half their friends and they're selling to the other half. If it's a con, then they're guilty, too. No one wants to think that about themselves, and no one wants to think that they've lost all their money."

He took a moment to think about it, opened his mouth, shut it again. I didn't have much hope. Deprogramming Ponzi victims is basically impossible, at least before the whole thing collapses. Sometimes, not even then.

"Sir," he said.

"Marty. Just Marty."

"Marty," he said, and grimaced. "I know you're trying to look out for me here, and I'm sure you know a lot about accounting, but *I* know Catalina Island. I'm sure it looks crazy to a mainlander, but people here are fucking *crazy* about fast food. It's like . . . *forbidden fruit,* you understand? It's romantic, it's the big city, it's the way normal Americans live their lives."

I did him the courtesy of taking that in and mulling it over. After really taking it in, I said, "I believe you. You are the expert on this. What's more, I've seen it in action. I'm sure there's a real market demand for fast food here, even frozen and microwaved fast food.

"So maybe we could call this a stalemate. You're an expert on Catalina, I'm an expert on accounting, and neither of us knows enough about the other's domain to declare themselves right.

"But there's one more thing I haven't told you about, the evidence I've seen with my own eyes, just a few minutes ago, in that condo over there." I jerked a thumb over my shoulder. "I'll tell you about it, if you're up for it."

He nodded slowly.

"You ever hear of a guy named Lionel Coleman Jr.?"

He nodded again. "That's the gentleman whose party you were at tonight, right?"

"That's correct. Do you know anything about his relationship to the Fry Guys?"

He concentrated for a moment. "I *think* I saw him at the depot, once. Maybe he's a customer?"

"He's the founder," I said, and let that sink in for a second.

"You think?" he said. *Denial, anger, bargaining, acceptance* . . .

"He just tried to hire me to run his books. He showed me the spreadsheets. You know how the point system keeps changing up?"

"Yeah," he said.

"That's on purpose. He's modeling all the things that you and the rest of the islanders might do to maximize your returns and changing the rules so it won't work, so he gets everything."

Clearly this explained some things for him. "That's fucking *bullshit.*" *Anger, bargaining, acceptance* . . .

"You know what 'leverage' means?"

His eyes flashed. "I'm guessing you don't mean using a long stick to pry up a rock."

"No," I said. "In finance, leverage is when you borrow money to make a bet. If you win, you pay off your bet. If you lose, you owe twice as much, and have to borrow a lot more."

He huffed a long breath out of his nostrils and I guessed he could see where this was going.

"So long as things are going good, you can pile up a lot of leverage. But when things turn bad, everyone has a margin call—that's when you have to pay off your debts. One person blows their margin call, so the next person blows it, and then the next one. Soon enough, everyone is busted. That's called 'contagion.'"

"Fuck," he whispered, with feeling.

"You know how you owe your upline some mix of food and money, and your downlines owe you, too?"

"Fuck." A little louder.

"The reason your hometown's burger mania is so big isn't that everyone loves burgers. There's enough debt swirling around to buy everyone a hundred burgers. That's just leverage. Junior in there has built a scam where he gets to clean out *everyone* and then fuck off back to the mainland."

He worked his mouth, but couldn't make another word emerge from it. He spat instead, a long, arcing gob that glittered in the Hamilton Cove parking lot lights.

"The worst part is that Junior doesn't even need the money. After he cleans you all out, it'll add maybe one percent to his net worth. He's doing this for the pure, sadistic pleasure of *winning*."

"He offered you a job?" Like an accusation.

"I turned him down." I looked around pointedly. *That's why I'm out here with you.*

"Fuck." He snorted a few more times. "He tried to hire you, though."

"Yeah."

"So you understand his system."

"Only the general shape of it. He's changing the rules all the time. It's his hobby. You guys are like a model train set he's programming to self-destruct."

"But you could understand it, if I showed you all the score-cards and my book, right?"

I tilted my head. I didn't like where this was going. "Maybe."

"You could help me beat it." *Bargaining, acceptance . . .*

"Beat it?"

"Turn the tables. That guy's so rich, we take him for ten percent of what he's worth, share it out. We all get whole again, and then some."

I shook my head, and before I could talk he said, "Come *on*, man, this is *bullshit*. If you're right, then this rich motherfucker mainlander is robbing everyone on this island blind."

"I'm right," I said.

"And we can't go to the cops about it."

I shrugged. "That's probably true. Gerry Ford basically legalized Ponzi schemes, back in the seventies. I don't suppose there'd be anyone at the FTC who'd take an interest in this, especially not with Shrub in the White House."

He snorted. "I'm not talking about the FTC. I'm talking about the LA sheriff's deputies, the only law on the island. Their job is to keep rich tourists safe from townies and low-class daytrippers, not to protect *us* from them."

I shrugged again. "I'm sure you're right. So yeah, I agree, going to the cops is out. But you're not going to beat Junior at his own game."

He glared. "Why, you think I'm too stupid to get one over on some Ivy League asshole?"

"No, Antonio," I said, softly. "It's because he's in charge of the rules of the game *and he cheats*. If you figure out how to beat his system, he'll change the system. He'll do it retroactively. He's the banker and the referee and the only way to beat his game is not to play."

He spat again, but I could see he was thinking about it. "So fine, I have to get everyone to quit this stupid scam. How do I do that?"

I squinted up at the ziggurat steps of condos climbing the hill, found Junior's balcony, squinted at the small distant people silhouetted against the party lights behind them, and thought.

"Well," I said, "I don't suppose you can convince everyone

to back out. It's hard to talk people out of scams. I mean, if you didn't know me personally, I don't suppose you'd have believed me when I told you what was what."

"No, I guess not." He sounded so demoralized.

"Jonathan Swift said that you can't reason people out of positions they didn't reason themselves into. Besides, like I said, even if you all decided to run a counterscam on Junior, he'd just fold up the operation. Any money you got out of him would actually come out of some islander's pocket. The thing about these operations is that the scammer doesn't need to keep any skin in the game. Junior might have put some of his own money in early on, as a pot-sweetener, a convincer to bring in other marks, but he's long since gotten it all back and more. It's gone. You won't get it back."

"Fuck." Antonio was back to whispering. Was this *acceptance*?

"But the longer this goes on, the more damage it does—that is, the more money Junior takes from you and your neighbors and puts in his own pocket. All you've got left to you is harm reduction—minimizing his take."

"How would that work?"

"Well, look, every game like this collapses in the end. Too much leverage, the whole thing falls over. One person tries to pull their money out, and that means there isn't enough to pay the next person, and so they pull their money out, and that triggers more defaults."

"Contagion."

"Exactly." I was getting excited now. "You know the saying 'Give me a lever long enough and a fulcrum on which to place it, and I shall move the world'?"

"Is that the same guy as the 'impossible to reason someone out of an idea' thing?"

"No, that was Jonathan Swift, the *Gulliver's Travels* guy. This one is Archimedes, the ancient Greek guy. But they call it leverage for a reason, because all that debt is balanced on the end of a very long fulcrum, and just a little pressure in the right place can catapult it to the sky."

He looked irritated. "I'm not following you. Just tell me, okay, without all the quotes?"

"Sorry," I said. "I know this is your life and your money and all your friends' money. I'm just thinking it through myself.

"Let me try it this way. The way that Junior has set up the Fry Guys, everyone has to keep hustling, putting money in, convincing other people to put money in. It's more money than anyone can afford, though, so everyone owes everyone else a big pile of dough, but everyone is also owed a big pile of dough, and all those debts accumulate fees and interest, so it feels like you're getting richer. Hell, maybe you're even plowing those 'profits' back into Fry Guys so you can get even bigger levels of debt and buy even more points in the scam."

"That's definitely happening," he said.

"All that leverage—all that debt—makes the whole thing really unstable. If a couple people cash out, demand all they're owed, and walk away from it, well, suddenly a bunch of their uplines stop getting paid, and they can't meet their obligations. Then the people *they* owe money to get margin calls—I mean, they have to settle their debts—and they can't do it either. Pretty soon, the whole thing falls apart, implodes, collapses."

"But it sounds like everyone loses everything."

I shook my head. "Antonio." I spoke softly, trying to calm him. He wasn't going to like this. "You've already lost everything. Every dollar was lost forever, the minute you put it into the system. It's what's called a 'negative sum' game. This isn't just about rearranging the dollars on-island, so you can stop the game and everyone gives back everything they took. There's a big vacuum cleaner at the top of the pyramid. That's Junior, and every time a dollar lands in *his* pocket, it disappears off the island. Far as you and your friends are concerned, all those dollars are gone—forever.

"Maybe a couple of you got ahead, got more money out of the system than they put in. Those people are the convincers, the Judas goats. Junior *let* them get ahead, so everyone else would think they stood a chance. But no one stood a chance. All the money is already gone."

"So what's the point?"

I took a deep breath. This wasn't going to be easy. *Anger. Denial. Bargaining. Acceptance.*

"The point is to shut it down. Shut it down now, before you and your neighbors and family and friends lose even more money."

He didn't say a word. Someone on Junior's balcony, high above us, laughed, a deep masculine guffaw, full of self-satisfaction.

Finally, he said, "You think you can do that?"

I let out the breath I'd been holding in. "I'm sure I can. You show me your book, maybe get a couple more from your friends, I'll figure out who needs to demand a cash-out, and in what order, to induce maximum instability. Junior might even flush some money back into the system to try to shore it up, but unless he's willing to cover all your losses *and* all the leverage, he's gonna fail."

The penny dropped. Antonio grinned. "And if he *does* make good on all that money people are trying to take out, everyone will get their money back!"

"Ye-e-s," I said, slowly. "But don't get your hopes up. I know Junior's type. Soon as he sees that there's a collapse coming, he's going to fold up the store. He takes risks with *other* people's money, not his own."

The front door of the condo opened and a silhouetted figure emerged, swaying slightly. He drew closer, but even before I could make out his features, I recognized Scott by his gait.

"Hey, buddy," I said, as he shuffled toward us. "Ready to head home?"

He snorted. Now he was close enough to see, and he was *bleary, at least* a couple of drinks over the line. I helped him into the golf cart's back seat and buckled him in, then slid in next to him.

"Back to the hotel," I said, just as Scott leaned out of the cart and threw up, noiselessly except for the splash of the used liquor on the pavement. "Slowly," I added. "Easy on the turns. And maybe we should stop on a beach somewhere and let Scott breathe some sea air." Scott belched and accepted the wet wipes Antonio offered him.

Scott loved the idea of crashing Junior's pyramid scheme. Even hungover, he grew visibly enthusiastic through his nausea as I explained the plan, over a pot of coffee on the terrace. It even brought his appetite back and we sent down for toast and toppings, and half an hour later, Antonio rapped at the penthouse door, burdened with a tray with three kinds of toast, pâté, cold cuts, cheeses, hummus, peanut butter, and fresh preserves. I relieved him of the tray and thanked him. He nodded but didn't go.

"Everything okay?"

"Sorry," he said, and started to go, then stopped. "It's just—" He flushed. "Were you serious last night? I know you'd had a few drinks, sir—"

"Marty," I said. "Not sir. And I'm serious as a heart attack. You busy now? Got other things you need to do?"

He looked flustered. "Not really," he said. "I have to meet a chopper in an hour, but I'm free until then."

"Great," I said. "Why don't you come help us eat this toast and we'll figure it out."

Eating three Tylenol and going through Antonio's book burned off the remainder of Scott's hangover. Antonio ate sparingly, but we managed to get him to put together a half-decent open-faced sandwich while we made up our own dagwoods.

"This guy?" Scott said, pointing to a name beside a column of numbers.

"My old running coach," Antonio said.

"You like him?" Scott said.

"I mean, I don't hate him."

"But you don't feel special about him, he didn't save your life or anything?"

Antonio put down his open-face. "I don't understand the question."

"It's just that this guy has a lot of exposure. If this guy over here—" Scott flipped through the notebook. "—demands payment, your coach is going to get squeezed hard and he'll probably miss a payment to one of these two." He referred to a diagram he'd drawn on a sheet of hotel stationery. "*They* have a bunch of exposure, too. Far as Jenga blocks go, your old coach is a good one to yank if we want to make the tower start wobbling."

"But he'll suffer worse than anyone else?"

I could see that Scott was thinking about this as a mathematical problem, while for Antonio, these were real people with names and histories and families. I cut in before Scott could really screw this up.

"Remember what I said, about how the money was gone the minute you put it in? Your coach wasn't ever going to be made whole again. No one was, except the lucky few who got in first, and maybe not even them, in the end."

Antonio squinted at me, like he was trying to peer through my bullshit. "But will he get it worse?"

I sighed. "Maybe, a little. But he'll also avoid getting in any deeper. In the long run, you'll be saving him money." I looked at the book. "Maybe a lot of money. He got in deep and fast. If we scald him now, he'll jump out and not jump back in."

I could tell Antonio didn't like this. I thumbed through his book, but Scott was right, the coach was the perfect guy, an ideal first domino to start the whole run. Maybe we could get some-one else's book and figure out another patient zero, but maybe not. Antonio had a rapport with us that was different from our relationships with all the other islanders.

One more shot. "Antonio, this problem you're having? It's not new. There's a name for it, even. It's called a 'bezzle.'"

"Embezzle?"

"No," I said. "Just *bezzle*." I could tell Scott didn't know the word, either. "It's a specialist term, comes from an economist, a famous guy called John Kenneth Galbraith. Taught at Harvard for fifty years, while serving under four presidents, including JFK, who made him ambassador to India.

"The word comes from 'embezzlement,' which Galbraith called 'the most interesting crime.' He had a way with words, and his definition of the bezzle was so great I memorized it. It's the 'weeks, months, or years' that 'elapse between the com-mission of the crime and its discovery. This is the period, in-cidentally, when the embezzler has his gain and the man who has been embezzled feels no loss. There is a net increase in psychic wealth.'"

Scott's eyebrows shot up. "Say that again."

I did.

"Oh, that's *good*," he said. "That's Yahoo! to a tee. All these companies they've bought, and no one realizes they're all dead in the water. Everyone thinks that because they paid top dollar for all the coolest web companies that they'll nurture them. No way—it's all a scam. They don't give a shit. They're gonna kill every single one of them. People fight so hard for the products they built, and no one knows that the product's *already* dead. Like you said, the company was dead the moment they signed the paperwork to sell to Yahoo!"

Antonio looked at Scott for a long time. "Didn't you tell me you sold your company to Yahoo!?"

Scott nodded, big enthusiastic head movements that clearly

triggered his hangover so he clutched his head and slugged more coffee. "I did indeed."

"Oh," Antonio said. "So this bezzle thing, you said, it's the time between the crime being committed and the crime being discovered?"

"Exactly. *You* know it's a crime. *I* know it. *Junior* sure as *hell* knows it. But none of your friends have figured it out. They're living the bezzle. They don't know they're broke. They think they're rich. If you go out and tell them they're broke, they'll get pissed off at you. They don't know their money is gone yet. They think it's in their bank accounts. They're in the bezzle. No one will thank you for getting them out of the bezzle."

Scott nodded. "Bezzle. I *love* that word. Such a *useful* word. When did you say it was coined?"

"Midcentury," I said. "The fifties."

He shrugged. "Who knew that Galbraith was such a futurist? He was clearly half a century ahead of his time. The 2000s are the Decade of the Bezzle."

Antonio knew a half dozen people who he figured were ready to be awoken to the bezzle. We set up in a cabana at the Descanso Beach Club and bought *micheladas* and gave economics lessons to them all day and the next, and then choppered home. A few months later, the island burned, a terrible fire that scarred the island. The die-hards came back. I didn't.

I never went back to Catalina Island.

6

But Scott did.

I hadn't heard from him for a couple of months, and I missed our penthouse weekends in Avalon, but I was keeping busy, having agreed to audit a very messy start-up bankruptcy where the VCs suspected (correctly) that the founders had absconded with about two million bucks. By the time I figured out which REIT they'd squirreled the money away into, the strip mall it owned had lost its big grocery store—part of Safeway's overall contraction—and the take was down to one mil.

But the founders fought the VCs and dragged the process out, and by the time the judge handed down her final order, a big Dollar General had taken over the Safeway space and the founders' share of the REIT liquidated at $1.3 mil. My 25 percent cut came to $325,000, which set me up for a whole year and then some.

I was just thinking of how I'd spend it when I got a text from Scott, saying he was in town and asking if I'd meet him at the Trader Vic's in Emeryville. I told him I'd be delighted and went to find a nice barkcloth aloha shirt in my closet before getting on BART, assuming that the inevitable mai tais would leave me in no shape to drive home.

I found him at a picture window overlooking the harbor, surrounded by day-drinking East Bay matrons who were noisily trading vicious gossip. He was drinking Scotch and wearing a faded U2 Zoo TV Tour tee. He looked miserable. My bright orange aloha shirt with its oversized hibiscuses felt very off-kilter.

I came in for a hug, but he stayed in his seat and offered me a limp handshake. I got into the dark wood captain's chair and scooted it forward, then asked a ramrod-straight, elderly Asian waiter in black tie to bring me a grog.

"Grog?" Scott said.

"Comes in a souvenir mug," I said. "I had one and I broke it."

That was before I came into the Unsalted Hash *and became a minimalist, back when I owned a home and collected things. Living on a bus—even a luxury tour bus like the* Hash—*makes that kind of collection impractical. There's no fun in collecting things if they just go into a storage locker.*

No, I don't miss living on the Hash. *I like life now that I've put down roots.*

What?

Yes, it probably does mean that I need another one of those Trader Vic's grog mugs. Yes, you can get me one. Sure, we can call it a birthday present. Why not? Get two, and I'll buy some rum.

"You look good," he said, after I'd had a long draw of grog, barely tasting the rum for the pineapple and passion fruit syrup, but getting enough of a kick to know it was there.

"Thanks," I said. "I've just come off a pretty sweet gig and I'm getting settled into some leisure."

"Thanks for not telling me I look good. I know I don't," he said. "It's been a shitty couple of months."

"I'm sorry to hear it."

He signaled for another Scotch and stared at the bobbing sailboats out of the picture window. "They look better from above," he said. "Down at this angle, you see all the scum at the waterline."

"How are things on Avalon?"

He frowned out the window, then told the view, "I don't go to Catalina anymore."

I waited for him to elaborate, then: "How about if I take you? I'm flush and I owe you one. Several, in fact."

He stared at the tied-up marina sailboats like he wanted to sink each and every one of them. Then he turned that glare on me.

"I *can't* go to Catalina anymore." His fresh whisky arrived and he made half of it disappear.

I waited for him to stop glaring at me. It took a while. He glared at his whisky instead.

"That sounds like a story," I said, gently.

"Not really," he said, into his whisky glass. Then, after a while: "Okay."

My crab rangoon arrived.

"Eat it," he said. "You can't interrupt me if your mouth is full, and I hate this story."

Antonio's plan to burst the Fry Guys bezzle went easier than expected. The tight-knit community of Avalon had more social cohesion than I'd banked on. I'd seen a lot of affinity scams, where people prey on their community, seen how they stayed afloat on the sea of petty resentments and grudges that fester below the surface in any community. But the people of Avalon overcame those long-standing grievances and didn't turn on each other.

Once it became clear that the bank was busting, word got around quick that any new money that went into the scheme would simply evaporate. The flow of real money dried up almost instantly, and that meant that there were no new suckers to buy up Junior's points-for-burgers, and the whole thing froze solid. It took mere days. The Fry Guys' landlord gave them the heave-ho and Junior's trusted lieutenants turned into instant pariahs.

It became an open secret that Junior had been behind the whole thing and he found himself on the receiving end of a lot of glares. He had to wait hours for shore boats when he tied up at the harbor, and a few times, he had to row himself ashore in a little Zodiac.

He was spitting mad, and it didn't take him long to figure out that I had kicked it off. Since I wasn't around to be angry at, he took it out on Scott.

His agents of retribution were the Los Angeles County sheriff's deputies who policed the island, thanks to its status as the farthest-flung tendril of LA County's sprawl.

Scott's troubles started the next time his chopper dropped him off at the heliport. He'd expected to see Antonio, but instead, he was met by two burly deputies, ruddy white guys in their fifties with flinty piggy eyes. The bigger one ordered him to a folding table under an Easy-Up that the heliport used to distribute water and snacks to boarding passengers.

The big cop talked like he was gargling rocks. The little one didn't talk at all. The little one dumped out Scott's bag while the big one tossed his stuff, seeming to relish it every time something fell to the ground. It took him all of five minutes to find Scott's shrooms.

He opened the bag and handed it to the little cop to sniff, then he had a sniff himself.

"You're under arrest," he said, and punched Scott right in the gut, hard enough that he saw flashing lights as he went over. As he retched, the little cop yanked his arms behind him and cuffed him while the big cop frisked him roughly. As he did, his uniform shirtsleeve rode up and revealed a forearm tattoo, right where a watch would hide it: the numbers 998, in neat letters.

"That rings a bell," I said.

"Yeah," he said. "I'm not surprised, knowing you."

The cops held him overnight before putting him on a ferry

the next morning, in cuffs. He was handed over to a Long Beach deputy, who handled his transfer paperwork without an extra word before giving him his phone call.

"My lawyer met with the prosecutor and they agreed to a conditional plea—I plead guilty, get no time, sealed record, and in ten years my record will be expunged, providing I don't get into trouble again."

"Plead guilty to *what*?"

He finished his whisky and signaled for another. "Felony assault on an officer and felony possession of a controlled substance."

"Jesus *Christ*," I said. "Scott, you pled guilty to a *felony*?"

"Two felonies," he muttered, and assumed custody of his next drink. The waiter in his tux took away my starter and pointed at my empty grog cup. I remembered that I wasn't driving and nodded.

"Buddy," I said, "I don't know who your lawyer was, but—"

"Yeah," he said. "Good lawyer. Bad cop. You know that 998?"

"Yeah," I said.

"You remember what it means yet?"

"No," I said. "I can look it up." I flipped open my HTC Dream, the smartphone I'd been obsessively fiddling with since I got it earlier that week. It was brand-new, the first Android phone, and I was willing to bet Scott hadn't seen one yet. It did get a brief rise out of him, and he leaned forward and stared at it for a moment as I thumbed a query using the little keyboard.

"Save your fingers," he said. "998 is 'officer-involved shooting.' It's the tattoo that a Lynwood Viking gets when he shoots someone."

Now I remembered. The Lynwood Vikings were one of the LA County deputy gangs, a bunch of neo-Nazis who were broken up and scattered when the LA sheriff shut down the Lynwood station house. They spent a decade murdering Black,

Latino, and Asian people—and anyone else who looked at them cross-eyed. A couple of them went to prison. The rest stayed on the job.

"The prosecutor and my lawyer both agreed that life would be better for all of us if I didn't end up on the stand in open court calling that cop a liar. Idea was, I'd take a plea, stay the fuck away from Catalina, and in a decade everything would go back to normal."

"Unreal," I said. "Un. Real. You think Junior sent him after you?"

He looked at me with real contempt. "He *told* me Junior sent him. But yeah, if there was any doubt, Junior's visit to my cell that night clinched it. He had a message for you, too."

My stomach curdled around the grog and the crabmeat. "Yeah?"

"He said, 'Tell that fucking bean counter that I know what he did to me, and I won't forget it.'"

"Jesus," I said, and grogged at my grog. "He sounds like a gangster out of a Cagney movie."

"He looked like he meant it," Scott said. "You should have seen his face. Made me glad there were bars between me and him."

I grogged some more.

"I haven't been back to Catalina since. I haven't crossed the LA County line since, except to sign some papers at the court-house, and I made sure my lawyer was with me the whole time." He closed his eyes and shuddered. "Those two cops, the whole system, it was like being caught in a gang war. Hell, it *is* a gang war. I don't know how Lionel got them to shake me down on his behalf, but honestly, I don't imagine it took much—he probably just cut them in for a piece of it. Real-estate guys are good at spreading it around."

He opened his eyes again. "They offered me early vesting at

Yahoo! Apparently I was a downer. I took the buyout. I'm a free man."

"Congratulations," I said, and raised my glass. He clinked.

"Yeah," he said. "Yeah." He put his glass down. "Anyway, I just wanted to tell you all that in person before I left."

"Where are you leaving *to*?"

"Rockport," he said. "Up the coast. Redwood country. I bought myself a little cabin up there, near the King Range Conservation Area. Sleepy place. Bad internet. Pretty sunsets." He flipped a handful of twenties onto the table. "I need a rest," he said.

"You've earned it," I said.

He stood. "Thanks, Marty. Look, no hard feelings. You were right, Junior was just fucking over that whole town, and it was chump change for him. He just got off on the power, on fooling them all, making them dance. Honestly, I probably wouldn't have stepped in if it wasn't for you, but I'm glad you did."

He pushed in his chair. "And I'm glad we went away together, all those times. It meant something. I needed a friend. Someone to trip balls with and run away from buffalo."

I smiled. "Bison."

"Right." He stuck out his hand. "Anyway. I just wanted to tell you."

I got up and stuck out my hand, too, but then, on impulse, went in for the hug. He squeezed me hard. He smelled like whisky. "You okay to drive?"

"Nope," he said. "I'm gonna walk awhile. Clear my head. Gotta go home and pack up my apartment. Movers are coming in two days."

"Be safe," I said. "Take care of yourself." He squeezed me once more.

"I'm going to try the Marty Hench plan. Gonna try and learn to relax. You ever find yourself up in the redwoods, drop me a line."

part two
three strikes

7

Genesius was a Roman comic actor who was famous for his plays making fun of Christianity. One day, the story goes, he was midscene when he had a religious revelation and converted to the faith. He was martyred when he refused Emperor Diocletian's order to renounce Jesus, and so became Saint Genesius, patron of comedians, torture victims, lawyers, converts, and clowns.

San Genesius State Penitentiary is located just outside of Vacaville, about three-quarters of the way between San Francisco and Sacramento, set far enough back from I-80 that they didn't have to post the usual signs about not picking up hitchhikers.

It's a brooding place, the way prisons tend to be, H-shaped, with an original 1930s cinder-block building as the crossbar, and two sixties-vintage wings on either end. Designed to house seven hundred inmates, home to three times that number. It smells, and the floors have lost their finish from prisoners' endless mopping, exposing rough aggregate surfaces that have absorbed an endless shower of fluids and misery.

The first time I visited San Genesius was in late 2012, four months after Scott surrendered himself to the California Highway Patrol detail in Redway, California. He was accompanied by his lawyer, a very expensive fellow from a Silicon Valley firm who specialized in getting diversion or other wrist-slaps for rich techies who got caught with Schedule II narcotics. He usually succeeded.

But not in Scott's case.

It wasn't even Scott's cocaine. I know, that sounds like the kind of bullshit anyone who got busted would say, but I believe him. I enjoy a little coke now and again, but Scott doesn't. I'd seen him pass on so many bumps and lines. For Scott, it was magic mushrooms as a daily driver, LSD for special occasions, and mescaline, peyote, salvia, DMT, and even ayahuasca when he wanted a true blowout. Scott just wasn't a coke kind of guy.

Scott wouldn't say whose cocaine it was. He wasn't a snitching kind of guy, either.

It was that refusal to throw someone to the lions that cost Scott his freedom. The cop who busted Scott—doing 95 m.p.h. on a winding stretch of the Pacific Coast Highway that was posted at 35, which was an idiotic thing that was (unlike cocaine) perfectly in character for Scott—found the coke when his dog "alerted" on Scott's car. It was down the side of the passenger seat, in a little baggie containing precisely 9.01 grams of powder cocaine of middling quantity. That 0.01 was important, because 9 grams is the threshold for an "intent to sell" rap, which is a Class B felony.

Scott's fancy lawyer could have gotten him diversion if Scott had coughed up the name of whatever friend had been riding in his passenger seat. Instead, he kept mum, and the prosecutor—furious with him and intending to "send a message"—made sure the judge knew that this was Scott's third felony rap: the felony assault on an officer and felony possession charges from Catalina filling out his rap sheet.

Three strikes. In 2011, a third felony conviction meant an automatic twenty-five-to-life sentence, under a vengeful 1994 law passed by state ballot initiative following the grisly murders of a teenager and a little girl. By 2012, that was softened, thanks to another ballot initiative motivated by a combination of horror at the state's bursting prisons and the cost of supporting so many young men who'd grown so old in those same teeming lockups.

Scott was arrested in late 2011, just after Thanksgiving. Bad timing.

Scott was serving twenty-five years to life in the minimum-security wing of San Genesius State Pen, and I didn't know about it until I sent him an email and got an autoresponse warning me that he was "away from my desk for the next quarter century."

I'd left San Francisco early, but I was still nearly late. I was twenty minutes en route when I remembered that I wasn't allowed to wear any "blue denim" and had to race home and change out of my jeans.

The rules for visiting Scott were so complex that I'd actually printed a checklist (e.g., "Spare key ring with only two keys"), but I'd forgotten about the jeans.

The checklist was just the latest hurdle in a series of bureaucratic steps, starting with mailing Scott a letter requesting that he send *me* a CDCR 106 visitor questionnaire, which I then had to send back to the prison administration, who took a month to approve it. I got five ten-dollar rolls of quarters at the bank and loaded them in a clear plastic bag, along with my driver's license. Everything else stayed in the trunk.

I handed in my CDCR 106 and submitted to a search and metal-detector scan, then sat tight in a visitors' lobby with the other visitors, waiting to be called into the visitation room. Mine was the only white face in the lobby, apart from the guard's. The largest group of visitors were young, sad women, often with kids; the second-largest group was older people with the wrung-out look of demoralized parents of adult children in crisis. Wives, kids, and parents amounted to three-quarters of the visitors. The rest were young men, friends or maybe siblings, staring hard at the floor or whispering to one another.

I was nearly the last one to be called. I followed a guard—an older white guy with volcanic acne and a pronounced limp—into the visitation room. It was crowded, and the ancient body-odor stink was overlaid with the odors of fresh-scrubbed kids and the desperately cheerful perfumes of the wives and girl-friends.

Scott and I were assigned a table right in the middle, between a young Black man and his sorrowing parents; a middle-aged Latina woman visiting a middle-aged man who looked enough like her that they were probably siblings; a Black woman and her teenaged son visiting their father, behind me; and behind Scott, a Middle Eastern boy, barely eighteen, visiting with a girl no older than he, tears coursing down his cheeks while her shoulders shook from soft, hiccuping sobs.

Scott was already at the table when I entered: shorn of his ponytail, with a few days' facial stubble, looking doughy and hollow-eyed, not so much scared as just *disappeared*. He registered me when I slid into my seat, a flick-flick of the eyes.

"Hi, Scott," I said.

"Marty," he said, in a numb voice, barely audible over the sounds around us.

"Jesus," I said. "Can you appeal?"

He shrugged and hitched a half grin in one corner of his mouth. "The lawyers will take whatever I give them and spend it. But the law's the law. Three strikes, you're out." His eyes flashed a little. "They didn't like that I wouldn't name names. They knew it wasn't my stuff, but they wanted to punish someone, and if I wouldn't give them a name, they'd make an example out of me. At least I was able to set things up so my lawyer would pay into my commissary." He patted his bulging stomach. "Keeps me out of the mess hall."

I was briefly at a loss for words. "Are you really going to spend *twenty-five years* here?"

Again with that half smile. Like everything else about that Scott, it was recognizable as a distant cousin to the happy-go-lucky guy I'd spent all those weekends with on Catalina, but only just. This Scott looked like a lossy JPEG of himself.

"They tell me I can get a third off my sentence for good behavior."

We talked inconsequentialities for a while, mostly just me quizzing him about how I could help him—what I could send, who he wanted to hear from, what I could relay to people on the outside.

Finally, I couldn't stop myself from asking, "But Scott, how the fuck are you going to do this? Brother, you look half dead and it's only been four months. Twenty-five years is a long time, but it's not forever. I don't want you to die in here. There's got to be a way for you to get through this. Can I sign you up for college classes? *Anything?*"

Again, the flash in his eyes. "It's not my job to figure out how you can help me, Marty. I'm the one in prison."

That rocked me back. It was right, of course. "I'm sorry," I said. "What if—" I stopped. What if *what*? "What if I go talk to some lawyers, some advocacy organizations? What if I get you some magazine subscriptions?"

He nodded. "I would appreciate that," he said. I think he meant it. Or at least that's what I told myself.

The drive home seemed twice as long as the drive up. I had to stop twice because I found myself crying. I was certain, absolutely certain, that Scott would not survive. I had just spent an hour with a man who was fixing to die. What's more, I didn't blame him. Not one bit. And that made me cry all the harder.

Six months later, he was a different man.

"Marty fucking *Hench*!" he said, grinning broadly and drumming the table with his palms. He threw his arms open—though he didn't rise for a hug—and gestured to my visitor's chair. Other prisoners and their families turned to stare at us briefly, then returned to their business.

"Scott Warms," I said, sitting down. "You look *amazing*." He did, too. Still pale, but fitter than last time, his prison-issue jumpsuit no longer bulging at the gut, clean-shaved, hair buzzed to an all-over half inch. "What's your secret?"

"Magic," he said. He grinned—the whole Scott Warms grin this time—and waited for me to bite.

I bit. "Do go on," I said, grinning back.

"We've got a *really* good Dungeons & Dragons group here," he said. "They've been playing for about ten years now. There's a guy who makes miniatures and dice out of toilet paper mâché, and when they sweep the cells and confiscate the dice, we draw dice-rolls out of decks of cards. The GM has been inside since the 1980s, but he actually knew Gary Gygax, and he's had people on the outside who've been sending him books and modules in his quarterly packages for decades. He's published two character classes in *Dragon* and four modules with Judges Guild while he was inside, though all the money they earned went to restitution for the liquor-store owner he shot."

"That is a *lot*," I said. "Give me a second." His smile widened. "Okay, maybe start with the liquor-store owner."

Scott shrugged. "It was a long time ago. Evan was strung out at the time. The guy lived. Evan's done twenty years and he hasn't touched heroin for decades. I'm not going to judge this guy by the things he did on the worst day of his life." He shrugged again, then the grin came back. "Man, that guy is a hell of a DM."

And then . . . he told me about his D&D games.

No, really. Scott was a pretty good storyteller, but D&D games are like dreams, more fun to have than to hear about. There were some pretty funny moments where Scott's cleric rolled up some consecutive critical fails and healed the boss troll his party was fighting, but for the most part, it was an eye-glazing half hour.

Not that I begrudged it. It was Scott's time, and he needed

the freedom to spend it the way he wanted way more than I needed to direct the subject of conversation.

When the story wound down, I got up to leave, and so did Scott. "We're allowed to hug," he said.

"Okay," I said. He always was a hugger. It went on for a while, and then I felt his fingers work at the waistband at the side of my pants, tucking something in there. I immediately felt like every person in that room was staring at us: guard, prisoner, and visitor. But no one seemed to notice. They were all wrapped up in their own drama.

I drove back to I-80, then pulled off at a truck stop, parking far from any of the other cars, before I fished in my waistband.

It was written on both sides of a quarter sheet of thin paper, folded twice. The writing was cramped, so tiny I had to squint.

Marty: My DM has an old friend on the outside who gets him sheets of blotter acid disguised as graph paper for games, a first-generation hippie chemist who learned his brew from Owsley. The D&D club plays, but we also have a monthly trip. I was skeptical at first, because I couldn't imagine having a bad trip while locked in a cage, but I was wrong.

It literally saved my life. We start our trip together in the day room, play awhile, get very silly, then we just start telling each other stories. We get pretty weird, but everyone who hears us just assumes it's part of the game. The DM has been making up his own variant rules for a quarter century, and honestly the stuff we say when we're tripping is not much weirder than the stuff we say when we're not. So long as we move our miniatures and roll our dice, everyone assumes it's all fine.

Then we go back to our cells and they lock us in, and we finish out the trip in our bunks or with our cellies. We don't tell them, though they probably suspect *something*.

But here's the deal: the DM is getting out, and he's not

going to risk his parole by sending contraband inside. The risk of getting caught is low, but he's a felon mailing graph paper back inside, so for him, it's a little higher.

Marty, I have a favor to ask.

He had a pretty clever method worked out: he'd start a book club, one where they'd take turns reading aloud to one another. Great works of literature, the kind of thing you could buy in a used bookstore.

I'd deposit a single drop of LSD onto the spine-side bottom corner of prime-numbered pages, so that any guard who riffled the book wouldn't handle the doctored areas. Plus, the tiny excisions at the spine would not be obvious to anyone who checked out the book after the acid had been extracted.

I understand that this is a terrible idea and you'd be an idiot to take me up on it.

But I still hope you'll do it.

Talking with my DM, I've learned a lot about the golden age of psychedelics research, back before the panic led to the pharma companies halting the supply of drugs and sent the FDA to ban it. There were *hundreds* of studies, Marty, and the results were really promising, especially for people with drug habits and people with trauma problems. As in, 99% of the people I'm locked in with here.

I've seen LSD make a difference. I know that sounds weird after decades of scare talk about drugs, when the only time you'd go tripping is when you're partying or at a festival. But the guys in here *need* this. They are benefiting from it. It's not just keeping them sane in a fucked-up situation, it's actually helping them get better. There's been a little underground club of psychonauts in here for decades and if it ends now, it will be a brutal turn for people who are living in the most brutal conditions.

So I understand if you won't do this, but fuck I really hope you will.

And then he promised to give me information for his DM's chemist, an encrypted email address at a Swiss privacy-focused provider, along with a "foolproof" dead-drop method: go to Redfin, find an empty house for sale, and have FedEx deliver an innocuous parcel containing a small vial of liquid LSD there, timing the arrival so that it shows up at a time when the Realtor wouldn't be there (but I would). That was a variant on an old trick that I knew for a *fact* worked, and it was clever.

I refolded the paper and put it in the armrest compartment, then I pulled out of the truck stop. It took a couple of hours to get home and the whole time I kept seeing phantom police cars in my mirrors, and every time I thought I caught a glimpse of one, my heart thundered so hard that I could hear it as loud as dubstep.

There was no way I could do this. No way. There were too many ways to get caught, and if I was, well, I'd be right next to Scott. Maybe I wouldn't get twenty-five years (I'd managed to make it that far without even one felony, let alone two), but it wouldn't be a short sentence, either. The Great State of California gets very touchy about people who help its prisoners smuggle contraband into its prisons.

Three months later, they turned me away.

"Your visitee is in the Special Housing Unit and is not eligible to receive visitors at this time." The guard at the reception looked at me like I was an idiot, and I realized I was just standing there with my mouth open, not saying anything, and there was a line behind me.

"He's in *solitary,*" the woman behind me called out. "You can't see him 'cause he's in solitary. Now move, *please*?" She had a toddler on her hip and she looked tired. I apologized and retreated to my car.

I sat there for a long time, hand on the key, not starting the ignition, until a guard wandered over and made me roll down my window so he could explain the policy against "loitering" outside the facility.

I drove home.

A month later, they turned me away.

He wasn't there. He was in the state medical facility, following a suicide attempt.

I didn't loiter in the parking lot.

A month later, he was eligible for his quarterly package.

I mailed him five books.

I had toyed with the idea of picking up some Carlos Castaneda, Ken Kesey, Hunter S. Thompson, and Philip K. Dick, but I quickly abandoned that plan (and later that night, got a momentary case of the shivers when I was struck by what an idiotic, self-sabotaging temptation of the fates that would have been).

I also contemplated sending the Bible, or hymnals, or something by Bill W., but I decided that was trying so hard it might wrap all the way around and seem suspicious on its own.

In the end, I went for high fantasy: all three Lord of the Rings books, *The Hobbit*, and *A Wizard of Earthsea*. It took me two full nights to prepare the books, working with a printed list of prime numbers and an eyedropper, wearing disposable gloves. When I was done, I packaged the books in a big bubble mailer and took it to a pack-and-ship across the Bay, with a handwritten slip giving Scott's prisoner number and address. As I expected, the bored clerk rekeyed the address, squinting at my nearly unreadable handwriting, and printed out a thermal adhesive-backed label.

I wore my uncle Ed's hat, pulled low. I paid cash. I parked around the block. I used store windows as mirrors on the way back to my car, hoping to catch a tail. I drove home to my place in Noe Valley and took the pork tenderloins, covered in salt and pepper and resting on a wire rack over a baking tray, out of the fridge and set them on the counter. While that came up to room temperature, I lit a chimney full of hardwood charcoal on top of the grill on my balcony. Once the coals were hot and covered in white ash, I slipped on a silicone cooking mitt and tipped the chimney onto one half of the grill, making a neat two-zone fire.

I burned up the bottle the liquid LSD had come in, the envelope it had been packaged in, the bubble wrap, and the gloves. The plastic stank and made black smoke. I let the coals burn for twenty minutes more until the plastic was nothing but residue. I threw on a couple more lumps of coal and a fist-sized chunk of cherrywood, then rested my oiled, cleaned grill on top of them. I carefully laid out the pork tenderloins in the cool zone, fat ends closest to the fire, and put the lid on tight, closing the vents up to slits. I washed and trimmed some asparagus while the timer on my phone counted down three minutes, then I flipped the tenderloins, putting sprigs of rosemary between them and the grill.

I flipped them twice more, then checked them with an instant-read thermometer, decided 135 degrees was done enough, and moved the tenderloins to the hot side of the fire for sixty seconds on a side, to develop a sear and crust. I moved them onto a plate and put a dish towel over it, then tossed the asparagus onto the hot zone and kept it moving around until it had a nice char, then moved it to the cool zone while I carved the tenderloins into thin medallions.

I transferred the asparagus to a fresh plate, sprayed it with aerosol olive oil, squeezed a lemon wedge over it, and sprinkled on a half pinch of flake salt. Then I added a medium-sized portion of tenderloin medallions and splashed them with some fiery mango salsa and got the plate nicely centered on my balcony's little bistro table, along with a wooden-handled Opinel steak knife and a nice fork, and four fingers of dark sipping rum—Bacardi Añejo.

I ate my dinner and stared at my neighbor's backyard garden while the sun went down, and I tried to appreciate every bite, just in case it was my last dinner as a free man.

Scott looked great.

Seeing him with clear eyes and a little smile, there in the prison visitation room, was a profound relief. It caused me to expel a breath I hadn't realized I'd been holding in, drawing a suspicious stare from the guard who escorted me into the room. I smiled apologetically at him and pretended I didn't see him scowl in return.

The last time I'd seen Scott, he'd been half asleep, doped to the gills on Haldol, one corner of his mouth and one hand ticcing in counterpoint with spasms. Slumped, fat, and listing, eyelids at half-mast, he'd seemed gone.

Six months and one more quarterly shipment of books later, Scott was back to his old self, with a wicked gleam and an easy laugh. He'd lost weight, or maybe his muscle tone was just better, and he radiated a kind of bemused air that I took for detachment at first, like he'd escaped us all, but which I decided was *engagement,* like he was right there with us, soaking up all the unintentional, undeniable *comedy* of it all.

"Hey, Marty!" he said, and launched to his feet and pulled me into a backslapping, crushing hug.

"Scott," I said, tensing up while I waited for him to slip another note into my waistband, but he didn't. We took our seats.

"Things are good, huh?" I said, then regretted it, because of course things weren't *good,* how could they be good when Scott had twenty-three years and change left on his sentence, maybe sixteen with good behavior?

But he nodded enthusiastically. "You wouldn't believe how good," he said. "The D&D game, the book club, they're going *so* well. The guys I'm hanging out with have become like brothers. It's completely changed how I relate to this place—how I relate to my *life.*" Which left me feeling incredibly exposed, like anyone could easily figure out this code: *Thank you for smuggling a Schedule I controlled substance to me, my fellow felon.* But of course, no one gave a shit about us or our discussion, and even if they had, that was quite a leap to make.

Scott saw my thinking on my face. "*Easy,*" he said. "I'm good. This situation"—he waved his hand around at the people, the walls, the vending machines, the buzzing lights—"is not ideal, but these guys aren't running a sci-fi gulag. No one's running speech recognition on our conversation looking for oblique references. They're just trying to warehouse a bunch of losers as cheaply as possible. Once you realize that, everything else becomes very straightforward." He snorted. "Very straightforward indeed."

He didn't feel the need to recount any of his D&D adventures that time, but we did have a long talk about the group's feelings on *The Hobbit.* Apparently they'd really identified with the all-male cast, and observed that Frodo and his dwarf pals got into exactly the kind of stupid, self-sabotaging trouble that lands guys in prison, chalking it up to the absence of female contributions to their deliberations.

"I never really thought about *The Hobbit* being such a sausagefest," I said.

"Spend enough time away from women, that kind of thing stands out. For guys in here, even reading about women is a treasure. Not just the straight ones, either. One of the guys in the book club is a Gold Star Gay, never so much as kissed a girl growing up, but he misses having women in his life as much as the rest of us."

"I wonder if women in lockup miss men the same way?"

"Not if they're smart," he said. "If I ever get out of here, I could happily spend ten years without ever seeing another man. No offense."

"None taken."

We stared at each other across the table. I had to remind myself that this serenity-radiating Buddha in khakis was the shattered zombie I'd seen just a few months before. I guess he didn't like thinking about that either. He got sad, his eyes drooping, and he said, "You need to know, Marty, that you're making a difference. I couldn't do this without your help."

Help, felony, what's the difference? I didn't say it.

But I mailed him another five books the next time he was eligible for a quarterly package.

The first time I got behind the wheel of a car, I was terrified. Objectively, I was right to be scared. Driving is just about the most dangerous thing you can do as an everyday American, and you'd have to be a lunatic to treat it like it was just a quick spin around the block. But that's *exactly* how we treat it, despite the fact that we are surrounded by people who are, *by definition,* lunatics, because they are all treating the experience like a spin around the block.

But if you do something dangerous and terrible long enough, eventually it becomes normal.

Over the next four years, I mailed twelve more packages. Mostly Zane Grey novels. Scott loved those. They reminded him of the good times on Catalina, helped him purge the bad associations he had with the place.

The chemist kept coming through and never charged me a dime. That might sound weird to you if all your drug experiences started in the post-Reagan, Just Say No era, but it made perfect sense to me. This was Silicon Valley, after all, where computers and psychedelics produced some of the strangest hybrids imaginable: hypercapitalist mystics who decried the material realm as an illusion even as they amassed billions of dollars.

Steve Jobs was a lifelong LSD evangelist (though Woz wouldn't touch the stuff). He called it "one of the most important things in my life." The Valley is full of billionaires who trip, and the proximity of the Stanford chemistry labs—and all the equipment they've discarded over the years, hoarded in the homes of chem grads who work in tech and only use their degrees to make dirt-cheap, lab-grade psychedelics—means there's never a shortage of extremely pure LSD kicking around. Also DMT, MDMA, 2C-P, and a whole alphabet soup of very small, very specific molecules.

Throw in one of the world's largest fleets of private jets, able to nip down to the jungles of Costa Rica or the Mexican desert and reenter the country with only the most cursory customs inspections, and you get a similar supply of ayahuasca, peyote, and mescaline.

Once you plug into the network, there's an effectively bottomless supply of this stuff for the taking, much of it in the hands of people for whom it is too cheap to bother selling. I had a friend around then who connected with an MDMA seller over the Silk Road and bought a *kilo* of pure MDMA for $3,000.

This was pure powder MDMA, and the recreational dose is something like 100–150 mg, which means that he had between thirteen thousand and twenty thousand doses in a double thickness of gallon-sized ziplock freezer bags in his sock drawer. He made his three grand back selling a generous scoop to a friend who had a friend who was heading to Coachella and then he just started giving the stuff away.

That's the thing. While the wholesale drug distribution networks were controlled by dangerous, organized criminals, the actual production side was often just some semiretired hobbyist engineer with a lab in their garage, who produced in so much quantity, so cheaply, that selling to anyone *except* those wholesalers made no sense. The cartels paid cash. Pals got freebies, in quantities that exceeded any sane personal usage.

So it never surprised me that I was getting drugs for free. I even helped myself to a dose or two. The first time, I got sloppy and managed to dose myself while I was infusing a collection of Steven Brust novels about a wisecracking assassin and his pet dragon. It was scary at first (the trip, not the novels—they're delightful), and then I figured out what was going on and carefully put away my workbench, changed into comfortable clothes, and headed down to Glen Canyon Park, where I spent the rest of the day hiking the rugged urban trails and looking *really* closely at leaves, bugs, and the occasional critter, which may or may not have actually been there.

The second time, I took a tin of Altoids that I'd dripped with three measured drops of liquid LSD with me when I went to stay with friends at a lakeside cabin in Napa. We took them at sunset, just as we were finishing up a couple of thick tritips over the charcoal grill. We ate as the doses came on, then stared into the firelight and wandered the woody trails while we peaked, finishing up with a 3 a.m. skinny dip in the cool, clear, sweet lake as we came down. We lay out nude on beach towels and watched the stars in the moonless, cloudless sky, murmuring conversations and giggling, sometimes reaching out to touch fingertips across the whirling void.

We slept late the next day, had pancakes and coffee at noon, went for another swim, and drove home. I was a little sleepy, so I went hunting up and down the radio dial for something to keep me alert on the empty, winding roads. I found a Sunday-afternoon news-roundup show where they had a panel about *Brown v. Plata,* and I stopped hunting.

I'd followed *Plata* ever since Scott went to prison: it was a lawsuit brought by California prisoners to argue that merely serving time in the overcrowded California prison system was a violation of their Eighth Amendment rights—the right to be free from "cruel and unusual punishment."

California's got a crunchy-granola reputation, but never forget, we're the state that gave America Richard Nixon, Ronald Reagan, and Darth Vader. The three-strikes rule was pure cruelty, a recipe for putting hundreds of thousands of Californians behind bars for decades, but those Californians who voted for the measure? They weren't going to vote for anyone who'd raise their taxes to build prisons to house all these prisoners.

By 1990, the prisons were already groaning and straining under their new life-servers. A class-action suit argued that these underfunded prisons were a danger to prisoners, so the prisons appealed. They lost. They appealed again. They lost again. That only took five years—an eyeblink to someone serving twenty-five years for possession of a single rock of crack cocaine.

The state's position was simple: We don't have money, and our judges *have* to hand out life sentences, so that's that. Unfortunately for several successive state attorneys general, none of that actually mattered as far as the Eighth Amendment is concerned. Unfortunately for prisoners, the California Department of Corrections was happy to ignore court orders and no one seemed to be in a position to make them stop.

By 2001, the original 1990 case had morphed into a new case, *Plata,* which got rolled up with *Coleman,* another prisoners' class action. By 2006 (sixteen years after all this started), Governor Schwarzenegger (remember him?) declared a state of emergency.

In 2009 (now nineteen years into the case), the courts ordered California to figure out how to release 40,000 of its 150,000 prisoners and reduce the state's prisons to a mere 137.5

percent of their capacity. That court order reads as *extremely pissed off* in a way that I don't often associate with judges writing about government agencies.

The anger was justified, because the state had no plan to get down to 137.5 percent of capacity—or rather, they had a *lot* of plans, each stupider than the last, like paying prisons in *other states* to house California inmates. The obvious solutions—releasing prisoners or building bigger prisons—never came up.

So it went. I'd followed *Plata* a little even before I had a pal inside the California state system, and once Scott landed behind bars, I'd paid more attention, setting a couple of news alerts. I knew that the case had gone to the Supreme Court, but that was months before. Now, they'd rendered a judgment.

The Supremes were *pissed*. The State of California had ignored *seventy* court orders to get its shit together. The time for court orders had passed. It was time for the Supremes to hand down . . . well, *another* court order. But while the previous orders had been about improving conditions—by increasing the number of doctors or decreasing the number of prisoners per cell—the Supremes were just gonna make the State of California release prisoners. *Fuck* that three-strikes rule. The California prison system was so badly run that merely *being incarcerated* constituted cruel and unusual punishment and so violated the Eighth Amendment.

As the Sunday-show panel debated the meaning of this order, I pulled off to the side of the road and just stared out the windshield at the whizzing cars.

Scott didn't talk about getting out of prison, and I didn't bring it up. We had both decided that we would spend the next quarter century of both our lives with me mailing contraband to him in San Genesius, both of us silently aware that even a relatively safe smuggling method wasn't perfect and that just one piece of very bad luck would be the end of it for both of us.

Now, unexpectedly, Scott had a path to freedom, and so did

I. This was true, despite Antonin Scalia's vicious dissent about the risks of releasing "fine physical specimens who have developed intimidating muscles pumping iron in the prison gym"—which shocked even the Sunday commenters—and Clarence Thomas's sadistic remarks about not "rewarding" healthy prisoners by releasing them early.

Scott and I might go free. So might thousands of other prisoners, and the families who were unfree the way I was, and in worse ways. The California prisons were so bad, they were literally indefensible. If the state had figured out how to make even a thin pretense of fixing the system, it might have escaped judgment. But no—it was so bad that it would now get good.

8

Let me give you a little life tip. If you are ever tempted to hold out hope that life will get better for America's prisoners, in even the tiniest ways, *avoid that temptation.*

America will *never* make life better for the millions of souls it has imprisoned. Never. It is not in our character. To be an American is to live with the festering background knowledge that you are in a land that imprisons more of its people than any country in the history of the world—a land with more prisoners than Stalin's USSR or Hu Jintao's China or P. W. Botha's Apartheid South Africa.

With so many in prison, either you have to believe that you are living in the midst of a great many secret criminals, or you have to confront the fact that you live in a place where the only thing standing between you and *decades* in a prison (running at two or three times its nominal capacity) is luck . . . and *connections.*

Most Americans don't have *connections* and luck is an inconstant companion, and so we have mostly decided that the truth is that a legion of secret criminals lurk among our neighbors and that our overstuffed prisons are so full only because so many of us deserve to grow old as caged animals.

To extend even the tiniest bit of mercy (or even empathy) to our incarcerated brothers and sisters is to admit the possibility that they don't belong there. If they don't belong there, then we are a nation that imprisons people who should be free. If that is true, than you or I or anyone else might end up in prison.

The belief in prisoners' just desserts is an emotional defense mechanism, as is the racism it depends on, because anyone who pays even a scintilla of attention to prisoners will know that the carceral state is not an equal-opportunity predator. It has an insatiable appetite for brown and Black flesh.

Sovereign Corrections and Rehabilitation assumed management of San Genesius State Penitentiary two weeks after the Supreme Court's *Plata* ruling. The timing wasn't a coincidence. The State of California was desperate to keep as many of its prisoners locked up as possible, because the voters of California wanted it that way.

But California voters did *not* want to pay higher taxes, and the Supreme Court wasn't going to let the state maintain the current crowding and understaffing. The state needed to free up money to build, renovate, and staff prison facilities, because that was the only way it could keep so many Californians locked up.

Enter SCAR. SCAR itself was less than a year old: it was a private-equity-funded "roll-up" of a dozen smaller prison companies—a grab bag of companies that supplied prisons with contract doctors and nurses or shrinks and counselors, companies that provided security systems from metal detectors to cameras and listening devices for prison phones, companies that ran commissaries or shipped quarterly packages from a thick catalog.

SCAR's private-equity backers bought and merged all of these companies and "rationalized" them by firing half their administrators and most of their IT people. They also borrowed heavily against the companies' future earnings and paid themselves a "special dividend" of half a billion dollars.

Ratcatchers used to speak of the king rats, when several sewer rats found their tails hopelessly entangled (in some versions, the ratcatchers would do the tangling, as a kind of journeyman project), fusing the vicious, swarming mass into a single, snarling spiderlike thing, a scuttling abomination that squirms and writhes and snaps as each formerly free rat finds itself part of a superorganism. Those individual rats are at war with one another, fighting for food, fighting for control over the direction of the whole. They are also at war with the world.

Behold, the private-equity roll-up: a king rat made of jealous, bickering companies, all vying to dominate each other and the public at the same time.

That was SCAR. That was who took over San Genesius State Penitentiary, with the mission of saving the State of California money by delivering prisoner "care" at lower prices than the state ever managed, while still realizing the profits that would allow SCAR to make its interest payments on the half-billion-dollar debt its corporate owners had extracted on their way in.

SCAR's press release promised that they would "realize efficiencies" that would result in the savings that would allow it to treat more prisoners better with less money while still making a tidy profit.

But: If the managers responsible for the prison failed to make a profit, the shareholders would fire them. If those same managers failed to deliver adequate care for their prisoners, well . . .

Well, they could file a class-action suit, just like those prisoners did in 1990. Twenty-one years later, they might just arrive at the point where they could . . . file another class-action suit.

The most obvious, immediate change was a halt to quarterly packages. From now on, all packages would be ordered out of SCAR's brick-thick catalog of gifts suitable for the incarcerated, like a Sears catalog where all the appliances were housed in transparent casings. The section of Father's Day, Mother's Day, and birthday cards (starting at $8.99) was prodigious.

If you were thinking of sending a hand-drawn birthday card, or even one with a handwritten message from a loved one, well, that was still an option—sort of. All you had to do was mail that card (or any other letter) to SCAR's postal facility and they would scan it and let your imprisoned loved one know where to get it.

The scanning was free! But receiving the scan was another matter.

SCAR had bought thousands of ruggedized Chinese Android tablets, ten-inch models with five-years-out-of-date processors. Each prisoner was given one of these absolutely free.

The tablets were free.

Every click cost money.

SCAR did away with the prison library, but they replaced it with an electronic library, containing thousands of titles, each one just a third more than Amazon's price for the same book. Prisoners who were lost in one of these good books could entertain themselves with some fun music chosen from a library of millions of tracks, each one a mere two dollars—double the price for the same music at iTunes.

And prisoners could get and receive as much email as they wanted, including those scanned handwritten birthday cards from their kids—at the price of a mere $0.25 per page.

Yes, per *page*. SCAR insisted that there was such a thing as a "page" of email—that being the amount of text that would fit on one of those ten-inch tablets' screens at a time. Call it two hundred words. Photos were extra—a dollar each—but in SCAR's defense, they *did* offer a discount on their per-page rate for ebooks, which cost ten dollars and up (instead of the hundreds of dollars they'd cost if the "per page" scam were applied to them).

The best part? SCAR was going to reconnect inmates to their loved ones inside. Not only would inmates be able to get emails from their kids and girlfriends and parents and wives (at twenty-five cents per page), but their tablets would let them make calls—including video calls—any time they wanted.

It only cost three dollars per minute. Eight dollars per minute if you turned on the video.

If that sounds like a lot of money, it is. If that sounds like a lot of money for a family whose loved one is in prison and not outside, working his job, contributing to the household finance: it *is*.

Now, driving all the way to Vacaville is pretty burdensome, especially if you're a mom on your own raising one or more kids while their father is locked up. But once you got there, you could have hours of face-to-face contact with your family member without spending another dime, except for whatever you fed to the vending machines in the visitation room.

At eight bucks a minute, you'd have to buy a hell of a lot from the vending machine before a video visit penciled out as a bargain. Getting poor, desperate family members of imprisoned men to spend their scarce cash on fuzzy videoconferences over slow prison Wi-Fi was always going to require some selling.

SCAR had an unbeatable sales pitch. They ended *all* in-person visits.

Because with no outside mail and no visitors, SCAR would be able to save a *bundle*. They could cut the hours of the guards who searched and supervised visitors. They could cut the hours of the guards who searched cells for contraband.

Beyond those savings, there were the earnings: Twenty-five cents per page for email. One dollar for a photo. Two dollars for an MP3. Ten dollars for an ebook. Three dollars per minute for voice calls. Eight dollars per minute for video calls.

That was how SCAR was going to do more with less, operating San Genesius State Pen for less than the California Department of Corrections ever managed, while still paying dividends to its private-equity owners and servicing the half-billion-dollar debt they'd saddled the prison with.

Scott didn't accept my first call. I'd created an account with SCAR's Prisoner Interaction Platform and lodged my credit card with them, a process that took a mere twenty-five minutes, thanks to all the times I needed to reload the SCAR website before I could complete the process.

After that, I was able to initiate a call. My browser spawned a postage-stamp-sized pop-up window and my computer's speakers issued a klaxon blatt, redolent of East Berlin in old movies. *Blatt,* it went, *blatt blatt,* and then there was a sad *bloop* and a DISCONNECTED message popped up on my screen.

I sent Scott an email asking when I should call and checked the box that let me pay the fees for him to read it and reply. A day later, I saw that he'd read it, but he didn't reply that day, or the next, or the next.

I tried to call again. This time, I didn't even get the DISCONNECTED message, just persistent *blatt blatt* until I gave up.

After that, I emailed him once a week and called two days after. Two weeks went by. Three. I was busy with a chewy new job that occupied all of my attention.

I'd taken it because it paid well, but it paid well because it was a rush: there was a merger hanging in the balance and one of the backers got cold feet when he saw the balance sheet, convinced there was a leak somewhere, going into someone's pockets. I could see why he thought that—the accounts did have a kind of funny and highly suggestive shape to them—but I was pretty sure it was just an anomaly.

You can't prove a negative, though, so the best you can do is imagine every single way your adversary could be attacking you and rule it out. It's time-consuming. As Goldfinger tells Bond, "Once is happenstance. Twice is coincidence. The third time it's enemy action." There were a lot of coincidences in those books. Were they the *same* coincidence? Because that would be *awfully* coincidental.

It was creative work. I had to pretend to be an evil genius, coming up with every plan of which I could conceive, then check for evidence that this scheme was actually taking place. I'd get into these reveries thinking of ways to steal from the company, my mind wandering, and then, abruptly, Scott would pop up in my mind's eye, and I'd check and confirm that no, he hadn't answered my email yet.

I found myself dwelling on Scott at bedtime when I was falling asleep. I found myself coming back to him when I was in the shower.

Fuck.

I was pretty sure the guy my client thought might be crooked wasn't crooked. If he was crooked, he was a lot smarter than me. I told my client that, and gave them a folder with all the different ways I'd come up with to scam them and showed them why I didn't think any of those methods had been used, and I told them if they thought of any scams I'd missed, I'd check it out.

They paid me—25 percent of the amount they thought had been stolen—and now I didn't have to work until June. It was January.

I started calling Scott more often. Back when I was a teenager, I'd built an autodialer: a blue box that I could insert between my phone and the wall. It would put the line in an off-hook state, dial my target number as fast as the telephone switch on the other end could receive it, wait exactly eleven seconds for an answering modem, then, if none arrived, disconnect and reconnect the line as fast as the phone system would register it and dial again. It was like an early drum machine making the world's least funky beat: buzz-boopboopboopboopboopboopboop-unh-unh-unh-click-buzz and repeat.

As unfunky as this beat was, there was something very satisfying about the buzz-and-boop-and-click-and-buzz rhythm in the background while I did homework or read a novel. As long as that beat was going, I knew that I'd be the next person who got through to the BBS I was dialing up, within seconds of the previous caller disconnecting. I also used this tool to win every concert ticket my local radio station gave away, until they finally barred me from participating in future giveaways.

Then, one 3 a.m., I rolled out of bed, fretful and bleary, made a pot of coffee, and created an autodialer to connect to Scott's SCAR tablet. I set it to run in the background, muting sound from the browser tab it was running in to silence that awful Soviet-sounding ringtone, and to unmute the tab and play a loud fanfare when and if Scott picked up.

I scheduled it from 7 a.m. to 9 p.m.—the window in which calls were allowed—and then I drove to the park and went for a walk. It wasn't the first time I'd found myself walking around a park in the hours between 2 a.m. and sunrise and truth be told, it wasn't a bad alternative to sleep. I often got good ideas in a park in the dark.

No ideas came that night, so I just walked and fretted and tried to imagine what it would be like if I were Scott, caged for decades to come, having found peace and then had it snatched away from me.

I stopped at a café for breakfast at 6 a.m., waiting while the morning barista unlocked and brought in the bakery trays and turned on the lights. The machines had been on for hours, she explained: "You gotta preheat the boilers, let all the expansion normalize, get the whole thermal mass evenly heated, so it'll produce a consistent extraction."

Her tattooed forearms bunched and relaxed as she dialed in her grinder, making a couple of shots while she watched a digital timer, adjusting the grind each time, then finally nodding and pulling herself a double and sipping it before making me my latte. I bought a flaky croissant to go with it—the hipsterization of San Francisco has its good points—and sipped and nibbled as I walked home.

It's always a little disorienting, the first couple of weeks after a big job. Every time, I have to learn how to do nothing all over again, and it gets harder every time. Sometimes, I worry that I'll completely lose the capacity for it and end up retired and restless for years and decades.

Yes, I eventually figured it out.
　No, I don't miss it.
　Yes, I'm not lying.
　Honestly.
　Okay, don't believe me, then. Your loss, toots.

I did a crossword puzzle, paid a couple of bills, and tried to read a novel. But my eyes kept sliding to my phone, where I was watching the time tick up to 7 a.m., and then, at 6:59, I opened my laptop and fired up my autodialer.

I don't know what I was thinking, honestly. Scott wasn't a hard-rock station giving away Jethro Tull tickets. He was a prisoner in a state corrections facility. The reason I couldn't get through to him is that he wouldn't pick up—it wasn't that his line was being clobbered by fast-fingered adolescents dying to dedicate "The Number of the Beast" to their schoolyard crushes.

I keep a list of between-job projects, though I don't like calling them that. I really want to get to the point where the paid work is between-project *jobs*, but my old man drummed his engineer's work ethic into me and I can't seem to get shut of it.

I went over the list. Half of it was things I had all the supplies on hand for but had no interest in; the other half was things I could easily have lost myself in, but needed to gather a lot of esoteric materials to try out (I'd been watching lockpicking videos on YouTube and I wanted very badly to try my hand at it).

So I took my project list and started a to-do list based on it, listing one next step for each of the projects, ideally something that could be done in just a few minutes. All the while, I kept my laptop at my elbow, speaker cranked up, autodialer tab in the foreground, waiting for Scott to pick up, jumping every time I heard a noise, convinced it was my call-connected tone.

There was a hot new pho place on Twenty-Fourth Street that I'd been eyeing up during my work crunch, promising myself a leisurely, noodle-slurping lunch, even if it meant standing in the long line that kicked off every day at eleven thirty and persisted until at least 2 p.m. Supposedly they had incredible broth. It *smelled* incredible.

But to go to the pho place, I'd have to close my laptop's lid. The thought made me anxious: What if the lid was closed during the window in which Scott would have answered?

My mental model of Scott's lack of response was utterly confused. Half the time I imagined him as a radio DJ with a busy line. The other half of the time I pictured him as a harried executive who had too many things to juggle and couldn't answer the phone.

And then I'd remember that he was probably locked in a cell, or at least in a wing, and if he wasn't answering me, it was probably because he was choosing not to. Or, perhaps, he couldn't: maybe he was in the hospital wing, or in solitary, or . . .

Scott picked up at 8:58 p.m., just as I was getting involved with a DVD box set of pre–Hays Code detective movies, noir pictures that predated the Hollywood morality police, where crime really *did* pay, good guys were chumps, and everybody smoked, drank, and boasted about screwing like rabbits, even if that action was mostly offstage.

I was just watching Clive Brook as "Rolls Royce" Wensel planning a jailbreak with Evelyn Brent as "Feathers" McCoy when my laptop made an old-fashioned modem squeal. I had finally managed to relax into the idea that I wasn't going to reach

Scott and my subconscious had stopped being vigilant for that sound effect, so when it detonated I jolted and swore.

I managed to drop both my laptop and the TV remote as I fumbled for both, and I got down on all fours to flip my laptop over and get my face in the camera's field as I scrambled for the remote and muted the movie.

My autodialer had foregrounded the browser and flipped to its tab as soon as it connected, so I found myself staring at a postage-stamp-sized video of Scott. I got into a cross-legged seat and positioned my laptop and zoomed up the video to a large, pixelated swarm.

"Scott!" I said. "God, buddy—"

He looked like shit, drawn and haggard, and it looked like his hairline had receded a full inch in just a couple of months. Even in pixelated blurrycam, he looked like death.

"Marty, what the fuck." His voice was flat and buzzed with compression artifacts. "What the fuck."

My mental model of who I'd been calling lurched 180 degrees. I'd been making his tablet buzz *all day* and no matter what he did, he couldn't stop it.

"I'm sorry," I said. "I was worried about you and you weren't answering me—"

"No," he said. "I wasn't." Tinny voices from the background leaked into the silence, shouting and talking and calling out. "Forget about me, Marty," he said at last. "I'm done."

The way he said "I'm done" made the blood drain out of my face and hands. "Scott, come on, we can figure this out—"

A buzzer sounded. "It's lights-out," he said. "Goodbye, Marty."

The lights behind him flicked off and the call terminated itself.

9

I couldn't forget about him, of course. I tried to enjoy my leisure, throwing myself into the project I'd picked—refurbishing a DEC PDP-11, a classic minicomputer that I'd bought on eBay from an estate sale. It had been in a leaky barn for years and there was mold on some of the boards, but it had good bones and they'd sold zillions of these so parts weren't hard to find. Never mind that the corner Walgreens sold singing greeting cards with more processor power: I'd have given a pinky finger and one ear for one back when I was twenty, when they cost $20,000—the same as a decent two-bedroom house in Colma.

But all I could think about was Scott. I'd retired my dialer, of course. I mailed him a letter, handwritten, posting it to the SCAR depot to be opened, scanned, and discarded. I included a completed credit-card form that paid Scott's fees to read it.

I emailed the mystery chemist and told him I wouldn't need a shipment. He wrote back to say he understood and let me know he would be there for me if I needed him again.

I still had a leftover LSD-doped Altoid rattling around in the tin, in a ziplock baggie that I'd sucked all the air out of and stored in a cool corner in the back of my bedroom closet. I had no urge to take it alone and wasn't sure who else I could invite along for a trip if I wanted to split it.

I got the PDP up and running and refreshed my knowledge

of VAX operating system syntax. I managed to configure a vintage network card and get it on the internet and then spent a fruitless couple of days trying to get a port of lynx—a text-only browser for Unix—to compile.

Eventually, I found a message board where the person who'd done the port admitted that they'd never gotten it to work and I gave up. Instead, I played through Adventure from beginning to end, really getting into it. It was as satisfying as ever, decades later. Interactive fiction is one of those genres that was basically perfected by the people who invented it.

I was so worried about Scott.

> Martin, my commissary autopayment has stopped. I wonder if you wouldn't mind poking around and seeing if you could get it started again.-Scott

That was how our correspondence began again. Those dry sentences turned out to belie a profound and desperate despondency.

SCAR had changed payment processors, so Scott's scheduled payments had been bouncing, sending messages to his unattended email account. Working by SCAR email, I got him to send me the necessary credentials to get into his account and redirect the payment. I also changed all the passwords, because of course SCAR was snooping on every word of this conversation and that meant that some random, underpaid contractor could gain access to Scott's bank account.

> Thanks. It's a relief to be able to get books again. When my account went negative, I got locked out of all my ebooks and other media (music, videos, etc). If it hadn't been for your prepaid replies, I'd have been stuck.

It was so normal, like any old email. I cautiously replied.

> I'm glad to hear it, Scott, and happy to help. What are you reading?

I prepaid for the reply and it came almost immediately.

> All the Brust books, starting with Jhereg. They're GREAT. Just plain ROMPS.

Jhereg was one of the books I'd sent in my first shipment of LSD-laced paperbacks.

I ordered copies of the book and the rest of the series and started reading them. Scott was right, they were romps, but by no means plain. What started out as a swashbuckling sword-and-sorcery series about a magical assassin and his wisecracking, psionic fantasy lizard familiar quickly turned into an extremely subtle social commentary.

I had never read a fantasy novel where the ratio of peasants to lords was more true to historical reality, and the books recapitulated a hundred years of Marxist revolutionary history in allegory that was at once thinly veiled and completely integrated into some extremely swashbuckling fantasy adventures.

Talking about *Jhereg* opened the door to more topics, and soon we became pen pals of a sort, with me pasting in newspaper articles and blog posts so that we could discuss them. Scott was fascinated by the foreclosure epidemic, as the banks that crashed the world economy and then got bailed out with public funds turned around and used it to take away their customers' homes.

He got into some truly epic rants on the subject and eventually I was able to talk him into letting me set up a pseudonymous blog to post them on. He attracted a modest readership and I pasted their comments into our email and pasted his replies back into the blog.

That led to our first video call. There was a troll on his blog who was chasing away the good commenters, but Scott wanted to argue with him, not block him. I emailed Scott that I found it very frustrating to watch him throw away his time on this bozo and he got pretty salty about how much time he had and how little there was to fill it, and I replied that *my* time wasn't nearly so abundant, and he called me some names, and I stopped replying, and then, the next day, he meekly asked if I had time for a call.

"I'm sorry," the postage-stamp-sized video of Scott said, his voice buzzing with compression artifacts that made him sound like a Dalek. He looked as sorry as a pixelated miniature could, but he also looked *good*. Seeing him released a huge knot of worry I only half knew I was carrying, left over from my brief glimpse of him before when he'd answered my war-dialer to tell me to fuck off already.

"It's okay," I said. "I don't mind. I'm having one of my extended vacations and I've already refurbished a VAX system, so I needed another project. It's just that arguing with this asshole, even by proxy, is no good for my mental health."

As I said the words, I couldn't stop marveling at how good Scott looked. I'd been convinced that he was as good as dead—he'd already made one attempt at it, after all. But he looked like he had it figured out: keep reading, keep writing, keep the connections alive.

He was visibly relieved. "You're right, you're right. I don't need to be arguing with that asshole. Just block him." He grinned. "Hey, I've been reading a book that's going to blow you away. It's called *The Information,* by James Gleick."

"The chaos guy?"

"Yeah," he said. "It's a history of information theory, but it's so much more than that. Imagine that those hippie-trippy Bay

Area cybernetic mystics actually knew what they were talking about, and that they could *write,* and then they turned out this incredible narrative that was also a super-deep philosophical inquiry into the very meaning of meaning itself—"

And we were off. I interrupted him partway through to order a copy for overnight delivery. We spent the next week exchanging emails about it, and then we had another video call, four hours' worth, where we dissected the book, chapter by chapter, with interludes to talk about everything else, from prison gossip to tech news. Scott had a morbid fascination with the rise and rise of Facebook, having known Zuckerberg socially and considering him "a fucking creep."

A week later, we were through with *The Information* and on to Bruce Schneier's *Liars and Outliers,* a popular information security book with an emphasis on the social dimensions of trust and security, which we both liked a *lot,* and also related to, given that I had logins to drain Scott's bank account and there wasn't a damned thing he could do about it if I turned on him.

After that one, I abandoned any pretense that I was doing a project with my time off. My project was Scott. The Scott and Marty Book Club. I started to paste the weekend book reviews from the *LA Times, San Francisco Chronicle,* and *NYT* into emails and Scott and I built out a long reading list.

We kept it up for four months.

Four months!

I've had some close male friendships before, but the relationship Scott and I built during those months was unlike any I'd ever had. There's something about having a pen pal who has all the time in the world to think about your last note and to compose his reply. It's weirdly flattering to have someone else pay that much attention to communicating with you.

But after four months, my reserves were pretty depleted, and I took a job auditing the books of a family IT consultancy whose founder had just died, and whose heirs thought they were being ripped off by his business partner. It turned out the partner *was* skimming, but just a little, and no more than the dead guy had—they both had a tacit agreement to pad their expenses, just not too much.

The actual reason the family got so much less than they'd expected was that the dead guy had been lying to *them* about how well the business was doing. We'd agreed to a fee of 25 percent of whatever irregularities I discovered in the books, which came out to a couple of bags of groceries for two weeks' work.

Win some, lose some.

My bank balance was dipping low and while I had a little cushion, I didn't want to touch it because it was tied up in tech stocks and everything was down. I hustled and ended up with some hourly contract work for a friend's start-up that needed a pinch-hitter CFO.

It wasn't quite a nine-to-five, but it was closer than I liked and I was profoundly relieved when I got a job for a Canadian company in Waterloo, Ontario, that had lost three million dollars' worth of investment capital that had been provided by a Research in Motion founder.

Turning the BlackBerry into a commercial success made you very rich, but not so rich that three million bucks didn't matter, especially since Apple and Google had sewn up the mobile-operating-system market for the rest of time, meaning there was no more Crackberry money on the way, so this guy took the losses seriously.

Fortunately for me, the start-up's founder had been siphoning funds off into his personal accounts. Unfortunately for Mr. Crackberry, the kid had already spent half of it at a Windsor casino. Fortunately for Mr. Crackberry, the kid had gambled the other half on Bitcoin, which was up a hair, and I was able to do some blockchain forensics to find it.

That gave Mr. Crackberry the ammo he needed to confront his problematic investee, who surrendered $1.5 million Canadian in exchange for a promise not to go to the cops. I got 25 percent of that, which took me out of the grind again.

Mr. Crackberry was actually happy in the end because the kid had an idea to combine offshore gambling and crypto that sounded absolutely ghastly and stupid to me, but exciting and lucrative to Mr. Crackberry.

These are not mutually exclusive, of course.

I declined their offer to come on board as a CTO, converted $375,000 Canadian to $368,000 U.S. (the U.S. dollar was in the toilet but I didn't want to hold the Canadian—I wanted to spend it). I put away 25 percent for my defined benefit pension contribution, 35 percent for taxes, and stuck the rest in my checking account: $147,200. I was flush again.

I planned to sleep in the next day but I found myself up and restless at 4 a.m. and went to the park and then the café and then got home with my croissant and realized that I could call Scott. I missed our book club.

The browser tab rang a few times and then Scott picked up. He was smiling and wide awake and I could tell something was wrong.

"Everything okay, buddy?"

He smiled wider. "Just fine."

"Okay," I said. "Only I think maybe it's not true. Talk to me? If you want to, that is?"

He closed his eyes and took a deep breath. "Look, I'm probably going to be okay, but it's the rest of the guys I'm worried about."

10

Something had changed with SCAR. It started with the food. It had always been bad. Now there wasn't enough of it. I know, I know: *The food here is terrible and the portions are so small.* But from what Scott could figure, the prisoners were on 1,500 calories a day, or maybe less.

Everyone started to get hungry. Always. Cellies shared their commissary, or begged family for more money in their accounts. Other guys got irritable, and then mean, and then they started to eat other prisoners' food. Mealtimes got *ugly*.

Commissary prices were up. Commissary portions were down. Somewhere, SCAR had found a contractor who would sell them a 4.32-ounce can of tuna that only had 3.9 ounces in it. They didn't even bother to make up the extra space with water. Prisoners built balance scales out of string woven from sheet threads passed through either end of a toothbrush handle teetering on a table corner, and weighed the new tuna against the old.

There were fewer guards, too, which had a ripple effect through prison life. Head counts took longer and sometimes cut into yard time or meal time. Fights didn't get broken up as quickly, or sometimes weren't broken up at all. The prisoners did all the important work around the prison, but they had to be supervised by guards, whether they were manning the commissary or mopping the floors. If guards weren't available, the work wasn't done.

The tablets started to break. They'd *always* broken, but they'd been the one thing that SCAR could be relied on to replace quickly, since a broken tablet was a tablet that stopped producing revenue for SCAR. SCAR wouldn't swap you a new tablet just because your screen was cracked or because the battery was so worn out that it only worked when it was plugged in, but once it was completely unusable, it would be sent to a depot for refurbishment and replaced with another refurb.

But one day, that stopped. A prisoner finally managed to snag one of the elusive guards and ask for a swap-out, and the guard took the old model but never came back with a new one. Days ticked by. A week. The prisoner caught up with the guard, who shrugged and said, "You'll get it when you get it."

Other tablets broke and disappeared. The tablets weren't just the prisoners' music, video, and book library, weren't just their lifeline to mail and voice calls and video calls, they were also their interface to the commissary. Fifteen hundred calories a day and no commissary made things *mean*.

There were more fights. The guards stopped pretending they were breaking them up. There were fewer guards anyway. Scott heard two of them talking about taking a buyout package from the new owners.

SCAR had new owners.

"What do you know about them?" I asked. Scott's camera had stopped working, so we were stuck on voice calls.

"Not much," he said. "No one tells us anything but the rumor mill says that we're getting a new warden next week and that nothing is going to change until he arrives. Maybe you can poke around SCAR's corporate filings?"

"I can definitely do that. You don't want me to try to talk to a journalist, though? This can't be legal."

"Buddy, from what you tell me, California is broke. No one's going to give a shit about what happens in a state pen. You're a forensic accountant, not a muckraker. Stay in your lane, all right?"

I pretended I wasn't offended. "Sure thing. Sorry, Scott. I just—"

He sighed. "I know. I'm just hungry. Makes a man irritable."

"I thought your commissary was still working? Aren't the bank transfers still good?"

"They're fine but getting food delivered right now is bad for your health. No one wants to admit to being able to get extra chow. Some of these guys are in a bad way, losing their judgment and their cool. They're looking at decades more time and thinking about what twenty years of starvation diet will be like."

"Shit," I said.

"Yup," he said.

"Okay, I'll get digging."

I figured out what had happened to SCAR the same day they announced. The private-equity firm that had rolled up SCAR and saddled it with a half-billion dollars in debt was just one of eight similar operations nationwide, and now *they* had been rolled up in an even *bigger* PE play, this one led by Thames Estuary Management.

You'd think that Thames Estuary was based in London, or at least somewhere in the actual Thames estuary, but you'd be wrong. The company was registered in Nevada and its actual headquarters were in Long Beach, CA. I *did* find a related Bermudan company, but that was just a vehicle for base-eroding profit-shifting: Thames Estuary had some registered trademarks that it had sold to the Bermudan company and licensed back for hundreds of millions of dollars per year.

The Bermudan company—Dark Gulch Holdings—siphoned off all the profits in trademark licensing fees, ensuring that Thames Estuary showed no taxable profits as far as the IRS and the California Franchise Tax Board were concerned.

This wasn't Thames Estuary's first rodeo. The year before, it had bought and flipped a hundred nursing homes. The purchases were 95 percent debt-funded to the tune of $450 million, meaning they were playing with other people's money. They laid off some staff and consolidated the homes' back offices, renegotiated deals with Hillrom, a giant company that made both caskets and hospital beds, and fired the unionized nurses in all their Illinois facilities.

This reshuffling paid off . . . a little. Thames Estuary sold its nursing homes to Live Street Capital, a front for the Bahraini royals, who paid them $475 million. A $25 million profit on an investment of $450 million might not sound like much, but remember, Thames Estuary only put up 5 percent, that is, $22.5 million, meaning it more than doubled its money. .

In reality, they had to use some of that to service the debt and pay transaction fees to their investment bankers, but don't worry! Half of what remained they paid to themselves as "carried interest" (a tax loophole invented by sixteenth-century sea captains and beloved of hedge-fund managers) and the rest got laundered through Dark Gulch and ended up bobbing in azure Caribbean waters in a state of tax-free grace.

The nursing-home caper made for a good calling card. Thames Estuary could have used it to raise cash from rich Silicon Valley "pioneers," wealthy dentists, and other usual suspects, but it changed tactics: it went public.

Now, taking Thames Estuary through an IPO would have been messy and potentially embarrassing. When you list your company on a stock exchange, you allow any schmuck to invest in it, and the SEC doesn't like to see schmucks get ripped off. An IPO means opening your books, making mandatory disclosures, and, in the wake of Enron, the possibility of prison sentences for lying or omitting on those disclosures.

But Thames Estuary was on the cutting edge of financial sleaze. They went public through a special-purpose acquisition company—a.k.a., a "SPAC." SPACs are "blank-check companies"—

companies that *have* no business and *do* no business. You'd think that having no business and doing no business would be a liability when it comes to attracting investors, but remember, if you have nothing and do nothing, you can disclose *everything* and still not fill a sheet of paper. Investors hate reading.

A SPAC is an empty vessel. A group of "smart guys"—say, the people who doubled their money while enshittifying a hundred nursing homes—file the paperwork to create a public company, one that any average schmuck can put money into. The paperwork is easy, because the SPAC doesn't do any business. It says, "We're a SPAC. We have nothing. We do nothing. Give us your money, and we'll buy a company that is doing stuff. We will apply our special genius to that company and make it more profitable, and when we do that, your ten-dollar shares will increase in value and you can sell them and make money, too."

The first time you hear about a SPAC, you may assume you're misunderstanding. It sounds like a scam. Normal IPOs require people to explain how their business works before they take it public. SPACs don't have a business until *after* they go public, which means they can skip all those tedious disclosures that are supposed to protect normal schmucks, rake in their ten-dollar share purchases, *then* use the money to go on a shopping spree.

No, you didn't misunderstand that.

SPACs are as obvious a scam as you could ask for, a completely transparent ruse to bypass disclosure rules. In fact, calling SPACs a transparent ruse is an insult to good, hardworking transparent ruses all around the world.

So why would anyone hand them their money? More to the point, why did average schmucks hand Thames Estuary's SPAC $750 million when it IPOed? Couldn't they see it was a scam?

I've talked to a lot of people who've invested in scams and I estimate that at least half the time, they know it's a scam, but they figure they're *in on it*. After all, what do you call what happened in 2008, when the richest bankers in the world crashed the global economy, got trillions of dollars in bailouts, and walked away even richer? It's a *scam*. Obviously, the fact that something is a *scam* doesn't make it a *bad investment*.

Flush with average schmucks' ten-dollar shares, the founders of Thames Estuary went to the banks that had financed their nursing-home scam and levered the money up to $11 billion. They paid themselves a one-billion-dollar special dividend, then made generous offers on those eight prison roll-ups and merged them into one *very* large private prison company—a private prison *system*.

That required disclosure, and they released a fat PDF full of ways to make money. For example, they were going to solve the California prison-crowding problem by sending California prisoners to Arizona, New Mexico, Colorado, and Utah.

Normally, this would be frowned upon because prisoners who are sent out of state end up isolated from their families, who can't get the time off work to drive across state lines to see their loved ones. Maintaining family connections is widely understood to be correlated with successful rehabilitation, and, contrariwise, prisoners who drift away from their families while they're inside are much more likely to reoffend after their release.

But the prisoners in Thames Estuary's care wouldn't have that problem: whether they were locked up in their hometowns or on the dark side of the moon, the visitation process would be the same—an eight-dollar-per-minute video call, or a three-dollar-per-minute voice call. That was pricey for a family whose breadwinner was serving fifteen years, but don't worry; Thames Estuary had a financing arm that was going to offer easy credit to those families. The APR was a strictly humanitarian *443 percent*. The same subsidiary was prepared to offer comparable terms to parolees and ex-prisoners who needed a loan to get back on their feet.

It was just one of the many synergies that were going to justify the giant SPAC cash infusion and safeguard the flow of debt payments to Deutsche Bank and JPMorgan, who had turned the $750 million in IPO money to $11 billion in total liquidity.

Reading through the documentation for the acquisition made my head hurt. It was needlessly, performatively complex—one of those deals that was complicated so it would be hard to understand, rather than being hard to understand because it was complicated. There's a certain kind of mark that assumes that any sufficiently thick prospectus *must* be a good buy, just as any sufficiently large pile of shit *must* have a pony beneath it.

I am good at slicing through that kind of document. I'd been at it so long—more than three decades, by then—that I did it by reflex and sometimes I didn't even realize that I was at it until I talked to some hapless civilian who professed bafflement or revealed their grave misconceptions about a scam whose contours I'd immediately grasped.

It wasn't the bafflegab and chaff that made my head hurt; it was the fact that it had *worked*. A lot of average schmucks had fallen for it, and so had the loan officers at two of the world's largest financial institutions—institutions that had been at the brink of collapse thanks to bad loans just a few years before and only existed today thanks to the public bailouts that rescued them.

When I started out in this business, my mental model was that 80 percent of business was real and 20 percent was scams. When the S&L crisis hit, I recalibrated to 70/30. After Enron, the dot-bomb, and the subprime crisis, I was at 40/60. Reading the paperwork from Thames Estuary, I felt like the *entire* economy had become a scam, and any real businesses remaining were incidental residue.

Thames Estuary had built a king rat without parallel.

The majority of prisons in eight states would be a machine for transferring billions from the public purse to Thames Estuary's executives and shareholders. It wasn't just their loan-sharking subsidiary, or the commissary subsidiary, or the quarterly-package subsidiary, or the subsidiary that sold cameras and monitoring tools. It wasn't the halfway houses, or the ankle-cuff monitoring, or the chain of bail bondsmen who offered "seamless integration" with the local jails Thames Estuary had acquired in its massive roll-up.

It was *all* of it. To hell with king rats, this was a *machine,* a million-armed robot whose every limb was tipped with a needle that sank itself into a different place on prisoners and their families and drew out a few more cc's of blood.

One of Thames Estuary's subsidiaries was Prisonsy, a former fintech start-up that pivoted to processing prison commissary payments, then expanded its offerings to ebooks, games, videos, and music.

All of that was sold in an app store that came locked to a tablet, which they would generously provide, free of charge, to every prisoner in their care. It would serve as the prisoners' portal to email, voice calls, and videoconferencing.

It would replace the tablets that prisoners had received under previous prison operators, including SCAR. Which was good, because for months, all of those prison operators had drawn down their maintenance programs, eventually killing them altogether, so that every prison in Thames Estuary's care had been transformed into a scrap heap of e-waste.

Giving all those prisoners shining new tablets was a kindness.

And if none of the media they'd previously purchased was carried over to their new devices, well, that was a small price to pay for a serious upgrade, wasn't it?

11

Scott was more philosophical than I was. "It was in the terms of service all along," he joked, and a half second later, his tiny, pixelated face flickered into a wry smile. "The fine print is very clear: we bought *licenses,* not books or music. The license was tied to our tablets. When the tablets went into the trash, the licenses went with them."

"I know you're joking," I said, "but it is just such an evil little scam. I know you can afford to replace your library, but what about the prisoners who don't have a couple million in the bank? From what you told me, they spent money on books and music they couldn't afford, and they *really* can't afford to buy them again."

Another half-second delay and Scott's face grew more serious. "Yeah," he said. "Yeah, that's right. There's guys in here who might not read another book for the next ten years at this point, unless their ex-wives take pity on them and throw them a little commissary." He sighed. "I guess that's truly the end of the book club." Scott's book club had rallied after the ban on print books, focusing on public-domain titles from Project Gutenberg, which were free on the SCAR tablets.

"Surely you haven't read every decent book written prior to 1923?" There were a few books that were in the public domain that had been published later than then, but figuring out which was hard. The SCAR system blocked access to the Gutenberg UK archive, where copyright tapped out at the life of the author plus fifty years, and so included everything from George Orwell to Ford Madox Ford, but the pre-1923 literary corpus had a surprising number of forgotten classics that spoke to Scott and his fellow inmates.

A half-second delay, then Scott pixelated further as he shook his head. "Blocked," he said. "If you want to read *Pilgrim's Progress* or even the Bible, you've got to buy a commercial edition from the Library Store." Another headshake. "I still can't believe they called it the Library Store. Jesus, what an Orwellian masterpiece of doublespeak. Which one is it, a library, or a store?"

"That's an excellent point. I suppose they like calling it a 'library' so no one claims that they eliminated the prison library. But they like calling it a store so their shareholders see that they're making money for them."

He nodded, another out-of-phase gesture. I realized I'd been holding my head unnaturally still out of a desire not to appear distorted on his screen, which must have been even worse than mine, given the three-generations-old processors in the free tablets Thames Estuary handed out.

"Just like the button on the old online bookstore said, *buy this book*. But then they turned around and claimed you were buying a *license* to the book. I guess they thought that even prisoners would call bullshit on a button that went *license this book*."

The conversation lapsed. I hated it when that happened. Every second of silence cost thirteen and a third cents. Scott insisted that he didn't care if he spent himself dry behind bars but I had looked up the statistics for what happened to prisoners who were released but couldn't support themselves. One month, I'd insisted that I pay for our calls and the bill was bigger than my mortgage payment. I mentioned it to Scott and he insisted on paying me back and wouldn't let me pay again.

"Well—" I said, prelude to making an excuse to end the call.

"Marty, you don't have to hang up every time there's a natural pause in the conversation. I can afford it."

I sighed. "I'd feel better about it if you'd let me pay some of the times. I'm earning income out here."

He shrugged. "My investments are doing okay, based on those emails you forwarded me from my broker." He smiled suddenly, and even with the blurrycam, I could see it was one of his wicked grins.

"Tell you what," he said. "How about if I hire you? You figure out how to get all of us our ebooks and music back and I'll pay you your customary twenty-five percent. Then you can use that money to pay for these calls."

"That's pretty baroque, Scott. You're saying that I can pay for the calls only if I let you pay me first?"

"Not just pay you—pay you to unravel a scam."

"I can't tell if you're joking or not."

"Neither can I. Look, Marty, it's a pleasure to watch you work, and from what you've told me already, Thames Estuary is a real, old-fashioned hive of scum and villainy. Someone like you should really kick over that rock and catalog whatever's living under there."

"Now you put it that way, I'm happy to do it. No need to maintain a pretense of being on a job."

His camera image suddenly flicked into a clear, high-rez stream, something that happened from time to time. The moment of clarity let me see what had been hidden by the distortion— beneath his joking tone, he was *furious*.

"Marty," he said, in clipped tones, "this company is *literally holding me prisoner*. They raised billions of dollars on the prospect of making me and millions of other people *hurt*. The worse we hurt, the better they do. I *want* to see them *taken apart*. Hell, even if that doesn't happen, I want to know who they are. I want to put names to my tormentors. I want to tell every guy in here who these motherfuckers are. The guys in here think that the prison guards are the ones responsible for their misery. I talked to one of those guys: he's twenty-six, making minimum wage, and he's contracted through a staffing agency so he doesn't get benefits. *That guy*'s not the one who's benefiting from this bullshit. I won't say he's a prisoner, too—no one knows better than me the difference between a prisoner and a guard. But even though that guy's got it a million times better than me in a million ways, he's still in a deeply shitty situation.

"Somewhere out there are some motherfuckers with mansions and ivory-handled back scratchers and they're making payments on them with the blood and tears of prisoners in eight states. I want you to *unravel* them, Marty, the way we did that stupid hamburger racket on Catalina Island, and for the same reason. It's *uncivilized*. It's *cruel*. It is *offensive*.

"So I want to retain the services of Martin Hench. I want you to be my economic assassin, my avenging angel of the balance sheet. I will pay you an hourly rate if this weird commission thing of yours doesn't sit well with you. I'll make it worth your while, however you want. Just say the word, Marty."

Oh. "Oh. Yeah, okay, Scott. Yes, I'll do this. And if taking twenty-five percent will let you let me pay for some of these calls, then we can do it that way. But you only had to ask. Like you say, I'm not good for much, but *this* is something I know how to do."

"Marty, you are competent in many domains, as you well know. But you are a virtuoso when it comes to spotting scams. A ninja. A superhero. A rock star. A—"

"Fine," I said. "Let's stop wasting your money on airtime. I have a scam to unravel."

12

Thames Estuary's SPAC had been filing its paperwork. If you weren't paying close attention, you'd think that they were coloring inside the lines. Certainly, the average schmucks who staked it with the collateral for its Wall Street loans probably thought that everything was fine. If you bought ten ten-dollar shares then and now they're trading at twenty dollars, you're going to be smug and happy about your extra hundred dollars, but not so obsessed that you're going to pore over those boring-ass SEC forms in its shareholder portal.

Just in case you *were* curious, the fact that the disclosures were all broken up into about a hundred files might deter you. Not me: I know the magic of wget, a decades-old Unix utility that can crawl a page and download everything linked off it. Took about a minute and then I had a hundred PDFs on my desktop and I was opening them quickly, categorizing them and saving them into subfolders.

Whoever had constructed those files was a good sleight-of-hand artist. The material disclosures were buried in extremely long, flowery, overwrought narrative statements about the company's probity and vision, running to multiple pages.

I found the intelligence that the Mississippi Department of Corrections contract was the subject of a lawsuit in a single sentence on page 11 of one such document, sandwiched between a disclosure of the "risk" that crime rates were falling in Maine and that the contract they'd inherited did not have a minimum-head-count guarantee and the "risk" that grain futures were trending high and that this might shave sixteen basis points off the projected profits from their food-preparation division.

Not that these weren't interesting disclosures. The caveat about the lack of a Maine head-count guarantee implied that they *did* have a minimum-occupancy guarantee in other states—that is, they would get paid the same whether their cells were full or empty, meaning that the state had a perverse incentive to arrest and imprison more people. After all, they were going to pay for those incarcerations no matter what.

The news about wheat futures tying in to their profit projections was also interesting, but only insofar as it confirmed that the whole enterprise was being steered by stone finance freaks, the kind of people who were more interested in placing bets on crop yields than rehabilitating the army of captive human beings who were utterly at their mercy.

But that lawsuit was more interesting still. I handed over my credit card to PACER, the federal court records site, and paid ten cents a page to download all the filings. Fifty bucks later, I was reading about all the ways that the Mississippi contract was deficient, including the fact that it came with a nondisclosure agreement, meaning that the people of the Great State of Mississippi couldn't actually find out how deficient it was.

Fortunately for those people, a blundering state senator on the Corrections Committee had posted the contract to his Facebook page, thinking that he'd marked it private to a friend, along with an exhortation to buy stock in Thames Estuary and dump stock in its main rival, Corrections Corporation of America. No one told Senator Kris Tac that the file was hanging out there for all to read until Biloxi Bill, the anonymous blogger behind the *Biloxi Times,* published a scathing, scatological analysis of the contract, which got picked up by *The Clarion-Ledger* in Jackson, whence the senator hailed.

The senator quickly deleted the Facebook post, but the file was still live on biloxitimes.blogspot.com. The senator sent a copyright complaint to Google, which owned Blogspot, and the file came down, but just as quickly it went back up, accompanied by an outraged article from Biloxi Bill. That prompted the senator to contact the Mississippi Bureau of Investigation, insisting that they uncover Biloxi Bill's true identity on the grounds that he was engaged in "espionage."

Unfortunately for Senator Tac, this demand was also inadvertently posted to his Facebook wall rather than being privately relayed to the head of the MBI Executive Protection Division. Once again, the leak was published on the *Biloxi Times*, and once again, the senator sent a takedown notice to Google, which once again caved—but not before the Internet Archive got a snapshot of the page for its Wayback Machine.

I found the takedown Senator Tac sent to the Internet Archive in the Lumen database, as well as the stiffly worded reply the Internet Archive's general counsel sent back to the senator, reminding him that DMCA 512(f) provided for "damages, including costs and attorney's fees," when takedown notices were "knowingly and materially" misrepresentations. The Lumen database didn't have a follow-up notice from the senator, so I guess he got the message.

The lawsuit didn't have anything to do with Scott's commission, but it was a loose end, and I'd learned a lot from pulling on loose ends. The parties to the suit had already exchanged documents and gone through a protracted wrangle over discovery, and PACER duly coughed up a hundred dollars' worth of internal memos and balance sheets from inside Thames Estuary. These were heavily redacted—there were whole black pages where the only unredacted element was the page number in the top right corner—but I printed them out and hole-punched them and stuck them in a fat binder that I took to the park with a red pen and a box of post-it index tabs.

It was a nice, brisk autumn day, a marked contrast with the mini heat wave we'd experienced the week before. There were cavorting dogs and frisbee players to keep me company, and a couple of panhandlers came and politely inquired about my reading material and could I spare a few dollars. I gave them the money and told them I was doing my homework for an accounting course, a surefire way to head off any further nosy queries.

The litigants were mostly interested in piercing the corporate veil—that is, figuring out who they were suing. Thames Estuary Ltd.—the public company—had a dual-share structure; the majority of voting shares were owned by Thames Estuary Capital LLC, a Bahamas company, and that company's owners were a secret protected by the legendary Bahamian discretion about the origin and destination of vast capital pools.

But the litigants thought that the real money might be wrapped up in the state senator's affairs in more ways, and they were hoping to show that these shadowy figures had corrupted Mississippi politics in many high-priced ways, which would give all Mississippi taxpayers standing to sue to recover the additional costs they'd borne in higher taxes and the necessity of paying cash for public services that were never delivered. That would make for a big, fat class-action suit.

The discovery documents were a bureaucratic game of Go Fish: "Give us all your documents related to dealings between the beneficial owners of Thames Estuary LLC and this state agency." "Go fish." "How about *this* agency?" "Go fish." "What about this senator? This judge? This retired assemblyman?" Go fish, go fish, go fish.

But they were careful, and they'd done the work, cross-referencing every agency and public official in a multitiered, floridly ramified series of requests that had the telltale signs of a giant database merge.

I checked and found that they'd filed an identical set of requests from the other side, using the Mississippi Public Records Act to demand any correspondence by any state agency or official with Thames Estuary.

I liked these litigants. This was stultifyingly dull work, and even with automation tools, it probably cost a fortune just in paralegal fees, hitting each of those agencies and offices through their idiosyncratic portals and procedures.

But they hit pay dirt. The public records requests revealed documents that had been suppressed in discovery, while the discovery documents found the dirty laundry that the state had hoped to keep out of the public eye. The judge was appropriately outraged about the discovery failures, and the state ombudsman refused to be outdone, publicly excoriating the foot-dragging state agencies in fluent Old High Dudgeon.

From what I could see, the plaintiffs were steaming toward a hell of a suit, likely to get certified for their class action, with a big payday for the law firm involved and a bunch of three-dollar checks for every Mississippian. Most of them wouldn't get cashed, but the law firm's fees would run to low seven figures. Good for them.

Good for me, too. They'd taken a weed-whacker to the tangled back end of Thames Estuary and made a hell of a lot of loose threads. As noted, loose threads are something of a specialty of mine.

Being able to cross-reference the public docs and the corporate docs was so useful here: both sets were heavily redacted, but each side redacted *different* passages. I paid some Mechanical Turk workers to compare these matching docs and reverse those redactions. I started with the names and businesses they uncovered, reasoning that anything my target wanted kept secret was something I should look at closely.

Cherrystone Holdings was a Nassau company. Its officers' names were not a matter of public record, but luckily, one of those officers had signed an email to a Mississippi Department of Corrections accounts payable officer with his name and title: Aldo Jaffe, Chief Operating Officer.

Jaffe was on LinkedIn, and while he didn't list Cherrystone

Holdings in his CV, he did list a half dozen other companies, and I was able to find *their* boards, which were all nearly identical— only the secretaries differed, and a quick search confirmed that they were contractors who specialized in Bahamian corporate compliance.

One name jumped out from all those boards—Lionel Coleman Jr., who was either the CEO or COO of every single one of them.

Hello, Junior.

13

"I'd say I didn't believe it except it makes such perfect sense," Scott said.

"It's definitely him," I said. "The whole thing is basically a scaled-up version of that nasty little hamburger scam. I've been digging into how Junior spent the past decade. He's really made something of himself. Went from REITs into loan origination and Collateralized Debt Obligations. Made hundreds of millions, got an award from the LA Chamber of Commerce for services to affordable housing."

"Let me guess," Scott said, "subprime loans?"

"Got it in one. Only the subprimiest. I chased down a random sampling of ten of them and all ten were in foreclosure."

He whistled. "That takes some doing."

I nodded. "Like Goldfinger says, 'Once is happenstance, twice is coincidence, three times is enemy action.'"

"And ten times is deliberate depravity."

We chuckled, then both of us remembered that the guy we were laughing at had Scott and millions more utterly at his mercy, and stopped.

"You think he's more than a bit player in this?"

I paused. "I don't think I could prove in a court of law that he was calling the shots, not without a subpoena. But based on the way that the shell companies that hold significant stakes in the Bahamian company are structured, I would say that he controls the majority of voting shares in Thames Estuary LLC, and even though they're a minority shareholder in Thames Estuary

Limited, the shares they do own are a comfortable majority of the voting shares."

"How does *that* work?"

"Oh," I said. "I must have skipped that part. The SPAC has a two-tier share structure. The ten-dollar shares they sold to everyday shmucks are called 'preferred shares,' but that's because they get liquidation preference—they're first in line to get paid if the company goes bankrupt. But the shares that the founders hold are 'voting shares' and they get ten votes for every vote the preferred shares have. All told, the preferred shares only come out to forty percent of the voting power, so even if every one of those ten-buck chucks voted in favor of something, the founders can veto them."

"Oh, it's the Google scam."

"Pretty much." I'd gotten a good belly laugh out of Google's pre-IPO letter to potential investors warning them that the company's "genius" founders were holding on to a majority of the voting shares to prevent their small-minded investors from joggling their elbows. It had sent me down a research rabbit hole and turned me into a half expert on the practice.

"The Google boys mostly copy-pasted the share structure of News Corp—and even Rupert Murdoch pieced his share-structure scam together from previous ones. Everyone wants to get the public's money but no one wants to be accountable to the public."

"Don't know that I can blame them, to be honest." There was some shouting down the cellblock from him and he paused a moment until it died down. "One thing I can't figure is why all the secrecy? I'm no Joseph Goebbels but I can think of easy ways Junior could spin this scam to make himself look good, like he's bailing out the mismanaged public system and the privateers who stepped in to loot it."

"Yeah, I don't imagine that all the skullduggery is motivated by shame. I agree that given half a chance, Junior would love to brag on this. I bet that guy goes to bed every night and masturbates furiously at the thought that more than a million of his fellow Americans are absolutely in his power. It would be very on-brand.

"Whenever I find someone hiding their interest in a company, there's only two explanations: either they're not paying taxes, or they're screwing their investors by selling to themselves at a fat markup."

"Not both?"

"Oh sure, both too."

"Sounds like the kind of thing that the SEC and the IRS might be interested in," Scott said.

"Indeed it does."

> Mr. Hench, this note is being sent to you because you are Scott Warms's emergency contact.

> Mr. Warms has been involved in a violent incident and has been removed to the California Medical Facility in Vacaville. He has regained consciousness and he can receive visitors.

> The link below will take you to a page detailing the conditions for prisoner visits at the CMF.

> This email address is not attended and replies will not be read. If you have further queries, please contact the CMF and cite Scott Warms's inmate number.

It was unsigned.

Three inmates known to be members of the Aryan Brotherhood cornered Scott in his cell while he was reading. They smashed his tablet and then used the sharp plastic fragments, along with their fists and feet, to beat him unconscious. He had a broken jaw, two broken ribs, and lost four teeth. He was concussed and his kidneys were bruised. He was pissing blood.

The beating came within forty-eight hours of our last conversation. Scott was unreachable for the next three days. I almost missed the email because it looked so spammy, but I'd written a mail rule that flagged any messages containing "Scott Warms" and moved them to a separate folder.

I was allowed to bring Scott up to three magazines and two paperback books. After dithering for a time, I doctored the books—a nice old copy of John D. MacDonald's *The Girl, the Gold Watch & Everything* and an oversized paperback of Ostrom's *Governing the Commons*. I was pretty sure he'd enjoy both of them, regardless of the chemical additions I made.

I didn't let myself ask whether he'd be able to enjoy any books, ever, with his head injury.

Scott was doped up. I hadn't been in his presence in a year, not since SCAR took over and killed in-person visits. I had braced myself for him to look bad—no one looks good with a broken jaw—but even so.

Even so.

The lines in his skin, seamed as an elephant's. The tone of his skin. Loose. Papery. His collarbones standing out, his wristbones knobby between his thin arms and crabbed hands.

He couldn't really talk, not with his jaw wired. So I talked, foolish and nervous small talk about the traffic and my houseplants and the neighborhood stray cat that turned out not to be a stray at all, just someone's pet who had figured out how to slip his collar and beg for a free dinner at a half-dozen houses.

Smiling hurt him.

A male nurse came in, burly and harried. He did something to Scott's IV. "He'll be out in five minutes, better say your goodbyes," he said.

Scott rolled his eyes, but then they started to droop.

"Buddy," I said. "I'll come back again soon. Soon as I can. Get better. Remember, you've got someone who cares about you.

Rest and get better." I'd said *get better* twice. I resisted the urge to say it a third time. I squeezed his hand but he was already dropping off and didn't squeeze back.

The elevator discharged me into a secure lobby; I'd have to pass through two security checks and two sets of doors before I was back in the parking lot.

Junior was waiting for me in the second lobby. The last time I'd seen him he'd been florid and chubby, manic and delighted about his hamburger scheme and then enraged that I wouldn't help him wrangle his spreadsheets.

Now, he was lean and rugged, enormously contented. He'd had his teeth whitened, or maybe capped—that Tony Robinson thing. Maybe he'd had botox; hard to imagine how else he achieved that look of supreme, smooth relaxation. He wore a stiff white shirt open at the collar, no tie, under a blazer that showed off rowing-machine shoulders and the trim waistline of a thirty-year-old. Dark Japanese denim jeans tailored to break over old-fashioned brogues, along with a short-back-and-sides, completed the look—wealthy hipster, equally at home on a TED stage or drinking a twelve-dollar bulletproof coffee in the Mission.

"Marty," he said, smiling broadly but without any other part of his face moving at all. Definitely botox. Those *teeth*. "It's nice to see you. I wonder if I might have a minute of your time." Not a question. There were two corrections officers between me and the door. They watched us with flat, bored eyes. I wondered how they felt about Junior's whole outfit. His shoes probably cost more than they made in a month. Maybe his haircut, too.

"Lionel," I said, catching myself before I called him "Junior." "This is a surprise." It was, but perhaps it shouldn't have been. I was rapidly reassessing the violence that befell Scott. I wondered if any members of the Aryan Brotherhood were recuperating in the CMF.

"The acting warden's a friend of mine. She lets me work out of a spare office when I'm in town. It's just this way."

One of the bored COs pressed a button, and a short buzzer sounded, while the latch of a steel door leading off to the side audibly clicked open as its solenoid fired.

"This way," he said again, holding the door open. He waited for me to pass through and then let it slam shut. The latch clunked again as it locked behind us.

He led me down a long administrative corridor of gleaming white tile and chipped particleboard doors with brass nameplates, stopping at one door where the nameplate had been removed, leaving behind two rectangles of dirty white two-sided tape. He swung the door open without an "after you" or even a gesture. Power move.

Inside: A steel desk in front of an empty bookcase. A steel-mesh security window looking out on an empty exercise yard. More power games: his office chair, behind the desk, was a tall, high-backed executive model, while I was expected to sit in a low, straight-backed, armless chair that would let him stare down his nose at me. I briefly considered sitting in *his* chair—after all, he'd sent me in first, why shouldn't I assume that he was giving me first dibs?

But Lionel Coleman Jr. had a dear friend of mine utterly in his power.

I sat in the low chair. The split vinyl seat sighed out a stale breath. Junior closed the door. It audibly locked. He sat in his high throne and peered down his nose. He looked great. He *glowed*. Whatever he was injecting or ingesting or rubbing in, it was working.

"How's Scott doing?" Those teeth. So white.

"Badly," I said.

"He could be worse," Junior said. Oh, those *teeth*.

"I suppose things could always be worse," I said.

"Oh," Junior said, "oh, I don't know. There's a point where things can't get any worse." He paused.

I was supposed to let the penny drop and gulp nervously. I didn't see any reason to play that role.

"You mean he could be murdered," I said.

He didn't say anything. Just showed me those teeth.

Then: "It could actually get worse," he said. "I believe you've had your own run-ins with the law. Something in Avalon, wasn't it? I only remember because it's so unusual. There's really no crime in Avalon. But given your own carelessness, I think it's fair to say that things could continue getting worse for you, even if things can't get any worse for Scott."

I'd had to surrender all my electronics and pass through a metal detector to enter the CMF. Junior would be very certain that I wasn't recording him.

Again, this was all supposed to be subtext. I didn't see any reason not to make it text. Subtext is like the thing that lurks in the shadows, always scarier for its ambiguity. Whatever is revealed by turning on the lights will never be as scary as what your fears attribute to the dark.

"You know I'm not recording you, so you're threatening to have me imprisoned if I keep investigating your business. You listened in on my call with Scott, so you know that I'm pulling it apart, the way I did your hamburger racket. You arranged to have Scott beaten nearly to death and you want me to know that you could do the same or worse to me.

"Do I have that right?"

He put his teeth away and I got to watch him test the poker-face limits of botox. It was impressive. He didn't look angry so much as a little constipated. Judging from his white knuckles and the pulse at his throat, I guessed that he was in a fury.

Pretty powerful stuff, that botox.

"Mr. Hench, I'm sure we both want what's best for Scott." It came out in a teakettle hiss. He hadn't liked being called out, not one bit. He swallowed. "A quick recovery, a safe incarceration, and a full rehabilitation." He swallowed again and unsheathed his teeth a little. "Research shows that successful rehabilitation is linked to strong support networks of friends and family outside of the prison environment. You're Scott's most frequent visitor—"

"I haven't visited Scott for more than a year. Haven't you heard? They shut the whole visiting thing down."

He acted as though I was confused, rather than angry. "Excuse me, most frequent *video* visitor. It's clear that Scott's safety and well-being matter to you."

He paused to see if I had anything snappy to interject. I didn't. I could see where this was going and I didn't like it.

"Prisons are intrinsically unsafe places, and no amount of oversight can eliminate all the danger. Now that he's involved in gang wars, that's going to be especially difficult. I hope you will be my partner in my efforts to prevent Scott from coming to any more harm."

I mastered myself, played it straight. "I would very much like him to be safe. How do you propose that we can keep him from coming to harm?"

"The Aryan Brotherhood doesn't administer beatings like the one that Scott suffered for nothing. I don't claim to have any special insight into the activities that brought Scott into their crosshairs. But if you have any influence over him, you can help him stay safe by encouraging him to avoid those activities in future. And if you happen to have any role in those activities, I can only suggest that you, too, should refrain from further pursuits."

I mastered myself. I mastered myself. I didn't master myself.

"You're saying that if I keep looking into Thames Estuary, you'll have your prison Nazis beat Scott to death."

"Mr. Hench," he said, "I don't think you grasp the scope of this crisis. The Aryan Brotherhood doesn't solely operate inside the prison system. It's entirely possible—likely even—that conflicts that begin within the prison system can spill out and affect involved parties on the outside."

"You're saying you'll have them beat *me* to death," I said.

"Mr. Hench," he said, "I want Scott to be safe. I want him to serve his time without further incident and to thrive upon his release." Teeth. Teeth. "And I want you to thrive as well." Teeth. "And I want you to be *safe*."

The smart-ass in me wanted to say, *You're threatening to have us both beaten to death, right?* But I mastered myself.

"I understand," I said.

He showed me out of that office and back down the hall. I retrieved my phone and wallet from the lockers. I got in my car. I drove home.

part three

ex libris

14

I've been threatened by better men than Lionel Coleman Jr.

Yes, Scott was in danger. Yes, Junior had a lot of money and pull. But I've found a lot of money that was stolen from powerful people and the odd government agency, and there are a lot of people who'll return my calls.

Scott was transferred to a rehab wing of the California Medical Facility after four months of care. They gave him a partial denture and speech therapy to teach him how to use his remodeled jawbone. I visited him twice more in the hospital. We were never alone, not even for a minute. We were chaperoned by stone-faced guards who didn't bother to hide the fact that they were eavesdropping on us. Most of our conversations ended when a burly nurse came in and sedated him. But I managed to slip him a note telling him what had happened and asking if he wanted me to keep running down Junior. The next time, he took my hand in both of his, looked deep into my eyes, and mouthed *Yes*.

I put out feelers. I called in favors. I made a dinner date with an investigator in the California AG's office, a woman whose boyfriend had gotten involved with a low-rent exercise-equipment cult whose leader talked him into taking out a second mortgage and emptying out his retirement savings to buy inventory.

This is not a smart move, not for the boyfriend and not for the guru either. She might have let it lie if it had only been the boyfriend's money, but he took out a bunch of credit cards in her name and maxed them out with the guru's merchant account. Smart woman, foolish choices.

She was smart enough not to investigate it herself, but she had colleagues who were only too happy to convene a grand jury, subpoena the guru's bank records and tax returns, and go to town on 'em. But the guru was better at funny accounting than he was at paying Vietnamese sweatshops to turn out Bowflex knockoffs. The overworked accountants at the AG's office bounced off of them and didn't have the time to tear them apart and build a crazy wall of red string and thumbtacks to peel open the guru's nesting companies and trusts.

My investigator friend knew my work from a few cases where it had been useful in recovering some good people's money from some bad people and she called me up: "Marty, there's no twenty-five percent in this one. Whatever comes out of this guy, it'll end up in escrow for his victims. I can't just hand you a quarter of it. But this guy is a bad guy."

"Send me the files," I said. Some jobs you do for the money. Some jobs you do for the satisfaction, like pitting your wits against a crossword constructor. The guru was good at his job. I was better at mine. My friend owed me a favor.

She breezed into the Battery Club with a clatter of heels and a confident stride. Everyone else in the private club was a tech executive, or wanted to be, and dressed in studied casualness, signaling their wealth and ambition by choosing hoodies and tees that sold for a thousand dollars or more, but to the untrained eye could be conference swag.

By contrast, Michelle Reim looked like the hard-charging government lawyer she was: dressed in a smart suit that did *not* look expensive—judges and juries found it suspicious if public servants arrived in court wearing Prada. Her hair was styled but not aggressively so, no artfully mussed rock-'n'-roller do or studiously careless ponytail.

"Marty," she said. "Let's get a table." The club wouldn't admit me until she arrived, so I'd been cooling my heels in the plebs' waiting room. Now she brought me inside the high-ceilinged room of well-fed, hungry people buzzing intensely at each other in overstuffed conversation areas or hammering at their keyboards while scowling at their screens.

We found a satellite room of dark blue walls and bookcases full of ornamental books, and she led me to a tiny table in a far corner. A server appeared a moment later and she ordered us both coffees and asked that we be left alone after they were delivered. The server—a poker-faced young Asian woman in a white shirt and green tie—didn't bat an eye. The coffees materialized a moment later.

"Nice place," I said.

She shrugged. "My husband joined." I'd noticed the ring on her finger, a pure reflex. "He's general counsel at a fintech company. The CEO is raising money from overseas investors and he wanted to be able to take them somewhere nice and he bought memberships for all the senior managers. I got in on the spousal package."

I took in the surroundings: fanciful taxidermy, brass-accented globes, large "statement" abstract oils. "Remember when tech bros tried to impress investors with how cheap they were? I never thought I'd miss those sawhorse desks."

She smiled. "They have those in their office. Ikea sells them as ready-mades: two sawhorses and a door for two hundred dollars. They take the investors to the office and show them how frugal they're living, then they take them here and buy them hundred-and-fifty-dollar shots of Pappy van Winkle."

"This is why I've never been a start-up guy," I said. "I don't have the cognitive capacity to reconcile those two signifiers."

"It takes a special kind of person. But hell, irrationality is very big these days."

We both paused for a moment. The 2016 campaign had been a roller coaster of high weirdness and low comedy, and the election

itself was the surreal punch line. But of course, that was just for
starters. The real fun had begun on inauguration day, with the
"American carnage" speech and the bone-deep realization that
we were in for four years of this stuff, and that it was going to get
a *lot* worse before it got better.

"Well, that's why I came to you," I said. "Ordinarily when I
find a grift like this one, crossing state lines and taking a couple
of loops through offshore havens, I go to the feds. Somehow, I
couldn't feature Lindsey Graham getting too worked up about
this one. And these guys are ripping off the State of California
for tens of millions. Real money.

"I thought, okay, no point in trying the feds, but Xavier Bec-
erra is an ambitious guy. I remember when he ran for mayor of
LA. Lost it, sure, but then he did a decade and a half in Congress and came home to serve as the new California AG. They
say AG stands for 'aspiring governor,' right? Busting open a big
scam like this one feels like an opportunity for him."

She was looking away, staring hard at a stuffed badger, face a
mask. She sipped her coffee. "Marty, do you know who Trump's
tapped to run the Bureau of Prisons?"

"I confess I don't. A lot of news these days, hard to keep up
with it all."

"This isn't in the news yet, just on the grapevine. Trump's top
warden is a general whose most recent career accomplishment
was running detainee operations in Iraq and Afghanistan." She
dropped her voice. "The guy's a torturer, Marty. A sadist. A war
criminal. They're gonna put him in charge of the prisons."

"Federal prisons."

She shook her head sadly. "Yeah, this guy won't have juris-
diction over the state pens, but you have to read the room here.
There's going to be so much bad stuff thrown at us for the next
four years—ugly immigration stuff, all kinds of surveillance
stuff, things that matter to *lots* of Californians, not just people
in lockup and their families. Remember, four and a half million

Californians voted for Trump, and there's plenty more who *like* to see prisoners suffer. It's supposed to be a punishment, after all."

"But it's not just that they're suffering—they're suffering while these guys take the California taxpayer for a ride. I've barely scratched the surface and I'm already at seven figures. Get me into their books and I'll find plenty more."

She was quiet for a long time. "Marty," she said, barely a whisper, "drop it, okay? I've been testing the waters all week, ever since you first messaged me, and *no one* wants to take these guys on. Everyone was underwater *before* the election, and now they've got weights tied around their ankles. You'd need to add another zero to these guys' take before anyone would take notice. No one wants to go out on a limb to help a bunch of convicts—"

"I told you, even if you don't care about the prison conditions, they're doing millions in fraud—"

"Honestly, Marty, it's gotta be hundreds of millions before you'll get priority on anyone's queue in my office." She sipped some coffee and put the cup down with a click. "I won't pretend I hate this as much as you, but Marty, believe me when I say I hate it *so much*. We are living in a golden age of grift. We just put a guy in the White House who brags about his criminal acts, says they 'make him smart.'

"People today, they think the government can't do anything right, so they want the private sector to take it over. Then, when someone like these Thames Estuary people come along and start stealing everything that isn't nailed down, those same people are like, 'You see? I *told* you the government was incompetent!' And then they slash *my* budget because I'm not doing enough to fight crime." She shrugged, her thin shoulders slumping on the downswing into a dejected slouch. "They got us beat, Marty. That's all there is to it. They got us beat."

"Ouch," I said.

She gave me a weak smile. "I like you, Marty. I like how

methodical you are. Even more, I like how you *care*. I like that you *believe*."

"You believe, too, Michelle. I know you do."

"Yeah." She sounded exhausted. "I believe. I care. But I gotta triage. You pick your jobs. I do, too. And when I take a job, I have to be able to make a case the AG can prove, otherwise I'm just wasting a lot of people's time that could be spent building a case against someone else."

"I hear you," I said. I could tell this was a dead end, but I had to try. I hadn't finished my coffee. "Michelle, I know for a *fact* that you don't just take the easy cases. That's what I like about you, you go after the big guys, even if it means you're maybe going to lose a few. You want to make an impact, not put notches in your gun barrel. You aren't afraid of an uphill battle. This is a fight worth fighting. These guys have more than a hundred thousand Californians at their mercy, and they're *torturing* them."

She got a cool look. "I thought you said the real issue was all the money they were stealing."

"That's the real issue for all the people you have to justify yourself to. But the *real* real issue? It's all those poor motherfuckers who are absolutely in the power of these looting sadists. That's why I care. I think it's why you'll care."

She put a twenty down on the table next to her coffee cup. "It's my treat," she said. "You're not wrong, Marty. It's a human tragedy. It's an outrage. But I've got more of those than I can handle. There's stuff at the border—" She broke off. "Marty, believe me when I tell you that I have checked this out every way I can and I just can't sell it. I can produce evidence but I can't bring a case. A prosecutor has to do that, and they're not home to your prisoners."

Now she looked me in the eye. "It's a disgusting mess, Marty. Thinking about it makes me want to crawl under the duvet and curl up into a ball. But I can't, because I've got a full dance card, too, lots of people whose only hope of justice is for me to show up and do my job. So that's what I've got to do. I'm really sorry about your friend. I'm even more sorry for the hundred thousand motherfuckers in California state pens. I'm even sorrier for their families. But I've got the wisdom to know the difference between things I can change and things I can't, and I . . . just . . . *can't*."

I picked up the twenty and handed it back to her, put my own down. "I've got this," I said. "I appreciate you doing all that, Michelle. I appreciate your taking the time to explain it to me. Most of all, I appreciate you doing what you can, for the people you can do it for."

"Thank you, Marty," she said.

"Thank *you*, Michelle."

She had to walk me out—no guests in the club without their members—but we didn't have anything else to say.

Between 1972 and 1978, Steve Soul (a.k.a. Stefon Magner) had a string of sixteen *Billboard* Hot 100 singles, one of which cracked the Top 10 and won him an appearance on *Soul Train*. He is largely forgotten today, except by hip-hop producers who prize his tracks as a source of deep, funky grooves. They sampled the hell out of him, not least because his rights were controlled by Inglewood Jams, a clearinghouse for obscure funk tracks that charged less than half of what the Big Three labels extracted for each sample license.

Yes, that Steve Soul. Yeah, he was pretty great. Not surprised you know his stuff. You've got excellent taste in music.

Even at that lower rate, those license payments would have set Stefon up for a comfortable retirement, especially when added to his Social Security and the disability check from Dodgers Stadium, where he cleaned floors for more than a decade before he fell down a beer-slicked bleacher and cracked two of his lumbar discs.

But Stefon didn't get a dime. His former manager, Chuy Flores, forged his signature on a copyright assignment in 1976.

Stefon didn't discover this fact until 1979, because Chuy kept cutting him royalty checks, even as Stefon's band broke up and those royalties trickled off. In Stefon's telling, the band broke up because the rest of the act—especially the three-piece rhythm section of two percussionists and a beautiful bass player with a natural afro and a wild, infectious hip-wiggle while she played—were too coked up to make it to rehearsal, making their performances into shambling wreckages and their studio sessions into vicious bickerfests. To hear the band tell of it, Stefon had bad LSD ("Lead Singer Disease") and decided he didn't need the rest of them.

One thing they all agreed on: there was no *way* Stefon would have signed over the band's earnings to Chuy, who was little more than a glorified bookkeeper, with Stefon hustling all their bookings and even ordering taxis to his bandmates' houses to make sure they showed up at the studio or the club on time.

Stefon remembered October of '79 well. He'd been waiting with dread for the envelope from Chuy. The previous royalty check, in July, had been under $250. The previous quarter's had been over $1,000. This quarter's might have zero. Stefon needed the money. His 1972 Ford Galaxie needed a new transmission. He couldn't keep driving it in first.

The envelope arrived late, the day before Halloween, and for a brief moment, Stefon was overcome by an incredible, unbelieving elation: Chuy's laboriously typewritten royalty statement ended with the miraculous figure of $7,421.16. Seven thousand dollars! It was more than two years' royalties, all in one go! He could fix the Galaxie's transmission *and* get the ragtop patched, and still have money left over for his back rent, his bar tab, his child support, *and* a fine steak dinner, and even then, he'd end the month with money in his savings account.

But there was no check in the envelope. Stefon shook the envelope, carefully unfolded the royalty statement to ensure that there was no check stapled to its back, went downstairs to the apartment building lobby and rechecked his mailbox.

Finally, he called Chuy.

"Chuy, man, you forgot to put a check in the envelope."

"I didn't forget, Steve. Read the paperwork again. You gotta send *me* a check."

"What the *fuck*? That's not funny, Chuy."

"I ain't joking, Steve. I been advancing you royalties for more than three years, but you haven't earned nothing new since then—no new recordings. I can't afford to carry you no more."

"Say *what*?"

Chuy explained it to him like he was a toddler. "Remember when you signed over your royalties to me in '76? Every dime I've sent you since then was an advance on your *future* recordings, only you haven't had none of those, so I'm cutting you off and calling in your note. I'm sorry, Steve, but I ain't a charity. You don't work, you don't earn. This is America, brother. No free lunches."

"After I did *what* in '76?"

"Steve, in 1976 you signed over all your royalties to me. We *agreed*, man! I can't *believe* you don't remember this! You came over to my spot and I told you how it was and you said you needed money to cover the extra horns for the studio session on *Fight Fire with Water*. I told you I'd cover them and you'd sign over all your royalties to me."

Stefon was briefly speechless. Chuy *had* paid the sidemen on that session, but that was because Chuy owed *him* a thousand bucks for a string of private parties they'd played for some of Chuy's cronies. Chuy had been stiffing him for months and Stefon had agreed to swap the session fees for the horn players in exchange for wiping out the debt, which had been getting in the way of their professional relationship.

"Chuy, you know it didn't happen that way. What the fuck are you talking about?"

"I'm talking about when you signed over all your royalties to me. And you know what? I don't like your tone. I've carried your ass for years now, sent you all that money out of my own pocket, and now you gotta pay up. My generosity's run out. When you gonna send me a check?"

Of course, it was a gambit. It put Stefon on tilt, got him to say a lot of ill-advised things over the phone, which Chuy secretly recorded. It also prompted Stefon to take a swing at Chuy, which Chuy dived on, shamming that he'd had a soft-tissue injury in his neck, bringing suit for damages and pressing an aggravated-assault charge.

He dropped all that once Stefon agreed not to keep on with any claims about the forged signature; Stefon went on to become a good husband, a good father, and a hard worker. And if cleaning floors at Dodgers Stadium wasn't what he'd dreamed of when he was headlining on *Soul Train,* at least he never missed a game, and his boy came most weekends and watched with him. Stefon's supervisor didn't care.

But the stolen royalties ate at him, especially when he started hearing *his* licks every time he turned on the radio. His *voice,* even. Chuy Flores had a fully paid-off three-bedroom in Eagle Rock and two cars and two ex-wives and three kids he was paying child support on, and Stefon sometimes drove past Chuy Flores's house to look at his fancy palm trees all wrapped up in strings of Christmas lights and think about who paid for them.

It was on one of those drives where Stefon learned about copyright termination. It was 2011, and NPR was doing a story on the 1976 Copyright Act, passed the same year that was on the bottom of the document Chuy forged.

Under the '76 act, artists acquired a "termination right"—
that is, the power to cancel any copyright assignment after
thirty-five years, even if they signed a contract promising to
sign away their rights forever and a day (or until the copyright
ran out, which was nearly the same thing).

Listening to a smart, assured lady law professor from UC
Berkeley explaining how this termination thing worked, Stefon
got a wild idea. He pulled over and found a stub of a pencil and
the back of a parking-ticket envelope and wrote down the professor's name when it was repeated at the end of the program.
The next day he went to the Inglewood Public Library and got a
reference librarian to teach him how to look up a UC Berkeley
email address and he sent an email to the professor asking how
he could terminate his copyright assignment.

He was pretty sure she wasn't going to answer him, but she
did, in less than a day. He got the email on his son's smartphone
and the boy helped him send a reply asking if he could call her.
One thing led to another and two weeks later, he'd filed the paperwork with the U.S. Copyright Office, along with a check for
one hundred dollars.

Time passed, and Stefon mostly forgot about his paperwork
adventure with the Copyright Office, though every now and
again he'd remember, think about that hundred dollars, and
shake his head. Then, nearly a year later, there it was, in his
mailbox: a letter saying that his copyright assignment had
been canceled and his copyrights were his again. There was
also a copy of a letter that had been sent to Chuy, explaining
the same thing.

Stefon knew a lawyer—well, almost a lawyer, an ex–trumpet
player who became a paralegal after one time subbing for Sly
Stone's usual guy, and then never getting another gig that good.
He invited Jamal over for dinner and cooked his best pot roast
and served it with good whiskey and then Jamal agreed to send
a letter to Inglewood Jams, informing them that Chuy no longer

controlled his copyrights and they had to deal with him direct from now on.

Stefon hand-delivered the letter the next day, wearing his good suit for reasons he couldn't explain. The receptionist took it without a blink. He waited.

"Thank you," she said, pointedly, glancing at the door.

"I can wait," he said.

"For *what*?" She reminded him of his boy's girlfriend, a sophomore a year younger than him. Both women projected a fierce message that they were done with everyone's shit, especially shit from men, especially old men. He chose his words carefully.

"I don't know, honestly." He smiled shyly. He was a good-looking man, still. That smile had once beamed out of televisions all over America, from the *Soul Train* stage. "But ma'am, begging your pardon, that letter is about my music, which you all sell here. You sell a lot of it, and I want to talk that over with whoever is in charge of that business."

She let down her guard by one minute increment. "You'll want Mr. Gounder," she said. "He's not in today. Give me your phone number, I'll have him call."

He did, but Mr. Gounder didn't call. He called back two days later, and the day after that, and the following Monday, and then he went back to the office. The receptionist who reminded him of his son's girlfriend gave him a shocked look.

"Hello," he said, and tried out that shy smile. "I wonder if I might see that Mr. Gounder."

She grew visibly uncomfortable. "Mr. Gounder isn't in today," she lied.

"I see," he said. "Will he be in tomorrow?"

"No," she said.

"The day after?"

"No." Softer.

"Is that Mr. Gounder of yours ever coming in?"

She sighed. "Mr. Gounder doesn't want to speak with you, I'm sorry."

The smile hadn't worked, so he switched to the look he used to give his bandmates when they wouldn't cooperate. "Maybe someone can tell me why?"

A door behind her had been open a crack; now it swung wide and a young man came out. He looked Hispanic, with a sharp fade and flashy sneakers, but he didn't talk like a club kid or a hood rat—he sounded like a USC law student.

"Sir, if you have a claim you'd like Mr. Gounder to engage with, please have your attorney contact him directly."

Stefon looked this kid up and down and up, tried and failed to catch the receptionist's eye, and said, "Maybe I can talk this over with you. Are you someone in charge around here?"

"I'm Xavier Perez. I'm vice president for catalog development here. I don't deal with legal claims, though. That's strictly Mr. Gounder's job. Please have your attorney put your query in writing and Mr. Gounder will be in touch as soon as is feasible."

"I did have a lawyer write him a letter," Stefon said. "I gave it to this young woman. Mr. Gounder hasn't been in touch."

Perez looked at the receptionist. "Did you receive a letter from this gentleman?"

She nodded, still not meeting Stefon's eye. "I gave it to Mr. Gounder last week."

Perez grinned, showing a gold tooth, and then, in his white, white voice, said, "There you have it. I'm sure Mr. Gounder will get back in touch with your counsel soon. Thank you for coming in today, Mr.—"

"Stefon Magner." Stefon waited a moment, then said, for the first time in many years, "I used to perform under Steve Soul, though."

Perez nodded briskly. He'd known that. "Nice to meet you,

Mr. Magner." Without waiting for a reply, he disappeared back into his office.

Stefon cooked Jamal another dinner and Jamal wrote another letter, this one more forceful, and addressed to Gounder by name. Two weeks later, Jamal wrote another letter without needing dinner because "that motherfucker went to Harvard fucking law"—Jamal had looked him up in the ALA directory—"and he knows you can't make legal problems go away just by ignoring them. Time for that piece of shit to put on his big-boy pants and be a goddamned *lawyer*."

The one thing Jamal wouldn't do was file a lawsuit. "You need a lawyer for that," he said. "I mean, I can help you with the paperwork, but a paralegal can't file the suit. And you shouldn't file your own suit, either. Those guys'll just hire some blow-dried asshole from a big law firm and they'll crush you like a cockroach."

"Well, *shit*," Stefon said. But it all made sense. Anyone doing business *with* Chuy Flores would do business *like* Chuy Flores—that is, crooked as hell.

"What you need is a *contingency* lawyer," Jamal said. "Someone who'll take the job for a piece of the action."

Which is how Stefon ended up being represented by Benny Caetani II, son of Benedetto Caetani, who graduated at the top of his Yale class, won a string of spectacular class-action suits, then got disbarred after someone leaked calls where he admitted moving money from one client trust account into another to cover a shortfall. No one seriously thought that Benedetto was stealing anyone's money—he'd had receivables due within a week that let him make the trust account whole—but he was also clearly guilty.

Equally, no one seriously believed that the high-powered surveillance that led to Benedetto's downfall was *random*. Benedetto had transferred more than a hundred million dollars from the balance sheets of America's largest, dirtiest corporations—poison-peddling pharma giants, toxic-waste-dumping chemical companies, a global chain of botox parlors with some very loose syringes indeed—and they were gunning for him.

Officially, Benedetto was out of the lawyer game. Unofficially, he was the brains behind Benny, and the two of them ran a *squeaky-clean* shop, making sure that everything that an actual lawyer had to do, Benny did—while Benedetto did everything else. Father and son got along well and they were a hell of a team. When Benedetto called me in to audit Inglewood Jams' books, I jumped at the opportunity. They were a delight to work for.

"They played tough," Benedetto said, as his minions arranged the bankers' boxes on the steel kitchen shelves he'd had installed on the long walls of the storefront he'd rented for me to work out of for the month. "At first. Told me they didn't owe Stefon a dime, and that they'd rather bankrupt themselves in court than pay some broken-down, washed-up disco king anything. Told me his problem was with Chuy, not Inglewood Jams."

"Well, to be fair, that Chuy guy sounds like a class-A piece of shit."

"A *broke* piece of shit. Guy's got a million-dollar nose and an empty bank account."

"So you had to go after Inglewood Jams."

Benedetto twirled around in his Aeron chair. He'd sent over a pair of them, asking if I needed more, because he had a storage locker full of them that he'd gotten as part of a settlement with a broke Santa Monica crowdsourcing company that stiffed its workers when it folded.

"I did. I went *after* them. That Gounder lawyer tried to bluff, then when that didn't work, he tried to dodge service. Which was such a *kindergarten* move. Plus he was no good at it. Caught him outside the rub-and-tug parlor he went to every Friday after work. Handed him the papers. Wore a bodycam. Didn't mention his wife. Didn't have to."

"You think he settled because he didn't want his wife to find out he was getting hand jobs at a massage parlor?"

"No, he held out awhile after that. But I could see it preying on him, every time I was face-to-face with him. Eventually, he musta told his bosses that they were gonna lose, and so they offered a settlement. It was trash. I laughed in his face. He tossed out some better offers, but none of them even in the *ballpark* of what we would get in court. Finally, I told him to get serious or send his court suit out to the dry cleaner's. That's when he offered to make Stefon whole and pay me a little for my trouble on top of things."

I suppressed a snort. I was sure that *a little on top* amounted to some real folding money.

"Even *then* he tried to pull a fast one, told me he'd calculate Stefon's royalties and send a check the next week. I was like, 'Hold *up,* there is *no way* you're going to be able to make an honest accounting for Stefon's royalties in a *week.* The dude's samples are in *hundreds* of songs. The mere fact that you claimed that you could come up with a fair amount in a week tells me you were planning to pull a lowball number out of your ass and pass it off as the audited total, so tell you what, I'm gonna get the best forensic accountant in the state of California to come down here to LA and crawl all over your papers, and you are going to send him everything he needs to do it, or we're going to *court,* motherfucker."

"And he agreed?"

"Hell no. He *refused.* We went to a preliminary hearing. Judge turned out to be a classic soul fan. It didn't go well for Gounder or Inglewood. The next day, he was back in my office, and now, well, here we are."

The last of the boxes had been shelved.

Benedetto rose from his chair. "Thank you, gentlemen," he said to the movers, and dug a roll of twenties out of his pocket and handed each of them two of their own. He turned to me as they filed out. "You wanna get sushi? The place next door is *great.*"

The empty storefront was in a down-at-heels strip mall in Eagle Rock. On one side, there was a Brazilian jujitsu studio that never seemed to have any students training in it. On the other side was Sushi Jiro, name on a faded sign with half its lightbulbs gone. Beyond that was a vaping store.

"The place next door is *good*?"

He laughed. "You San Francisco motherfuckers got *terrible* LA restaurant radar. Put Sushi Jiro in the Mission and it'd have a Michelin star and a six-month waiting list. Here it's in a strip mall and only the locals know how good it is. Bet you never had a decent meal in this town, am I right?"

"I've had a few," I said, "but I admit my track record isn't great."

"Let's improve it."

The sushi was amazing.

Inglewood Jams had the kind of books that were *performatively* bad, designed to foil any attempt at human comprehension.

But whoever cooked them was an amateur, someone who mistook *complexity* for *obfuscation.* Like *cross-referencing* was a species of transcendentally esoteric sorcery. I don't mind cross-referencing. It's meditative, like playing solitaire. I had Benedetto send over some colored post-it tabs and a big photocopier with an automatic feeder and I started making piles.

One night, I worked later than I planned. Sushi Jiro was becoming a serious hazard to my waistline and my sleep-debt, because when your dinner break is ten yards and two doors away from your desk, it's just too damned easy to get back to work after dinner.

That night, I'd fallen into a cross-referencing reverie, and before I knew it, it was 2 a.m., my lower back was groaning, and my eyes were stinging.

I straightened, groaned, and slid my laptop into my bag. I found my keys and unlocked the door. The storefront was covered with brown butcher's paper, but it didn't go all the way to the edge. I had just a moment to sleepily note that there was some movement visible through the crack in the paper over the glass door when it came flying back toward me, bouncing off my toe, mostly, and my nose, a little. I put my one hand to my face as I instinctively threw myself into the door to close it again.

I was too late and too tired. A strong shoulder on the other side of the doorframe pushed it open and I stumbled back, and then the guy was on me, the door sighing shut behind him on its gas lift as he bore me to the ground and straddled my chest, a move he undertook with the ease of much practice. He pinned my arms under his knees and then gave me a couple of hard hits, one to the jaw, one to the nose.

My lip and nose were bleeding freely and my head was ringing from the hits and from getting smacked into the carpet tiles over concrete when I went down backward. I struggled—to free my arms, to buck off my attacker, to focus on him.

He was a beefy white guy in his late fifties, with watery dark eyes and a patchy shave that showed gray mixed in with his dark stubble. As he raised his fist for another blow, I saw that he was wearing a big class ring. A minute later, that ring opened my cheek, just under the orbit of my eye.

Apart from some involuntary animal grunts, I hadn't made a sound. Now I did. "Ow!" I shouted. "Shit!" I shouted. "Stop!" I shouted.

He split my lip again. I bucked hard but I couldn't budge him. He had a double chin, a gut, and he was strong, and used that bulk to back up his strength. It was like trying to free myself from under a boulder. That kept punching me in the face.

The strip mall would be deserted. Everything was closed, even the vaping store.

Shouting wouldn't help. I did it anyway. He shut my mouth for me with a left. I gagged on blood.

He took a break from punching me in the face, then. I think he was tired. His chest heaved, and he wiped sweat off his lip with the back of his hand, leaving behind a streaky mustache of my blood.

He *contemplated* me, weighing me up. I thought maybe he was trying to decide if I had any fight left in me, or perhaps whether I had any valuables he could help himself to.

He cleared his throat and looked at me again. "Goddammit, I messed your face up so bad I can't tell for sure. I hope to fuck that you're Martin Hench, though."

Even with my addled wits, this was an important piece of intelligence: *he came here for me.* This wasn't a random act of senseless Los Angeles street violence. This was aimed at *me*.

I was briefly angry at Benedetto for not warning me that Chuy Flores was such a tough son of a bitch. Then I had the presence of mind to lie.

"I don't know who the fuck this Mark Hendricks is." My voice was thick with gargled blood, but I was proud of *Mark Hendricks*. Pretty fast thinking for a guy with a probable concussion.

The guy slapped me open-handed across the face, and as I lay dazed for a moment, he shifted, reached into my back pocket for my wallet, and yanked it—and the seat of my pants—free. Before I could react, his knees were back on my biceps, pinning my arms and shoulders. It was a very neat move, and fast for an old guy like him.

He flipped my wallet open and squinted at it, then held it at arm's length, then smiled broadly. He had bleach-white teeth, a row of perfectly uniform caps. Los fucking Angeles, where even the thugs have a million-dollar smile.

"Shoulda sprung for botox," I slurred.

His grin got wider. "Maybe someday I will. Got these in trade from a cosmetic dentist I did some work for." He dropped my wallet. "Listen, Martin Hench, you stay the fuck away from Thames Estuary and Lawrence Coleman."

"It's Lionel Coleman," I said.

"What the fuck ever," he said. He labored to his feet. I stayed still. He looked at me from a great height, and I stared up his nostrils. Without warning, he kicked my ribs hard enough that I heard one of them crack.

"You've been told," he said to my writhing body, and let himself out.

The storefront had an old break room with a first-aid kit, and a bathroom with a sink. I sponged myself clean in the mirror, ate two expired Aleves and three 200 mg expired Tylenols out of the kit. The ass was ripped most of the way out of my pants, so I moved my wallet to my front pocket, which my massage therapist had been nagging at me to do for years.

I opened the door more carefully this time and limped out into the parking lot. My rental—a little red Civic—was the only car left in the parking lot, except for a rusted junker with no tires that was the perennial sentry of its farthest corner.

I bipped the doors open with my fob, checked the back seat, then slid inside. I checked my reflection in the rearview mirror and winced, which pulled at my bruises and set blood oozing from my lip and cheekbone again, which made me wince harder. I was already halfway to Quasimodo and I tried to remember if there was a 7-Eleven on the route home where I could buy a couple of bags of frozen peas for the swelling.

I reset the mirror and backed out of my spot. The pain was increasing. They'd have Advil at the 7-Eleven, and I'd remembered where there was one on the way back to my Airbnb.

As I waited for a red light at Eagle Rock and Colorado Boulevard, I watched as a homeless man labored across the road with his shopping cart. I was still watching him when I realized the light had been green for some time and had just toggled yellow. I made the turn and headed up Colorado, but I was barely a hundred yards down the road when I heard a siren blat and saw the police lights. I checked my mirrors and saw the LASD cruiser directly behind me, racing right up to my bumper, slowing only at the very last moment. The cruiser's high beams blinked insistently and the siren whooped.

I pulled over.

I waited while the officer slowly got out of his car and walked to my driver's-side window. I kept my hands at ten and two. The officer tapped my window and made a roll-down motion, so I hit the button, moving slowly, putting my hand back.

I got a light in my face, squinting and thus reopening my cheekbone and lip.

"Everything all right, sir?"

"Yes," I said, feeling the blood ooze down my chin. "I was beaten up," I said, stating the obvious.

"That is unfortunate," the officer said. "License and registration."

I got my driver's license out of my wallet and found the rental papers in the glove box and handed them over. He crunched back to his cruiser and I watched him in the side mirror. He'd left his cruiser's headlights on and in the glare it was hard to tell, but it looked like there was another cop in the car whom he was conferring with. After a long delay, he came back.

"Step out of the car, please."

I did. He turned me around and had me plant my hands on the hood, kicked my feet apart, and roughly frisked me, getting his hand inside the rent in the seat of my pants and patting my boxer shorts and giving my balls a hard squeeze.

"Sir, do you know why I stopped you?"

"I don't," I said.

"You proceeded unsafely through a traffic signal. Have you been drinking, sir?"

"I haven't."

"Have you consumed any cannabis or other drugs?"

"I haven't."

He turned me around and shone his light in my eyes. "If I search your car, am I gonna find any drugs?"

"No, sir."

"Because I am gonna search that car and if I do find drugs and you've been lying to me, this is gonna be a lot worse than it needs to be."

I didn't dignify that with a response. My head hurt. My face hurt. My back hurt. This was a bullshit stop.

I expected the deputy's partner to get out of the cruiser while my tormentor tossed the rental car, but he stayed put. I did, too. Obviously. I wasn't going to take off on foot. I'm a forensic accountant, not a gang kid getting fifteen minutes of fame on *Cops*.

He spent long enough on the rental that I started to worry. Who knew what some previous driver might have shoved between the seats? But after pulling out the floor mats and tossing them onto the grassy verge beside the car, he finally stood up.

"All right, sir. I'm going to go and get a breathalyzer test. You can refuse it and I will then suspend your license for twenty-four hours. I will arrest you for a suspected DUI and bring you in for a blood test. If you fail that test, you will be subject to additional criminal penalties. Do you understand me?"

He had old coffee on his breath. My face hurt. "I'll take a test."

Back to the cruiser. It had been half an hour at least. Once the breathalyzer was done—fifteen minutes, if memory served—I could go to the 7-Eleven for painkillers and frozen peas. I decided I'd add a six-pack, I was so tired. My face hurt. I knew that mouthing off to this cop wouldn't make things go faster, quite the opposite, but as he took his leisurely time coming back to me, I was hard-pressed not to.

I blew. "May I sit down?" I asked. "My face hurts."

He didn't bother to look up from his phone. "Stay where you are, sir."

I stood. My face hurt. Time crawled. Finally, the breathalyzer beeped. He held it up and squinted at it, then used his phone to light up its face.

When he did, his sleeve rode up and revealed the "998" tattoo on his forearm.

Suddenly, I didn't care so much about the pain in my face. The cop looked at me. He was an older guy, but quite a silver fox, in a Clooneyoid sort of way. Had the same smile lines at the corners of his lips and eyes. But on him, they looked mean. Dangerous. A man who would smile at you while he beat your face in.

"All right, sir," he said. "I'm going to write you a citation for reckless driving and you will be free to go." He smiled. "Thank you for your cooperation." It sounded like "fuck you."

Back to the cruiser again. When he was done writing, he switched off his headlights, and the bubble light inside the car lit up his partner. Heavyset. Smiling. *Excellent* teeth. He gave me the same look as he had just before kicking me in the ribs. I gasped involuntarily and my ribs burned. His smile got bigger.

The Clooneyoid deputy returned with my ticket. I looked at it and then I realized he'd said "reckless driving"—*not* "dangerous driving." This was a *summons,* not a *citation.* For a misdemeanor. Two points off my license and I'd have to go to court. Depending on the judge, I could be in for fines or even a jail sentence.

Clooneyoid saw me figuring this out and he smiled, too. Everyone was having a great time tonight except for poor old Marty Hench.

"See you in court, sir," he said.

I exercised *extreme* care on the drive to the 7-Eleven, even backing out of my parking spot and reparking so that I was perfectly centered between the white lines. The clerk didn't bat an eye at my hamburger face. I gave myself five minutes to bury my bruises in the frozen peas before I backed out and drove the rest of the way to my Airbnb.

I drove five under the limit the whole way, and when I got out of my rental, I looked long and hard up and down the street for an LA Sheriff's Department cruiser.

Benedetto was outraged by my face and swore he'd sue the Sheriff's Department on my behalf. He got even angrier when I got stopped again, the following week, as I was leaving my concussion checkup at the Kaiser hospital on Sunset by a sheriff's deputy who had me pull over in front of the big Scientology building.

This deputy was a little bantam rooster of a fellow, with a shiny bald head and mirror shades and no neck. He strutted up to my car, got me out of it, ran my ID, and frisked me.

"Do you know why I pulled you over, sir?" he said. He had that cop knack for making "sir" sound like "motherfucker."

"No, sir," I said, trying it out myself.

He didn't like that and leaned in close enough for me to smell his aftershave and the scented sunscreen on his bare scalp.

"I stopped you, *sir*, because you were using your phone while driving."

I must have looked surprised.

"I personally saw you tapping at your phone screen. That is a misdemeanor, sir. Reckless driving."

He stopped as if waiting for me to respond. I made myself go mild. "Sir, I did not use my phone."

He was waiting for that. He narrowed his eyes and leaned in closer. "Are you telling me I didn't see what I saw?"

Mild, Marty, mild. "I don't know what you saw, sir, but I didn't use my phone."

He rocked back and tilted his head. Patients went by with crutches and walkers. Nurses and doctors passed in scrubs. Scientologists scurried in and out of their gigantic temple. A fruit cart man labored past us.

"Well, sir, this should be simple enough to resolve." He reached for his belt and pulled out a generic ruggedized cop-rectangle of gear, and unspooled a multiheaded cable from its side. He leaned into the rental and retrieved my phone, and squinted at its I/O port, then attached the cable to my phone. The rugged rectangle beeped. "I'm gathering forensics on your mobile device, sir," he said.

I'd figured that out already. My phone—like yours and everyone else's—was a trove of my most intimate information, a record of all the places I'd been and people I'd spoken to and all the things I'd said to them. It was full of photos and passwords and client files and voice memos. It was more information than any judge would have granted a warrant for on a reckless-driving rap.

The little man smirked as he held my phone and his gadget. I stayed mild as milk. I was running full-device encryption. I'm no computer security expert, but I spend a lot of time around them, and they'd been insistent on this point, and had made reference to this very scenario in describing why I would bother to dig around my phone's settings to turn this on.

God, my face hurt. I didn't know how long the gadget was supposed to take, but from the cop's increasing impatience, I could tell it was going long.

Beep. The cop shaded the gadget's little screen from the punishing LA sun with one hand and peered at it.

"Sir, I need you to unlock this device, please."

My face hurt. *Be mild, Marty.* "I invoke my right to counsel," I said.

He pursed his lips. "Sir, if you would please enter your un-lock code, we can verify whether your device is in use and we can both be on our way."

"I invoke my right to remain silent." I said it straight into his bodycam.

He sighed and looked irritated. I had known Benedetto for so long that I had once had to dial his number from a landline. I'd long ago memorized his office's number, 1–800-LAWER4U. He'd bought it early, back before 800 numbers got expensive, and he'd had plenty of offers for it. He'd kept it.

15

"That DA sure doesn't like these guys," Benedetto said, by way of an opener once we'd been served our steaks and martinis. He had a regular table at Musso and Frank, and the headwaiter had greeted him by name. He insisted that we get the porterhouses, and confirmed that we wanted *both* the creamed horseradish *and* the raw stuff.

"I can't imagine why not," I said. The martini was very cold, and came with a little carafe for a top-up, in its own little ice bucket. My face hurt, but between a couple of Aleves and the martini, it hurt a little less. At least my lip had stopped bleeding.

"Jesus, you look like a rubber Halloween mask."

"It feels worse than it looks." I drank half the martini. I wasn't driving. On Benedetto's advice, I'd switched to Ubers.

"DAs, they mostly don't mind when a cop is a little playful, but these deputies gangs are something else. You know they were pit-fighting prisoners?"

"Jesus."

"They made book on the fights. Couple of the prisoners died. One of them was the junkie kid of someone who mattered, and it got messy. DA isn't going to go to war to make the sheriff clean house, but when they run a gladiator ring and some A-list producer's son dies in it—" He clasped his hands like he was holding an egg in them, then opened them up in an expanding motion. "Well, things *breach*. They break out of the realm of people you can fuck up with impunity, and into the realm of people who you *can't*.

"So the DA doesn't like these guys and she's assured me that the reckless-driving charges will be reduced to dangerous-driving charges—" I started to object and he raised his hand. "—and I will be paying your fines, as part of the expenses for your services to my client Mr. Magner."

"I can pay my fines, Benedetto."

"I'm sure you can," he said, "but you have already paid a high price for being in Los Angeles." He gestured at my battered face. "So it will be my pleasure to cover this expense for you. I intend to take a deduction against it and I'm fully prepared to defend it to the IRS, on the basis that I am buying your goodwill against future contracts that may redound to my benefit and that of my clients."

I snorted. "All right, Benedetto." The steaks arrived. The waiter wore a fire-engine-red tux jacket with wide black satin lapels, a starched white shirt, and a narrow black tie, and he had a mustache like a Mexican cowboy in a 1930s oater. He fussed with little ramekins of ketchup, Tabasco, two kinds of horserad-ish, and French mustard, then wished us a good meal.

"How are things coming with Stefon's royalties, anyway?"

I already had a mouthful of beef—from the strip-steak side of the porterhouse, saving the tenderloin for last—so I chewed and washed it down with some ice-cold vodka that the bar-tender had whispered the word "vermouth" over.

"It's coming," I said. "They liked to aggregate their accounts, so you'd get a song with three samples in it and all three would be billed out collectively, even though they had three separate rights holders. My guess is they were ripping off Chuy for years."

Benedetto set down his fork and his eight-inch gleaming steak knife. He dabbed at his mouth with his napkin and set it back down on his lap, folded into a triangle, the corners tucked into his pants pockets. "Chuy should hire you to audit *his* statements."

"I wouldn't work for him," I said. "Thankfully, I get to choose my own clients. But I *have* been keeping a tab of how much money I think they stiffed him for. I figure you can take it to Inglewood Jams when you're trying to get them to cough up for Stefon. You can say to 'em, 'Look, you stop arguing and pay what you owe my guy or I'm going to Chuy with this and then you'll have to fend *him* off.'"

Benedetto was jowlier than he'd been when I first met him a couple of decades before, but he still had those brooding good looks, like a Roman gladiator. The years only gave him gravitas. He'd been married and divorced twice in those years and I'd noticed that the lock screen on his phone was a bombshell blonde, probably the same age as him, with a long, elegant neck and shrewd eyes—a starlet aged into something more substantial than mere model looks.

He shook his big anvil of a head. "I won't threaten to take that money to Chuy, Marty. I'll tell those assholes, 'Look, you know that Chuy was stealing from my client, and I know you were stealing from Chuy. I'm gonna treat every dime you held back on from Chuy as escrowed funds that you set aside for Stefon, and you're gonna pay him that, too."

"It's a lovely idea, but why on Earth would they agree to pay you any of that?"

"Because I'll let it be known that if they don't, I'll sue them on Chuy's behalf, just for shits and giggles, you know, pro bono. So they either pay Stefon, or they pay Chuy, plus a six-figure bill for outside counsel and a public record of their scumbag accounting that every other rights holder they rep can use to launch their own action."

"You're a smart man, Benedetto."

He downed the rest of his martini. "We're both smart guys, Marty, just we each got our own skill sets. Division of labor." He studied my face for a moment. "Though maybe you could expand your skills into martial arts or something?" He looked harder. "Or marksmanship." Shook his head. "God, I hate to see you like this." He paused, opened his mouth, shut it.

"Marty, I don't want to spook you, but I don't think those guys are gonna let up. I also don't think they're doing this as a favor to this asshole you told me about, the prison-industrial-complex guy, what's his dick, Junior. The way these guys are on you, I'd say it's personal. Did you do something to them, personally?"

My first impulse was to blow the question off. I obviously hadn't done anything personally to crooked LA sheriff's deputies. What could I have done? Audited their tax returns on behalf of an angry ex-wife chasing child support? I did that kind of work from time to time, but I'd remember if I'd peeled open a cop.

But I gave it a hard think, and saw Benedetto watching my face as I did. At least he knew I was taking him seriously. No one likes to be given a brush-off.

"Honestly, nothing," I said. I thought some more. "You say this feels personal, but I can tell you one hundred percent that these guys are happy to do dirty work for Junior. I don't know why, but it's true." I told him the story of Scott's rousting and felonization on Catalina Island.

"You mentioned this to me before," Benedetto said, nodding. He'd ordered us a fresh round of drinks and bread pudding for both of us. They were delivered by a slim young waitress with her hair center-parted and pulled back into a shining ponytail. He smiled broadly at her and thanked her. "Headwaiter's kid," he said. "I remember her quinceañera like it was yesterday. Shit, time goes by fast.

"This island thing, that shakedown, what was it about? How did you guys piss in Junior's cornflakes? Was it a drug thing?"

I'd told him the bison story. I'd told a lot of people that story. It was a great story.

"No, not drugs," I said. The bread pudding came with a scoop of snow-white vanilla ice cream, which was melting rapidly from the pudding's warmth, mixing with the surface crust of browned sugar and dough. I picked up a spoon with a bowl like a small ladle and got a mix of both melted and frozen ice cream and a large mouthful of the bread all floating in it, then let it kind of dissolve on my tongue until I couldn't help but chew it and swallow it.

"Jesus Christ, Marty, that's some X-rated table manners you got there. You need a cool cloth or anything?" I ignored him and enjoyed tracing the dessert's passage down my gullet.

"Okay," I said, after a sip of martini, "it wasn't drugs, it was hamburgers."

"Hamburgers."

"Eat your bread pudding before all the ice cream melts and I'll explain it."

"Marty, for a smart guy, you're a dumb guy," he said, as I scraped up the slurry of the few remaining dissolved crumbs and melted ice cream for a final half mouthful.

"You'll get no argument from me there, except maybe about the smart-guy part."

"Those cops who went after your friend on Catalina weren't Junior's hired goons, they were his business partners."

Oh. "Oh."

"These gangster deputies didn't roll you because Junior booked them for one regulation beating for hire. They came after you because they are co-owners of Thames Estuary. They weren't just roughing you up, they were creating shareholder value."

"Fuck. You've gotta be right."

"You know I am," he said. "But if you wanna be sure, I advise you to find a good forensic accountant and ask him to confirm it."

16

Junior liked to spend other people's money. The capital for Thames Estuary's private-equity incarnation came from a syndicate of rich investors, who entrusted him with a mix of loans and equity shares that he could use to buy and destroy a bunch of nursing homes. One of those investors was an Orange County cosmetic dentist who sank a million bucks into the project and then got wind that Junior had used his investors' cash to charter a private jet for a "business trip" to the Bahamas, and decided he wanted his million bucks back.

The irony is that the private flight to the Bahamas might *actually* have been a business trip—some of that shell-company paperwork needs a wet signature. It's possible that Junior flew to Nassau and went straight to a lawyer's office on Bay Street and signed his name fifty times in a row.

But it's also true that Junior proceeded to bill three nights in a suite at the Fowl Cay to the fund, including a five-figure room-service bill, which may sound extreme, but it's surprisingly easy to do if you have a taste for rare wines. The Fowl Cay has a great sommelier and a superb cellar, and specializes in in-room tastings for guests.

Junior was affronted by the accusation that he acted with anything less than perfect fiduciary probity and sent the dentist a letter saying so. The letter was an exhibit to the lawsuit that the dentist filed the next day.

The lawsuit failed. The law is surprisingly tolerant of private-equity managers who fuck over their investors. In the hierarchy of American finance, the people who *have* the money are a full rung below the people who *spend* it.

The lawsuit failed, but not before the dentist had used the discovery process to prize loose a list of the other investors in Junior's fund. These weren't people, they were LLCs (the dentist wasn't technically a shareholder, either—he'd formed a special-purpose LLC). The dentist wanted confirmation that everyone had been given the proper disclosures about Junior's expenditures.

They had. Junior was shameless, and his other investors didn't care. The dentist had a stick up his ass about expense-padding.

But that list of LLCs was useful. It was exactly the kind of thing that I loved. These were all of Junior's loose ends, and if I tugged on each of them in turn, eventually I'd loosen up the knots and it would all start to unravel.

When you think of "the law," you probably imagine the text of the bills that Congress passed. That's the *Schoolhouse Rock!* "I'm Just a Bill" ten-thousand-foot version of "the law," and it's not wrong, but it is *woefully* incomplete.

The law is also court records. Every time a judge decides a case, it becomes a precedent. If all you know about the law is what Congress wrote, and not how the judges that came afterward interpreted the law, then you don't know the law. Reading the law won't tell you whether you broke it (or whether someone else did when they harmed you). You also need to be able to consult the relevant case law.

In a just world, we'd all have access to all the case law. It's not the law unless everyone can read it. That's a principle that goes back to the Magna Carta. To the Charter of the Forest. To the Ten. Fucking. Commandments.

The law isn't the law unless the law is public. The law that

Congress made isn't the law without the court records that flow from it. Unless those court records are available, then the law isn't the law.

The law just *isn't* the law. You can't get at the case law without paying for it. Back in 1998, the U.S. federal courts set up a server to host court documents, called PACER. It was 1998, so PACER was pretty primitive, just a giant folder full of PDFs. You couldn't search those PDFs, and downloading them came at a high price—seven cents per page.

How could the courts justify charging you to read the law? Congress *told them* they could—they authorized the Judicial Conference of the USA to run PACER on a break-even basis. A giant drive full of PDFs connected to a web server was reasonably expensive, back in 1998.

But giving the world access to a folder full of PDFs only got cheaper every year after that, and PACER only got more expensive. By 2012, PACER cost ten cents per page to access. That's not much if you're a partner at a white-shoe law firm billing $1,500 per hour.

But if you're a working-class stiff trying to figure out whether your deadbeat ex owes you alimony, or whether your scumbag boss illegally dismissed you, or whether you should pay a settlement to the jerk who says you rear-ended him, ten cents a page can really add up. Especially if you're a working-class stiff who doesn't know what you're looking for and spends a lot of time doubling back over your own trail.

The court system makes *hundreds of millions of dollars* in profit off PACER, and they justify it by saying that the excess goes to pay for stuff like big TV screens in courtrooms. I don't know whether courtrooms need TV screens. Maybe they do. But those TV screens shouldn't be subsidized by a break-even program that stands between everyone in America and the laws they are supposed to obey.

I'm not the only one who feels this way. Back in 2009, a

group of civic-minded geeks created RECAP, which is PACER backward, in every way. RECAP is a browser plug-in that notices every time you download a page from PACER and submits it to an open archive that anyone can access for free. If RECAP notices that the PDF you're trying to download from PACER is already in the RECAP archive, it saves you the ten cents per page and sends you the free copy.

RECAP exists because the law belongs to all of us. U.S. law— like all works created by the U.S. government—is in the public domain. It has no copyright. That's where the "Thumb Drive Corps" comes in. In 2007, the PACER people tried to mollify their critics by giving seventeen public libraries free access to PACER, and the Thumb Drive Corps was born: these volunteers visited these libraries with thumb drives and downloaded as many important PACER docs as they could, then bulk-uploaded them to RECAP.

One Thumb Drive Corpsman was Aaron Swartz, a brilliant kid who helped invent the tech behind podcasts when he was twelve years old and went on to cofound Reddit. Swartz believed in liberating government docs, and he was a skilled programmer, so he wrote some code to speed up the retrieval of PACER docs from his local library. He pulled down 2.7 *million* documents totaling *20 million pages*—about two million dollars' worth of legal documents that he made free.

The FBI and a local prosecutor named Steve Heymann tried to shake Swartz down for the caper, but Swartz was a smart kid and he knew a bunch of smart lawyers and they sent 'em packing, and RECAP got 2.7 million documents.

Of course, hell hath no fury like a fed scorned, and a couple of years later, Heymann threw the book at Swartz when he was caught downloading a bunch of scientific articles from MIT's network. Swartz had permission to access these articles, but he violated MIT's terms of service by using another little computer program to download them, and according to Heymann, that was a felony violation of the Computer Fraud and Abuse Act.

Actually, Heymann charged Swartz with *thirteen* felonies and threatened him with *thirty-five years* in prison. Swartz went back to his good lawyers, but the feds dragged out the proceedings until Swartz was out of money and had tapped everyone he could. Facing prison, Swartz hanged himself. He was twenty-six.

That law they tried to pin on Swartz? The Computer Fraud and Abuse Act was signed by Ronald Reagan in a panic in 1986 after he watched the movie *War Games* where a young Matthew Broderick nearly starts World War III by hacking into a secret government computer. True story. Well, not *War Games*. That was fiction. But the part where Ronald Reagan used it to justify signing a law that could turn a terms of service violation into a felony? That part's true.

I made sure the RECAP plug-in was running and fired up PACER and started searching for cases that mentioned any of the LLCs that were shareholders in Thames Estuary. It was laborious work—the PACER search interface was slightly better than nothing, but not much better.

But I got some hits. There was an LLC that was involved in a cryptocurrency pump-and-dump, both as victim and perp (they got scammed into buying worthless shitcoins and then tried to unload them on another sucker). There was an LLC that got sued by an insurance company for filing a fraudulent claim for flood damage to a garage that wasn't actually flooded.

And then there was Jimkelly Holdings LLC, which was already in RECAP, which meant that someone had already looked up the case while running RECAP, because they were either a cheapskate or an open-access advocate (or both, I suppose).

Jimkelly Holdings was a California LLC with two fifty-fifty

partners: Jim Mandoyan and his wife Kelly Mandoyan. Ex-wife, eventually. That's how the LLC ended up in a court record: it was part of a divorce proceeding in which Kelly accused Jim of transferring his assets to shell companies to hide them from the court. To be fair, that's exactly what he'd done.

But that wasn't the interesting part. The interesting part was that Jim Mandoyan was an LA sheriff's deputy. A Lynwood sheriff's deputy. I'd bet anything he had a "998" tattoo somewhere on his person.

Benedetto was right. Junior had made a bunch of armed, untouchable corrupt cops into his shareholders, and they, in turn, were his private mercenary force.

It was time for me to leave LA.

Benedetto agreed, and he arranged to have the dozen or so banker's boxes I hadn't fully parsed through sent to my apartment in San Francisco. I could go through them there just as well as I could in LA, now that all the heavy lifting was done and I was just mopping up around the edges. I caught the next Southwest flight out of Burbank to Oakland and found my sphincter clenching every time I saw anyone in anything like a cop uniform. It didn't fully unclench until we were in the sky. It was a short flight—only forty-five minutes—but I downed a double Bloody Mary off the drinks cart anyway.

Benedetto drove me to the airport himself. He was pensive the whole way. When we came off 101, he turned his head and said, "So what, you'll never come to LA again?"

I'd been thinking the same thing. "I thought Junior and I had an arrangement. He keeps my friend hostage, I stop digging into his accounts."

"Junior sounds like the kind of guy who doesn't like loose ends. Maybe if he'd already gotten clear of this scam and was working on the next one, he'd be willing to let go, but Marty, I don't feature him laying off until such time as you don't represent any kind of threat to him."

I sighed. "I know," I said. "I know."

As I stood at the Oakland baggage carousel waiting for my free checked bag to come around, I thought about this some more. I would have to do something.

At least I was out of LA. Whatever else Junior could do to me, he couldn't send his hired goons out after me.

I comforted myself with that thought on the long BART ride back across the Bay, and then on the long uphill slog to my apartment.

As I worked my key in the lock, my neighbor's apartment door popped open. Duy had offered to water my plants and take in my mail, and he appeared in the hallway with a laden Safeway bag full of junk mail and bills.

"Are you okay?" he said. My face was a lot better, but it was still a *lot*.

"It's fine," I said. "Looks worse than it feels. Nothing permanent, anyway." I took the bag from him. "Thanks—I owe you one."

"It's nothing," he said. "You return the favor when we go to Fire Island next month, we call it even."

"Deal," I said, and went into my place. I opened the blinds, checked the fridge for leftovers that had turned into science experiments, kicked off my pants, and sat on the sofa in my underwear and went through the mail.

I was three-quarters of the way through it when I got to the registered letter from the California Franchise Tax Board, which Duy had signed for. It was a regular letter, not a thick envelope full of forms. I got a bad feeling.

I worked my thumb under the corner of the flap and opened it up and then unfolded the single, machine-font sheet of paper. I read it and then read it again, just to be sure.

I was being audited.

17

Hassan Aziz had only been working for the California Franchise Tax Board for a year. He'd graduated from USC's Business and Finance program third in his class, and gone on to Ernst & Young to work in the consulting arm, where his job was to create "tax efficient" structures for blue-chip companies that would then be run past the EY auditors who signed off on the books the company sent to the IRS.

Hassan's job was a simple, rote task: sit down with the finance team of a local division of a billion-dollar company that bottled soda or mixed cement or fixed airplanes, review its supply chain and payroll, figure out which of about forty tax dodges most closely fit the situation, pull the appropriate template, spend an hour or two "customizing" a "report" that he pulled down off the EY server, and then take the next two weeks off.

Two weeks later, he would turn in this "report"—slathered in "COMMERCIAL/CONFIDENTIAL" and "TRADE SECRET" notices—to his opposite number at the client and spend a couple of hours walking him through it.

The next day, EY's billing department would send an invoice for two weeks' work at $1,500 per day to the client. The client would pay it, because that $15,000 was a bargain compared to the millions it stood to realize in "tax efficiency." After that, Hassan's only job was to check in with his contact at the company on behalf of the EY sales team, to help them close a mid-six-figure deal for the software and consultants who'd implement the strategy for them.

Hassan only made it through three of these before he quit.

The thing was, the "tax optimization" strategies were idiotic. Id. I. Otic. Transparent *nonsense*. The only way an auditor could possibly sign off on them was if they absolutely, positively did not give a single shit, either about doing their job or getting caught.

Now, the auditors who were signing off on these books *also* worked for EY, but supposedly there was a "firewall" between them and the consultants like Hassan. That "firewall" was even more laughable and paper-thin than the tax optimization strategies. The Sacramento EY office was only five stories tall, and even if Hassan worked on a different floor from his auditor counterparts, he saw the same faces every day in the elevator, at the Crunch Fitness on Douglas Boulevard, or at the Monk's Cellar for after-dinner drinks. A couple of them had been in his class at USC, and he met more of them at various work Christmas parties and team-building retreats. Some firewall.

One night he found himself at the Monk's Cellar at a table with Lynn Kabaroff, who'd been one year ahead of him at USC. They were two of the only brown-skinned people in the bar and in their respective divisions at EY (Lynn worked on the audit side). They had a curious relationship with one another: neither wanted to seem standoffish to their white colleagues, but both of them caught the foolish utterances that those colleagues made and when they did, it was natural that they'd seek out each other's eyes for a shared, silent moment of *can you believe this shit?*

"The thing that gets me," Hassan said, lowering his voice below the noise-floor of the busy bar, "is just how *weak* these scams are. I mean, the clients don't know any better. Even their finance departments are a bunch of bookkeepers led by a guy who knows how to talk to rich investors.

"But *our* people should know better—I mean, *your* people.

They see this bullshit on the balance sheet and they still sign the audit report. That shit could come and bite *them* on the ass. Did they sleep through the CPA ethics exam?"

Lynn laughed a lot harder than this merited, and Hassan gave her a quizzical look.

"You don't know?" she said.

"If I knew, I'd be laughing with you. What's so funny?"

"If you're ever going into an ethics exam or any other continuing-ed exam, you just talk to your supervisor and they'll give you the answer key. They bribe someone at the National Association of State Boards of Accountancy and they've got a full set."

"They *cheat* on *ethics* exams?"

She giggled, then shook her head. "Yeah, I guess it's more funny-oh-shit than funny-ha-ha."

The news made Hassan sick in a way he couldn't quite put into words. But at least it explained why none of the EY auditors who reviewed his work flagged it for the obvious bullshit it was. Later on, he wished he could have said, "I quit my job on the spot." But that's not the case: he showed up for work every day for about a month until, one morning, he found himself hitting the snooze button on his alarm clock over and over again.

He finally got out of bed after 11 a.m. and made coffee and a home brunch before checking his phone and seeing all the messages from his bosses and colleagues and client contacts asking where he was. He didn't answer them. Instead, he drove to the big Century Arden multiplex and bought a ticket for the next movie showing. Coincidentally, that happened to be *The Wolf of Wall Street,* which impressed him for its accuracy as to the total incompetence of financial regulators and the shameless sleaze of the finance bros they were nominally supervising.

That's when he finally quit his job. He told the whole story to the California Franchise Tax Board Audit Division subchief who interviewed him. She was charmed by his story but warned him that people who went into the job with a mission had a tendency to burn out and made sure he understood the warning signs. Partway through the checklist, he realized that he'd just been hired.

I learned all of this *after* my audit. I called Hassan immediately and let him know that I was a CPA and would represent myself at the audit. I told him that I had been scanning my receipts and other financial paperwork since 2002, and that they were all cross-referenced to my quarterly cashbooks, which I used to generate my returns.

There was a long silence. "I see," he said, at last.

"I can make a password-protected zip of them and read you the password now. Then I'll stick it on Dropbox and then send you a download link. You want ten years? Or all the way back?"

"Mr. Hench," he said, "I appreciate your cooperative suggestions, but we have a procedure for this. I've prepared some Information Document Requests that specify the documents I'm seeking. You can upload them to our secure portal."

"Okay," I said, "but I've used that portal and it's pretty clunky. If you'd like, I can messenger you a hard drive or—"

"Again, I appreciate your offer, but if you wouldn't mind using the portal."

"No problem," I said.

The CFTB does a certain number of random audits every year, but the majority are triggered by suspicious numbers that don't pass the giggle test. I had a few oddball expenses, but nothing outrageous and never more than a couple percentage of my total income. What's more, I reported every *dime* of income.

As my Intro to Tax I instructor explained on the first day of class, back in the Stone Age: "If your client takes a deduction and it gets disallowed later, he just has to make up the tax liability. If he fails to disclose his income, he's committing a big-boy federal crime and they can send him to *prison*."

I filed all my documents using the CFTB's terrible portal, selecting the files one at a time, watching as each progress bar crawled with aching slowness across the screen, verifying that the file had transferred, then doing the next one.

Four days went by, and then I got another email from Hassan with more IDRs for more files. A *lot* more. I rearranged my afternoon and uploaded a couple of hundred documents. It was the bureaucratic version of *FarmVille,* a game where you attained victory by waiting for semi-random periods and then clicking your mouse a few times, then more waiting.

A week later, my phone rang. "Mr. Hench, this is Hassan Aziz at the California Franchise Tax Board."

"Nice to hear from you. How's the audit coming?"

"Mr. Hench, we're going to send you a mass storage device and a return shipping label. Will you be at your home address today?"

"I can be," I said. "Anything for my friends at the CFTB."

They wanted everything—all the stuff I'd proposed sending in on day one. That meant they were digging deep. That was fine: I kept very, very good records, and I didn't cheat on my taxes. Not even a little.

A month later, Hassan called me again. "Mr. Hench, I'm about to send you an IDR for some of your original paper receipts." He sounded embarrassed and uncomfortable. "These go back quite a long way, and there are a lot of them. Normally, we'd ask you to produce these within two weeks, but if you need more time—"

"I won't need more time," I said. "I pulled my originals out of storage right after I spoke to you the first time. I've got a living room full of banker's boxes filled with envelopes filled with receipts. I'm afraid the thermal-paper ones have faded, but they're all labeled. You want me to messenger you all of them, or a representative sample, or specific years, or—"

"I'll specify which records in the IDR."

I admit it. I enjoyed this.

The State of California paid for me to messenger six banker's boxes to Sacramento. Two weeks went by. The phone rang.

"Mr. Hench—"

"Hassan! How are you?"

"I'm fine, Mr. Hench, thank you for asking. I'm afraid that I'm going to need more of your records. I just wanted to give you advance warning before I filed this next IDR." He sounded decidedly uncomfortable.

"Tell you what," I said. "The remaining boxes will all just about fit into my car. I've been meaning to try the new branzino at Q1227. Gourmet burgers are just social media fodder, but Q Bennett is a legitimate genius and I can't wait to see what he does with fish. How about I pack the remainder up and drop them off in person while I'm there?"

"Mr. Hench, there's no need to go to that trouble—"

"It's no trouble at all. I'm sincerely coming for the fish. I can save the California taxpayer a couple hundred bucks in courier charges on the way."

There was a long pause at the other end. I had an instinct about Hassan. I thought he was a good guy. I thought he was being leaned on to fuck me over. I thought he resented it.

"All right, Mr. Hench. When do you think you'll be in town?"

I was right.

"I can drive down this afternoon and be at your office tomorrow morning."

"I'll be in at nine a.m."

"See you then."

Q1227 didn't have any tables, but I slipped the maître d' twenty dollars and she found me a spot at the bar, which was fine because it gave me a view of all the fine bourbons Q Bennett kept in stock. I'd found a Comfort Inn within walking distance and I had three, including a George T. Stagg that was exceptional.

The next morning, I parked in the visitor lot of the California Franchise Tax Board building, got the hand truck out of my trunk and pulled up the handle, then balanced the remaining five banker's boxes on it in a tall stack. I bungeed them in place and wheeled them into the building.

The receptionist was both confused and visibly alarmed by the sight of a taxpayer in his lobby with such a large and ungainly load, but he called Hassan, listened momentarily, then took my ID and printed me a visitor label. I stuck it to my chest and waited patiently.

Hassan was a well-turned-out, fit young man, olive-skinned, with a blade of a nose and a strong chin and smart, shrewd eyes. He wore a shirt and tie and black shoes with a high shine. His socks were orange-and-black-striped, a small act of rebellion, but he was otherwise a short-haired, clear-eyed, even-toothed picture of administrative probity.

"Mr. Hench," he said.

"Mr. Aziz," I said, and patted my stack of boxes. "Personal delivery."

He stared at the boxes with a grimace of dread, then reached tentatively for the dolly's handles.

"I'm going to need the hand truck back, I'm afraid. Why don't I take these up to your office for you and unload them and then I can get out of your hair."

He could have said no, could have made me unload there

in the lobby and then called for help or ferried the boxes up in shifts, but he didn't. He just nodded and pressed the elevator call button.

"Jeez, it probably would have been easier for you to just bring a truck down to my storage locker."

He looked around his crammed office, piled high with banker's boxes bearing my name in laser-printed sheets taped to their sides, grimaced again. "We normally get to requisition a special audit room rather than using our offices, but they were all full."

"Busy times," I said. There was a picture of a pretty Arab woman on his desk that I took to be a girlfriend, not a sister. A clean suit in a dry cleaner's bag hanging from a hook next to the door. A good chair. A docking station with a big screen. A laser printer on a low table with two boxes of paper beneath it.

"Where do you want them?" I asked, prompting a sigh.

"I cleared a space for them here," he said, pointing to a tiny patch of floor next to his chair.

"You sure you'll still be able to get in and out of here?"

"Pretty sure," he said. He had to step out of the office to give me room to unload the boxes.

"Newest ones on top, or oldest?"

A long pause. I stuck my head out into the hall. He opened his mouth, shut it, shook his head. "Oldest," he said.

"Oldest it is."

He let me watch him lock his office doors and secure my documents, then he escorted me to the elevators. He stepped into the elevator car with me at the last minute.

"I just want to say I'm sorry about this," he blurted. "I'm getting a lot of pressure here, but it's bullshit. I'm really sorry."

We had seconds until the elevator touched down. "I figured," I said. "You've got my cell. If you want to get a drink and talk about it, just message me."

The doors opened. He nodded very slightly at me and I wheeled my hand truck out.

I'd had room in the car for one of the last remaining boxes from Inglewood Jams, and I spent the rest of the day cross-referencing it with my existing files and then finalizing my report for Benedetto and Stefon. It had taken more than a month, and I'd found Stefon enough money to make a pretty big difference to his dotage—a couple of bags of groceries every week with enough left over to help his kid pay for college.

I knocked off around three and threw a load of laundry into the coin-op machine and then went for a walk around McKinley Park. Hassan's text came through after I got back, just as I was feeding quarters to the dryer.

> Mr. Hench, it's Hassan Aziz. If you'd still like to meet up, I'll be free after 5:30PM.

I liked a man who punctuated his SMSes.

> You know where the geese swim at McKinley Park?

A long pause.

> I believe so.

> How about there at 6?

Another pause.

> See you there.

I appreciated the spy-movie drama of meeting by a pond in a park, but it was also a very pretty spot and I'd marked it that day as a likely place to watch the sunset. Plus it was less unseemly than meeting at a bar, which had the reek of unprofessional chumminess.

By five thirty, the geese had moved on, for the most delightful of reasons: that same spot turned out to be the evening haunt of McKinley Park's enormous herd of feral cats, who prowled the grass, chasing squirrels and crickets, and, occasionally, each other. They frolicked. They *gamboled*. A couple of bold fellows joined me on my park bench and demanded scritches. I obliged. I couldn't have picked a better spot.

Hassan appeared at six on the dot, startling away a lean orange tabby that had been enthusiastically shedding all over my lap while I massaged the ruff around his neck.

"Unbelievable," he said, as the cat disappeared into some rushes.

"I wish I could take credit for them, but I had no idea. I looked them up on my phone and it turns out there's a bunch of locals who feed them and take them to the vet and make sure they're all fixed." A black furball pounced on a cricket and then peeked cautiously under its paws, releasing the panicked insect in the process. It gave chase. We both laughed.

"Well, if nothing else, I've found my new favorite park bench. Thank you, Mr. Hench."

"Can we make it Marty? After work hours?"

He stopped smiling and stared at the pond for a long moment.

"Marty," he said. "All right. Marty, I want to tell you something. But it's sensitive."

"I am discreet," I said. "Part of my job."

He looked at me, looked back at the pond, gave a tiny nod for his own benefit.

"I know it is. I suspect what I'm about to tell you won't be any surprise, either." Another long pause.

"Look, Hassan, I can tell you take your job seriously. My guess here is that you're in a professional bind. You've been asked to do something you know is wrong, but if you tell me about it, you'll be violating a different rule. Is that about right?"

He sighed. "Yeah, this won't be any surprise to you. Fuck it. Marty, I've been told to find problems with your taxes. Not to look for them, but to *find* them. But there's just one problem."

"I don't cheat on my taxes."

"No," he said, "you don't. I was hoping that some of those thermal receipts would be so faded I could disallow the expenses and hit you for fines, but I was just able to make them out." He squinched up his face. "Besides, that wasn't the kind of pain I was supposed to be inflicting on you. Too small-potatoes." He watched as a pair of cats got into a wrestling match, rolling around in the grass until the big tortoiseshell longhair pinned the black-and-white shorthair and yowled a victory cry.

"Mr. Hench—Marty—who the hell did you piss off, and how did you do it?"

The shorthair squirmed free of his tormentor and streaked off into the bushes, ears flat and tail low. "It's a long story," I said. "Probably one that's best told over a drink. Or six."

"You ever try Zankou Chicken?"

"I've driven past it a bunch of times in LA," I said, "but never went in."

"Do you like garlic?"

"I love garlic."

"All right then."

We got a whole bird and an extra pot of garlic sauce, a modified *toum* that thickened the mayo and olive oil with pureed potato. The chicken was perfect to begin with, but the garlic sauce made it *transcendent*. Hassan poured mezcal-and-grapefruit-juice palomas as we ate at his small, neat bachelor condo kitchen table. In between, I explained, starting with Catalina Island, and Scott, and Junior, proceeding carefully.

By the time we moved to his sofa with little plates of baklava, I had my laptop out and was showing him spreadsheets.

"I'm not keeping you from anything, am I?"

The sofa was a big sectional, the short leg of the L piled high with medieval history books.

"No," he said. "My girlfriend is out of town so I was pretty much at loose ends tonight anyway."

The long sections showed signs of having been slept on. He had a giant TV and three different game consoles.

We got deeper into the spreadsheets.

"This motherfucker is stealing millions," he said. "Millions." He glared at his screen. I'd copied my Thames Estuary folder onto a thumb drive and he'd got out his own personal laptop and loaded them up so he could work on his own.

"Tens of millions," I said. "And I bet he's not paying taxes on it. Plus he's figured out a way to convert all that extra money into juice with the Franchise Tax Board."

"Are you sure of that?" he said, but it sounded like he knew the answer. "I gather you've made a lot of enemies over the years. Maybe the pressure is coming from someone else you've pissed off."

I shrugged. "I can only make an educated guess here, but this is very much Junior's approach. Most of the scumbags I chase think the government is a *problem*. Junior thinks of it as a *tool*. Plus he's clearly got it in for me right now, and I wouldn't be surprised if some of his crooked deputies had connections with state agencies. There's a real spirit of collegial cooperation there."

"Ugh," he said. He flicked around a spreadsheet some more. "The temptation to look this guy up on my work system is incredible."

"Worried about getting logged?" I guessed.

"Exactly," he said. "They keep good forensics. Insider threats are my boss's worst nightmare."

"Don't punitive audits count as insider threats?"

He closed his laptop lid. "Not really. They care about peons like me selling access to the system for beer money. The order to track you down is coming from up high. If it turns into a scandal, it won't be my boss's problem—it'll be his boss's boss's boss's problem."

"Shit flows downhill," I said. "Remember Abu Ghraib? A whole goddamned torture chamber with thousands of prisoners, and it all turned out to be the fault of a single twenty-year-old private who worked at a chicken-processing factory until her reserve unit was sent to Iraq."

"Yeah, shit does indeed flow downhill." I got the distinct impression he was remembering incidents from his life where this principle had been demonstrated.

He picked up the mezcal bottle and poured himself two fingers. "Want a minimalist paloma?" he said.

I held up my glass and received an inch or two of golden, smoky booze. We clinked.

"Fuck it," he said. "Better to go down in flames for doing the right thing than doing the wrong thing."

"Meaning?"

"Meaning, I'm going to audit Thames Estuary. And Junior."

I offered to help, of course, but Hassan refused. At least, he refused my help with the accounting. He was happy to take my advice on getting set up with a burner phone. I had him leave his phone at home, drive to a suburb, street-park, pay cash for a local bus to a mall, and pay cash for a generic Android phone and a stack of prepaid SIM cards at a Best Buy. Maybe it was overkill, but if you're going to do some of it, why not all of it?

We used Signal and turned on disappearing messages, and he sometimes sent me pings asking me to look things up discreetly. It was a very honorable way for him to be sneaking around—asking me to tell him things, rather than telling me things he knew that I wasn't supposed to know.

But it was also frustrating, because I was left to try to infer the state of his audit from this fragmentary, one-sided conversation.

I spent a lot of time talking to Scott. He was recovering slowly, and had been paying a fortune for speech therapy visits over videoconference, but the progress was slow. His jaw had healed crooked and he looked a little like a sawfish, and he drooled if he wasn't careful.

But he was still Scott. He wanted to talk about the books he was reading. He relished the news about the Trump scandals, kept a series of notebooks filled with tiny writing, tracking the destiny of each swamp-monster's rise and fall. The guy who sent his staff out to drive around DC all night looking for good deals on cheap hotel mattresses and a specific brand of hand lotion just delighted him.

"It's wild," he said. "I mean, it sounds like one of those dope-stories the tweakers tell, you know, 'That time I drove around all night looking for hand lotion.' This guy is running the EP-fucking-A?"

"Yeah, and he sued the agency *fourteen* times!"

"Holy fuck," he said. "You can't make this stuff up."

There followed one of those silences that made me wonder if the janky service had dropped the call again. But then I heard some distorted sound through the speaker.

"Scott?" I said, softly.

He scrubbed at his eyes and took a breath. His voice was choked with tears. "Marty, it's so *broken*. I'm locked up with three thousand guys who are supposed to be the worst criminals in the world and even the worst of them hasn't caused *nearly* the damage of just one of these motherfuckers. Hell of it is, the worse those crooks in DC do, the *better* they do. They don't even bother hiding the crimes. It's just so eternally, totally, utterly *fucked*."

I started to make some soothing noises, but he cut me off. "Don't even try, Marty—don't even *try*. Back when I was a free man, I could pretend that there was some law left besides the law of the jungle. But once you're in here, you can't pretend anymore.

"I'm sure you don't want to think about this, but the only difference between my cage and yours is the spacing between the bars, not the captivity." He barked an angry laugh. "Makes it easier to live with the fact that I'm not getting out of this place."

I didn't have anything to say to that, but I tried anyway: "Scott, I know it's brutal in there, but there's people out here who care about you. When you get out—"

"Forget it," he said. "Forget I said anything." He snuffled up his snot. "I'm sorry, Marty. You don't need to worry about me. I'm breathing, I'm upright, and I've got millions in the bank still, right? What's a decade in a gulag to a man who's got all that?"

I almost blurted out the news about Hassan and the audit then, but I'd been operating on the assumption that Junior could—and probably did—monitor every call and message. I'd been bursting to spill the beans, but if Junior knew the audit was coming, he could lawyer up in advance, and if he knew I had a hand in it, he could trash Hassan with the Tax Franchise Board, make it seem like a revenge plot (which, to be fair, it was). And of course, he'd come after me, too—he had lots of direct options that were a lot more kinetic than getting me audited.

Someone off camera said something indistinct to Scott and he gave a lopsided smile with his broken face. "Yeah, all right," he said. "I'm gonna go, Marty. Yard time."

"Be safe," I said.

His smile got broader and as it stretched out his face, he briefly looked like his old self. "Safe? Marty, I'm just locked up with the drug dealers and the killers. You're the one out there with psychos like Junior."

18

After months of looking over my shoulder for Junior or his minions, it felt very weird to be seeking him out. It took some nerv-
ing to do it. Call me a coward, but the thought of contacting
Junior gave me a little tremor in my gut, a little sweat under the
pits.

"Mr. Coleman isn't available. Can I take a message?" His secretary had a Filipino accent and I could hear other people with
the same accent murmuring in the background—a virtual PA,
then, working from a call center in Manila. Classic Junior: cheap
as hell.

"I'm afraid I need to speak to him about a confidential matter."

"If you would like to leave a name and number, I can tell him
you called."

"I'll think about it," I said. The woman in the call center
sighed. I felt her pain.

"Thank you, sir. Is there anything else I can help you with?"

"No, that's all. I appreciate your help."

"Have a nice day." She was reading a script, but she sold the
line. I hoped she was getting paid well.

But I doubted it.

I didn't want to give Junior my number. I wanted to talk to him.
I wanted to explain where we stood. It was imperative that he
know about my deterrent. I needed a go-between, but was there

anyone who knew both of us? Well, sure, any number of people knew us both. All the regulars at Junior's Avalon parties. But did I trust any of *them*?

I'd been waiting for Facebook to die since I first tried it. It wasn't any one thing that turned me off, it was *everything*—it was like someone had taken all the things I hated about technology and stuck them together into a grotesque Frankenstein's monster. I resigned my account and blocked it at my router.

But I kept a burner account and used it with a VPN, because Facebook was purpose-built for invading people's privacy and sometimes, it was my job to do that. Junior had a dormant Facebook account, and it was still "friends" with a couple hundred more accounts. I scrolled through these looking for familiar faces, people I knew from his parties.

There: fiftyish, face a tanned botox mask. Broad shoulders. No neck. The name: "JK Scheinberg." I'd never known his last name, but I remembered JK, oh yes, and his Tommy Bahama shirts.

I clicked on JK and scrolled *his* contacts. I didn't spot who I was looking for. But now that I had a last name, I could search for "jk scheinberg katya." I started on Google Image Search, because I'd be able to spot Katya from a thumbnail. Those cheekbones and bee-stung lips and long neck were unmissable and unforgettable.

A little scrolling and I had her. Katya Belousov. Her Facebook profile was old and dusty, but her Instagram was filled with bikini shots and pictures of handbags that cost more than a car. The pictures were from all over the world, but ones from a severe white-walled bedroom dominated by a California superking and double doors opening onto a walk-in closet were geotagged in Dallas.

A data broker sold me a profile on Katya Belousov of Glen Abbey, a luxury gated community of million-dollar McMansions in a suburb that was most of the way to Plano. The property was registered to a Montana LLC whose officers were all offshore LLCs. Katya was living her best life, clearly.

She still had an LA cell phone number, though.

> Hi, Katya. My name's Marty Hench. You and I met at a party in Avalon a decade ago, and spent some time with my friend Scott. I'm sorry to reach out to you out of the blue, but I wanted to ask you a favor. I know this sounds weird, but could I call you?

It was a long shot, but I like to cover all the possibilities. Still, I was surprised when, only a few seconds later, my phone rang.

"Hello, Marty," Katya said.

Katya knew how Scott felt about her, but that was okay. He didn't let it get in the way of their friendship, so she didn't, either.

He'd discreetly asked for her number, that day at the gardens, and she wasn't surprised a few weeks later when he texted her asking if she was free for the coming weekend. She asked what he had in mind and he sent her a link to a Sonoma wine-country luxury inn with a Michelin-star kitchen, and she said she'd check her diary.

The weekend was mutually pleasurable, though not in the way that either of them had expected. From the moment he picked her up at SFO, they'd fallen into an easy, joking cama-raderie, discovering many mutual interests—both were fans of obscure Krautrock, both could quote long passages from Alexandra Kollontai from memory, and both agreed that the 1927 edition of *Red Love* was superior to the '77 translation. Katya did her impression of Kollontai's fierce stare and it was so spot-on perfect that Scott nearly swerved off the road and into a drainage ditch abutting a vineyard.

They made each other laugh, a lot. Scott had the weekend

papers dropped discreetly at the door to their room and they spent half of Saturday in bed next to each other, reading out bits of the paper. It was so much fun that they did it again on Sunday.

What they didn't do was fuck each other.

Scott tried, but the arrangement didn't work for him. He'd been riveted by Katya for months, confessed that he'd fantasized about her nonstop, but something about knowing that he was paying for her time made that part of his erotic imagination go AWOL. She tried a few things—she was good at her job and this wasn't the first time a customer had this kind of contradiction to resolve—but in the end, they both agreed that they were having too much fun to risk it with a bunch of heroic measures.

She actually offered him a discount on the weekend, something she'd never done before. She regretted the offer as soon as she'd made it, but he justified her trust by refusing it out of hand.

After that, they had a few more weekends away, and then one time when Katya was in San Francisco, she called *him* and they went out for a long night of boozing in the Mission, hopping from bar to bar and ending up at Zeitgeist, where they drank draft beer and ate thick burgers and made friends with a long table of off-duty burlesque performers who'd just come from practice.

The next day, Scott sent her a long message telling her that he knew she was a professional and that he didn't expect freebies forever just because she'd comped him for an evening out. She replied that she'd think about it and then the next time they got together, she kissed him on the cheek and told him this one was on her, too.

She didn't even notice that her cocaine had fallen out of her handbag and rolled beneath the passenger seat. She had started the trip with ten grams and had horned most of a gram over the weekend, leaving precisely 9.01 grams of cocaine in Scott's car for a California highway patrolman to discover a week later, when he pulled Scott over for doing 95 m.p.h. on a winding stretch of the Pacific Coast Highway.

If she'd only had one more bump, Scott would have been caught with less than nine grams, and they couldn't have made his possession into an "intent to sell" Class B felony.

"Yes, of course I can get in touch with Junior," she said. "Whatever it takes. Anything for Scott. Oh, Marty, I wish he'd let me call him."

"Why won't he?"

"Before his trial, he told me not even to try, because he didn't want me to think I owed it to him for keeping his mouth shut. He didn't want me feeling like I was in his debt."

"What an idiot," I said. "Maybe we can change his mind, after I talk to Junior."

"I'll get him."

I thought about insisting that Junior meet me at McKinley Park at dusk. It was a good meeting place, simultaneously private enough that we wouldn't be overheard while being public enough that he couldn't get away with having some of his cop-mafia buddies jump me.

But Junior was a busy man and he was only free to meet me in his offices in Long Beach, his PA informed me. She booked us thirty minutes at 5:30 p.m. on a Wednesday night, and warned me that Mr. Coleman had a dinner reservation that he'd need to leave for at six sharp.

Going back to LA was not a fun prospect. I took what precautions I could: I borrowed a friend's car—a three-year-old silver Prius C that looked exactly like a million other cars, whose license plate couldn't be connected to me. I street-parked it half a mile from Junior's office and walked in, watching closely for guys with the beefy look of retired LA County deputy sheriffs. I didn't spot any, but I did see Benedetto in the window of a café across the street, along with his son and one of their paralegals.

In an aggressively air-conditioned lobby, I let a bored rent-a-cop scan my driver's license and check my name on a list of visitors before buzzing me in and directing me to a specific elevator car that was preprogrammed to go straight up to the seventeenth floor. The ride was excruciating, and the doors took an eternity to part. I was braced for a fist, but the seventeenth-floor hallway was deserted.

Behind locked glass doors, Thames Estuary's offices were dark. I tried peering through the glass but only made out shadowy rectangles—a reception desk, a sofa, a coffee table. There was a keycard reader, but no doorbell. I tapped at the door, waited a beat, then tapped harder, using my borrowed car keys so the glass made sharp ringing noises.

A human figure emerged from the shadows behind the glass and drew up to the door. A man, with an impatient gait. Junior. He unlocked the door and stared at me. He had poker-player eyes and a wooden face.

"Lionel," I said.

"Marty." He opened the door and I stepped into the twilight of the office lobby.

Without a word, he walked past me, deep into the office. I followed, my eyes adjusting to the dim light enough that I avoided the lobby furniture.

Junior's office was a showpiece, with a vast Federal desk topped with dark red leather, a boardroom table big enough for a banquet, and a conversation corner with a love seat and a couple of overstuffed chairs arranged around a walnut coffee table. Brass lamps with Tiffany shades lit the scene in pools of warm yellow light, enough to show off the furnishings without washing out the twilit view through the picture windows, a view that stretched all the way to the distant twinkling lights of Catalina Island.

He sat down in one of the armchairs and I took the love seat, drawing my laptop out of my bag and setting it down on the table.

"I appreciate you meeting with me like this," I said.

"Katya was persuasive," he said. "She said it would be worth my while."

"I think it will be," I said. I looked at my laptop, back to him. I'd rehearsed this, but that didn't stop my heart from thudding. My hands wanted to shake; I put them in my lap.

"Here's a thing about the California Franchise Tax Board," I said, and his poker face slipped just a little. "Some of their auditors really care about their jobs. They got into the job because it meant something to them."

"I have the highest possible opinion of the entire CFTB," he said in careful tones.

"I'm not recording," I said. "I could strip naked if that would put you at your ease, but I thought we could get to the same place if I confessed to a felony."

"How do you know *I'm* not recording?" The poker face slipped further. He loved playing eleven-dimensional chess, even if he wasn't very good at it.

"Are you?"

"I'm not," he said.

"Good," I said, "because after I tell you my secret, I'm going to tell you some of yours. I think you'd prefer not to manufacture any evidence of what I say then."

A flash of worry, a grin, the poker mask. Oh, Junior. You are living proof that turning a large fortune into a vast fortune requires nothing more than low, vicious cunning.

"For several years, I mailed quarterly packages to Scott. Each of these packages contained large quantities of illegal hallucinogens, which Scott shared with other inmates."

I'd said that line into the mirror a hundred times, until I could say it without a quaver. I'd repeated it until it became a nonsense phrase, a collection of phonemes in a foreign language. Despite this, as I heard myself pronounce these syllables, I recoiled from them. My tongue thickened in my mouth and I had to articulate with the exaggerated care of a drunkard.

Junior gave up on the poker face, gave me a wolf's smile, bared teeth ready to rend and tear. I was done for.

"Junior," I said. He didn't like being called Junior and I knew it. The provocation was deliberate, to interrupt his train of thought, which was barreling toward how he would use my statement to put me in a cage next to Scott. At least we could save money on videoconferencing. "I have some more things to tell you."

"Say it." Impatient. "You've got ten minutes." It was more like twenty-five, according to his secretary, but I had a feeling we were going to go long.

I opened my laptop's lid and began to read him line items from the spreadsheet I'd gone full-screen on before putting the machine in sleep mode. Each line had an LLC, then the beneficial owners, then a dollar figure, which was the sum that the LLC had shuffled into Junior's Maltese accounts. These were the kickbacks that Junior's own affiliated companies paid to him for their subcontracts to Thames Estuary. They were the primary mechanism by which he had both stolen from the State of California and avoided both federal and state tax on the loot.

I read five lines and looked up. His expression was incredible, a furious toddler who's just had his ice cream confiscated by an intransigent parent. Clenched fists, lips skinned back from teeth, nose wrinkled like he'd smelled something dead and rotten.

I read five more lines. My voice got stronger and calmer, even as he started to make little choking noises.

"There's more," I said, "but in the interests of time, I'd like to move to the second sheet."

This one traced double-dip accounting, where Thames Estuary and a secretly held subsidiary masquerading as a separate company both claimed the same expense for deductions. I'd sorted it by dollar figure. The first line had six zeroes.

I was seven lines into that sheet when he reached across the table and slammed my laptop lid down, hard enough that he risked cracking the screen. Thankfully, I was expecting this and my fingers were clear.

He stood up and went to that big walnut Federal desk, moved a folder and retrieved a phone.

"That's what you were recording on?" I said.

He made an incoherent snarling noise.

"I'd reformat it if I were you. Reset it to factory defaults. But check to make sure your voice-memo app isn't synching to the cloud first. You'll want to delete that copy, too."

His hands shook as he stabbed at the glass rectangle.

"It's under Settings, then General, then Transfer or Reset Phone," I said. I'd looked it up. "Then you tap 'erase all contents and settings.' But don't forget to check for a cloud backup first. Everyone forgets those cloud backups. They're a menace."

He wrestled with his phone some more.

"It's Manage Storage, then Backups. Find the name of your phone and tap Delete." He glared at me. I shrugged. "Or don't. It's just that I figured we'd both be happier without that recording floating around out there."

I gave him time. The sun was going down outside the window, bathing the sea and the office walls in red-orange light. I got lost in the lights, floating above the scene. All the worry I'd felt melted away. We were locked into the script, and it would work or it wouldn't.

He sat back down in his overstuffed chair. It was meant to be a big, serious piece of furniture, but it made him look like a little boy. "I can't let your friend out," he said. "That's up to the parole board. Out of my hands."

"I understand," I said. "Scott understands, too. You keep Scott safe, call off the thugs you sicced on him. No one hurts him. He lives out his time safe and sound."

"Fine. Done. It was never personal, Hench. It's just business."

"I'm not done," I said. "You refund him the money he lost on his ebook and MP3 collection, and all the money he spent on video calls and email. I can give you a full accounting of it."

He barked a laugh. "You got it, buddy. Sure. Send me the bill, I'll get a credit to his account."

"You give him back books. Real books. I mail them, you pass them on to him. Letters, too. And visits. I want to visit him."

The little boy made a pissy little face. "That's a security measure. It keeps the inmates safe."

"You don't have to give everyone their in-person visits and letters back," I said. "You can keep making money for your investors off of that one. You've loaded up on a lot of debt. You can't afford to interrupt those cash flows. But you give them back to Scott. I get to see that he's safe, and he gets to go back to the kind of time he was doing before these scams took over."

"It's impossible. There's no way to make it work. We don't even have the facilities anymore. The visitation room is a break room for the guards now. Impossible."

I shrugged. "I guess we're done here, then." I stood up and grabbed my laptop. "Your books were a tough nut to crack until you sent that CFTB auditor after me. He was able to get pretty deep, fast."

He glared at me. I could tell he didn't think I was serious. "There's more, I'm sure. This was just the first cut. He's a smart guy, that auditor."

I was struggling with the office-door lock when he caught up with me.

"You can call the auditor off?"

"He and I have an understanding," I said. "You don't need to know the details."

He pushed my hands away from the lock. His palms were dripping. "Fine," he said. "Stop fucking around. It's fine. We'll make it happen."

Yeah, I bet you will. You're scamming tens of millions here, you can afford to staff a visitation room for me and my pal so I can be sure he's safe and well.

19

The rehab wing of the California Medical Facility smelled like a high-school gym: a humid place of old sweat and fresh perspiration, as men inched their way painfully along on rebuilt legs or worked their badly knit arms against a rubber thera-band. The physios were visibly disinterested in their progress, barely looking up from their phones to tell a patient-inmate to switch to the next tedious set of reps.

Scott and I sat on scuffed step stools we dragged out of a pile of equipment. His face was mostly healed now, and it wasn't quite so crooked as it had seemed the last time we'd been together. His dental appliance clicked a little when he talked, but despite this, his speech was clearer than I'd heard it since before the attack.

"That's the deal," I said. "Junior gives you back your music, your videos, and your ebooks. He refunds all the money you spent on teleconferencing and email. You get in-person visits. I can give you *paper books*." I made eye contact as I said these last two words, so that he'd know exactly what I was talking about.

He didn't say anything for a long time.

"Marty," he began, then stopped. He took a few deep breaths. "I'll be back in a second." He headed off to the men's room. His limp was barely noticeable. When he came back, his face was shining with the cold water he'd splashed on it.

"Marty," he said again. "I just want to make sure I understand something, okay, so I'm just going to say this. Is that all right?"

"Sure."

He dropped his voice to a bare whisper. "You traded some treats for me in exchange for laying off Junior and calling off the state tax investigation. Is that right?"

"That's about the size of it," I said. "A mutual friend of ours had a bigger name for the state tax authority, someone even dirtier than Junior, if you can believe it. And going after Junior would have been . . . political. My friend in the Franchise Tax Board decided he could get more mileage out of this new name."

Katya had a lot of dirt on JK, because JK was *very* dirty. He ran a chain of charter schools up and down the state that had extracted hundreds of millions in public money, and he'd off-shored it through a half-clever vehicle that used a trademark-licensing business to realize all the income in the Caymans, where IP income was taxed at zero percent.

Hassan understood that making an example out of JK would scare a lot of smaller roaches out from under the fridge and he was looking forward to squashing a lot of them. Junior was a small fry in comparison, and JK didn't have the same friends in high places. Hassan understood how to maximize his efforts to do the most for the taxpayers of California.

"That's not how it was supposed to go," Scott whispered, but now it was more of a hiss. His broken face contorted into a rictus of grief and rage. "*You were supposed to get him.*"

I rocked back. Was that true? Maybe. He'd asked me to go after Junior, but I'd always assumed that getting Junior was a means to an end—the point wasn't to bring down Junior, it was to keep Scott alive and well until he finished his time.

Had I been wrong all this time?

Evidently, I had. I'd been concerned with Scott's survival. Scott had somehow transcended concerns about his own well-being and committed himself to the greater good. I hadn't gotten the memo.

"Marty, fuck, don't you understand what life is like inside for the people who *don't* have millions in the bank and useful friends who can blackmail the warden into handing out privileges? More than a hundred thousand poor assholes are locked up and under that bastard's authority. What they're enduring isn't even punishment. The cruelty isn't the point. The point is to make Junior and his pals millions of bucks.

"Did you ever stop and think about what a family on food stamps has to give up to have a one-minute, eight-dollar video call with a dad on the inside? A husband? A son? How often do you think those guys get to talk to their kids, their brothers and sisters, their wives? I know a guy who couldn't afford two minutes of video time to say goodbye to his ten-year-old son when the kid was dying of leukemia.

"I don't give a shit about myself or my future inside, Marty. The life I've lived, I've had more than any ten of those guys. I've had my share. You were supposed to help *them*, not me."

The right thing to say was *Of course, you're right, Scott, I'll go back and get Hassan to reopen the books on Junior.* I was supposed to say, *Scott, you are a better man than me, and those people deserve better, and if it's in my power to help them, I have a duty to do so.* I should have said, *Thank you for helping me understand what I owe my fellow man.*

I *wanted* to say, *You fucking asshole, I just saved your life and you're going to throw it back in my face?*

Across the room, a man with his leg in a brace hobbled along, white-knuckling a railing, face contorted and unseeing as he stared past me into infinity. His physiotherapist scrolled on his phone. The man gasped and stopped and dropped his head. He was done for.

But then he looked up again, set his mouth in a straight line, and walked the rest of the way, turned, and started hobbling back. Even from across the room, I could hear him hiss with pain with every step. He didn't stop until he made it all the way back.

I found a 1982 paperback edition of Zane Grey's *The Vanishing American* on the discount table in front of Dog Eared Books in the Mission and bought it on the spot. The original 1922 serial saw the much-abused Navaho Nophaie dead of influenza in the final chapter. In the 1982 revised edition, Nophaie lived. It made for a worse ending, but it was still better than the 1925 Paramount film, which Jesse Lasky convinced Grey to neuter, turning it into a tale of noble savages and well-meaning settlers having innocent disagreements.

There were 342 pages in the revised edition. It had been so long since I'd last done this that I had to print out a table of prime numbers and then carefully drop three drips of extremely fantastic LSD onto the inside bottom-right corner of the pages.

I gave the book three days to dry, until there was not even the slightest sign that it had been altered. Then I took BART to Oakland Airport and caught a flight down to Daugherty Field, the tiny airport in Long Beach, and caught an Uber to Junior's office.

Junior met me in the lobby. I handed him the book.

"I'll see that he gets it," Junior said.

"I'm sure you will," I said. *You'd better.*

priorities

The guards at San Genesius State Penitentiary knew me. I was that weird guy who got to come and visit a prisoner in person, the exception that everyone knew about and no one was supposed to talk about.

Normally, they treated me like an administrative procedure: sign here, walk through this metal detector, wait here, time to go.

But that day, six months after I brokered a deal on Scott's behalf that he clearly disapproved of, the guards had no idea how to handle me. I was damp from the dash in the pouring rain from the parking lot to the old visitors' entrance and I sat uncomfortably on a scratched plastic chair they seemingly kept solely for my monthly visits.

There had once been dozens of chairs like it. Now it sat all alone in the dim waiting room under a patchwork of light provided by overhead fluorescents, only half of which were working.

Behind a heavy door at the other end of the room, murmured conversations. Twice, the door opened and a guard looked out at me and scowled. Different guard each time. The first was an older Black guy who looked like a lifer. The second was a white kid so young he could have been in high school. He had a frightened air and kept one hand on the pepper spray on his belt.

Time crawled by. I shifted in my wet pants and wiped at the drips of rain that slid out of my hairline and crawled down my face and neck. I'd left my watch and phone in the car. There was nothing of interest in that waiting room. I counted the lights—

eighteen—and the number that were burned out—thirteen—
and then the percentage that were working: 27.7777 percent.

I waited. It had been a long time since anyone had held a
murmured conversation on the other side of that heavy door,
much less looked in on me. I realized there was no reason for me
to stay in my seat. I got up and paced, touched my toes, rolled
my head around. It was a long drive and the stretches felt great.

I was leaning up against a wall, doing calf stretches, when
the door opened again.

"Mr. Hench." She was at least sixty, iron-gray hair in a careful cotton-ball arrangement atop her head, blue pantsuit, low
heels, subdued makeup. Her face was a sheer stone wall, where
no sympathy would ever find purchase.

"That's me," I said, springing away from the wall and wiping
my hands clean.

"I'm sorry to have kept you waiting. Mr. Warms is not available today. You should have been informed, and I regret the
oversight."

"Not available? Is he all right? I mean, he's not hurt, is he?"

"Mr. Warms is in good health."

"Then why can't I see him? It's not like he could have gone
out for groceries."

"I'm not at liberty to discuss the details of our inmates with
the public." She paused, gave me dead eyes. "I'm sure you understand."

This felt bad. Very bad. My hands started sweating. "Can
I speak to Junior? I mean, Lionel Coleman? Please? I'm sure a
quick phone call will sort this out. I'll go out to my car and give
him a ring and—"

"Mr. Coleman is on a leave of absence," she said. "I'm sorry
you came all this way. Mr. Coleman's departure was quite sudden and we are still adjusting our operations." She waited. I
didn't leave. Pointedly, she repeated, "I'm sorry you came all
this way."

I pushed down the fear I was feeling and the rage it provoked. Making my voice very calm, I said, "But I *did* come all this way. I would like very much to see my friend now."

"I'm afraid that's impossible," she said.

"Then *I'm* afraid we're at an impasse, because I have no intention of leaving until I verify my friend's safety. You may not be aware of it, but Scott has faced serious violence at this facility before and this . . . *arrangement* I have to visit him in person is in response to those administrative failures to ensure his safety."

She blinked a slow lizard blink. "Mr. Hench," she said, in a voice like the synthesized speech on a BART platform, "you can wait here for as long as you'd like, but it won't change the fact that Mr. Warms is no longer at this facility."

Scott's lawyer declined to speak to me on the phone. His receptionist made an appointment for me to see him the next day, and I pulled off Highway 80 somewhere by a Napa farmstand to make a note of the time and address. I bought a bag of peaches and a couple of ears of corn from the kid at the stand, and then went back for a fat, soft wheel of his chèvre. It seemed polite and I was starving. I got peach juice all down my shirt on the way back.

The law offices of Wilson, Brayton and Buncombe occupied both floors of a renovated warehouse building near the Presidio. They had their own parking valet. It was that kind of white-collar, white-shoe criminal defense firm. I tipped the valet five when I handed him my keys.

Laurie Buncombe was a grandmotherly woman in her early sixties with short brown hair and twinkling brown eyes. She wore a cardigan over a high-necked blouse and relaxed linen trousers that swished as she walked me from the reception desk back to her office, lined with family photos, a framed Stanford diploma, and a decree from the state legislature thanking her for her pro bono service.

We sat kitty-corner to each other on her brown leather L-shaped sofa and waited for her assistant to bring us cups of tea and coasters to protect the Danish wood coffee table between us.

"Mr. Hench, the first thing I want to convey to you is how grateful Scott is to you for the friendship and advocacy you've provided during his incarceration. Not just Scott, either. I know from long experience that it's hard to remain committed to an incarcerated friend, no matter how much respect and affection you may bear for him, as the years go by. There are so many factors in our daily lives that drag us away from the people who are locked away from us, and for all but the most devoted friends, out of sight eventually translates to out of mind. You are a commendable, true friend."

"I sense a 'but' coming on."

She gave me a kind smile that went all the way to her eyes. "There is indeed a 'but.' To get to it I need to tell you that I have Scott's explicit permission to convey the following to you, and Scott has asked me to ask you to treat this as confidential."

She stopped. That was my cue.

"I will treat it as confidential," I said. I put my hand over my heart. "I do solemnly swear."

"That's good to hear," she said.

The federal agents that visited San Genesius State Penitentiary without warning at 6 a.m. included two FBI field agents, two DEA diversion investigators, and an investigator from the Bureau of Prisons Western Region. As a courtesy, they were accompanied by observers from the California Department of Corrections and Rehabilitation.

The private cops at the door didn't want to let them in. They wanted to talk to their supervisors, who were still in bed. But the feds weren't half-trained rent-a-cops; they were federal agents, and they knew how to cite 18 USC 1511 (Obstruction of State or local law enforcement) with a bloodcurdling calm that had the mall cops falling over themselves to welcome them into the facility.

They proceeded in a tight formation directly to Scott Warms's cell, where they found Scott already dressed and waiting for them. They directed the rent-a-cops to unlock the door. The neatly excised inside-right corners of select pages from the 1982 paperback edition of Zane Grey's *The Vanishing American* were waiting for them on Scott's folded-down writing desk. The DEA agents quickly gloved up and moved them to an evidence bag.

They gathered up Scott's personal belongings (neatly folded and ready for transport on the end of his cot), the book and the pieces in their baggies, and Scott himself. They proceeded in formation back out of the San Genesius facility, handed over a thick folder of paperwork, and drove Scott downstate in a convoy of black SUVs, all the way to the maximum-security federal prison at Victorville, where he was confined to the prison's Special Housing Unit.

"Solitary confinement?" I said. "Jesus, we've got to do something, that's completely—"

"Mr. Hench," she said. "Marty. It will be easier if you just let me tell the story. Scott knows you're a good friend and that you care about his welfare. But in the final analysis, Scott is the final authority on his relationship with the State of California and the United States of America."

"Of course," I said. "Sorry."

At 6 a.m. on that same day, another fed quartet—two FBI field agents and two DEA investigators—presented a warrant to the gate guard at Bel Air Crest, who let them drive on to the property without incident. At the agents' request, the guard did not notify Lionel Coleman Jr., who lived in a ten-million-dollar, ninety-five-hundred-square-foot, six-bedroom mansion on Lancelot Lane, with a million-dollar view of the Pacific, the Getty, and the mountains of Topanga State Park.

The housekeeper who answered the door was instructed to wait outside. The team entered the house swiftly and ascended the commanding curved stair up from the marble-floored, high-ceilinged "lawyer-foyer" and to the second floor, then down a long hallway to the master bedroom, whose location they'd confirmed by consulting a two-year-old Zillow listing for the house.

Coleman slept in Calvin Klein jockey shorts. His companion, a woman substantially his junior whom the agents identified as Lora Palfrey, was given a robe and escorted back onto the front porch by one of the FBI men while the others helped Junior find track pants, a T-shirt, and tennis shoes. They allowed him to bring his wallet and a pair of socks to put on later. Out of respect, they did not handcuff him. He was allowed to call his lawyer once the convoy arrived at the Federal Building on Wilshire Boulevard.

"Normally, someone caught trafficking drugs into a California pen would be referred to the state police," she said, sipping her tea. I tried mine. It tasted like nothing at all. "But because of Mr. Coleman's multistate prison interests, the prospect that he was involved in trafficking narcotics to prisoners attracted federal scrutiny."

"Ms. Buncombe," I said. "I understand that the things I say to you are not within the client-attorney privilege. With that understanding, can I ask you whether Scott has discussed how he came by the LSD-doped papers?"

She put her tea down and looked at me for a long, long time.

"You're right," she said. "You aren't covered by the client-attorney privilege. I can tell you that Scott truthfully informed the federal authorities that Mr. Coleman personally delivered the drugs to him." She gave a long, slow blink, then went back to staring at me. Was that supposed to mean, *and then Junior turned around and told the feds that he got the book from you?* My mouth was so dry. The tea didn't help.

"Mr. Hench. Marty. Mr. Warms has also given me permission to disclose to you that, acting on his behalf, I have been in conversation with Mr. Coleman's team of attorneys, and that we have come to an arrangement."

Scott was sentenced to an extra ten years by a judge who didn't even look up from his paperwork when he pronounced the sentence. He was escorted from the room in a hail of glared daggers from the federal agents present, who muttered to each other. Feds don't like it when informants recant, and they'd leaned hard on Scott to get him to change his testimony back and testify against Junior. But Scott now said that he'd found the papers behind a loose brick in the San Genesius's exercise yard. He'd even showed them the brick.

The very same day, Junior announced that Thames Estuary was selling all of its prison holdings, at a substantial loss, to a variety of buyers. The SPAC shareholders were furious and threatened suits. The institutional investors were incandescent and filed suits. Junior announced his retirement. To Thailand. When the press release dropped, he was already on a plane.

Scott's video was grainy, his audio poor, his face tired. His voice: triumphant.

"Hello, Marty."

"Scott, are you okay? Jesus Christ, buddy. I mean—just, *Jesus Christ.*" I'd caught his eye momentarily as he was escorted out of his sentencing. Though his face was stony, his eyes had twinkled. I imagined I could see that twinkle again, through the postage-stamp-sized video.

"I am supremely fine, Marty. They're moving me to San Quentin tomorrow. It's got a computer lab. I'm hoping to teach classes."

"For the next twenty years."

"No," he said. "My skills will be out of date long before then. But maybe I can take some classes from someone else, further down the line."

We stared at one another through a long, uncomfortable silence.

"You did it," I said. "Was it worth it?"

"Fuck yes. I'd do it again. In a heartbeat. I *won*, Marty."

"But you got an extra *decade* on your sentence."

He shrugged. "And I gave every other motherfucker behind bars in this state some relief. No one else was going to do that. No one." He looked right out the camera, at me.

"Yeah," I said. "You're right. I guess I was thinking about you and you were thinking about everyone." I sighed. "You're an inspiration, Scott. Seriously."

"Come visit me at San Quentin?"

"Of course," I said. "I'll bring books."

BUSINESSWIRE | HOME | SERVICES | NEWS | EDUCATION | ABOUT US

PINEWOOD BROOK FUNDS ACQUIRES DISTRESSED CORRECTIONAL ASSETS

Correctional services firms to shed debt, restructure for new synergies and efficiencies

November 28, 2017

LAS VEGAS—(BUSINESS WIRE)—Pinewood Brook Funds (Malta) today announced a deal to acquire distressed assets, including operational contracts, from the receivers in bankruptcy of Thames Estuary Capital LLC. The assets include the exclusive right to supply communications services, educational and entertainment materials, correspondence and gifts to inmates in four U.S. states and American Samoa.

Creditors to Thames Estuary agreed to a debt restructuring that puts the firms on a robust, sustainable footing; the all-stock deal closed yesterday.

The new holdings enjoyed a bullish launch, announcing contracts with corrections departments in New Mexico, Montana, South Dakota and Louisiana.

Pinewood Brook CEO JK Scheinberg assured investors that the new venture would have his full attention, citing the recent release of all claims against him and his firms by the California Franchise Tax Board . . .

And that's the story.

Wait, are you asleep?

You were, you were totally sleeping.

It's okay. I'm tired, too. Let's hit the sack.

Big day tomorrow.

acknowledgments

For all the hardworking people who made this series possible: Patrick Nielsen Hayden, Mal Frazier, Terry McGarry, Russell Galen, Laura Etzkorn, Caro Perny, Sarah Reidy, Lucille Rettino, Jamie Broadhurst, Elena Stokes, Brianna Robinson, Nic Cheetham, Polly Grice, Sophie Whitehead, John Scalzi, Oriana Leckert, Roz Doctorow, Gord Doctorow, Alice Taylor, and Poesy Taylor Doctorow. I literally couldn't have done it without you and everything you did mattered.

THANK YOU!

Readers who've followed my work know that I have waged a decades-long war on "digital rights management"(DRM)— encryption that stops you from moving your books from one reader to another, giving tech giants like Amazon enormous power over readers, writers, and publishers.

To its credit, Amazon doesn't require DRM for ebooks, and my publishers—Tor/Macmillan in the USA and Canada and Head of Zeus/Bloomsbury in the UK, Australia, NZ, India, and South Africa—have gone to great lengths to ensure that my ebooks are sold DRM-free.

However, Amazon's audiobooks division, Audible (a monopolist with a greater than 90 percent market share), requires DRM for every title. Naturally, none of my books are for sale on Audible, which makes them effectively invisible to the majority of audiobook publishers.

I produce my own, high-quality audiobooks (the audio edition for this book and *Red Team Blues* were read by the marvelous

Wil Wheaton) and presell them on Kickstarter, in campaigns where readers can directly support this effort by buying audiobooks, ebooks, and hardcovers.

But many backers of the *Red Team Blues* Kickstarter did one better: after I posted an update noting how powerful a personal recommendation from a friend can be, these backers posted their reactions to *Red Team Blues* to social media, blogs, and book review sites. In so doing, they delivered the greatest boon an author can receive: an honest reaction from one reader to another.

Below are the names of those generous backers. If you enjoyed this book (or *any* book!), please consider telling the people who matter to you about it. There is no greater way to promote good books and sustain the authors who write them.

Matt Haughey, Sean "seanbseanb" Berry, John Paine, Katherine Shipman, Chev Eldrid, Spencer Greenhalgh, Jeff Rhyason, Mitch Silverman, Nick Radonic, John Bridges, James Boyle, Jeremiah Miller, Meejum Kaufman, AJ Voraman, Dennis Boesgaard Petersen, Rod Bartlett, Vincent Waciuk, Chris Hall, James Kasson, Case Harris, Brian Conner, Irfan Kanat, Daniel Morgan, Amber D. Scott, Justin Zheng, Derron Simon, Chris Swan, Marcus Ganley, Miki Menghini, Francis O'Donovan, Sagebrush, Luis Blackaller, Fauns, Mark Lyken, Skylar Reiner, Jason Douthit, Bryan, Larry Kuperman, The Revd Dr A K M Adam, Penny Ramirez, Gianfranco Cecconi, Katarina Bosnjak, Dean Lea, Ray Berger, Ben Ramsey, Beaches, Hadas Nahshon, David Simeone, Michael P. Sauers, The Happy Anarchist, Calder Fertig.

For James Boyle and Jennifer Jenkins, as ever, for their wise counsel and clarifying ideas about copyright, fair use, quotation and epigrams.

Turn the page for a sneak peek at
Cory Doctorow's next novel

picks and shovels

Available February 2025

Fidelity Computing was the most colorful PC company in Silicon Valley.

A Catholic priest, a Mormon bishop, and an Orthodox rabbi walk into a technology gold rush and start a computer company. The fact that it sounded like the setup for a nerdy joke about the mid-1980s was fantastic for their bottom line. Everyone who heard their story loved it.

As juicy as the story of Fidelity Computing was, they flew under most people's radar for years, even as they built a wildly profitable technology empire from direct sales through faith groups. The first time most of us heard of them was in 1983, when *Byte* ran its cover story on Fidelity Computing, unearthing a parallel universe of technology that had grown up while no one was looking.

At first, I thought maybe they were doing something similar to Apple's new Macintosh: like Apple, they made PCs (the Wise PC), an operating system (Wise DOS), and a whole line of monitors, disk drives, printers, and software.

Like the Mac, none of these things worked with anything else—you needed to buy everything from floppy disks to printer cables specially from them, because nothing anyone else made would work with their system.

And like the Mac, they sold mostly through word of mouth. The big difference was that Mac users were proud to call themselves a cult, while Fidelity Computing's customers were literally a religion.

Long after Fidelity had been called to the Great Beyond, its most loyal customers gave it an afterlife, nursing their computers along, until the parts and supplies ran out. They'd have kept going even then if there'd been any way to unlock their machines and use the same stuff the rest of the computing world relied on. But that wasn't something Fidelity Computing would permit, even from beyond the grave.

I was summoned to Fidelity headquarters—in unfashionable Colma, far from the white-hot start-ups of Palo Alto, Mountain View, and, of course, Cupertino—by a friend of Art's. Art had a lot more friends than me. I was a skipping stone, working as the part-time bookkeeper/accountant/CFO for half a dozen companies and never spending more than one or two days in the same office.

Art was hardly more stable than me—he switched start-ups all the time, working for as little as two months (and never for more than a year) before moving on. His bosses knew what they were getting: you hired Art Hellman to blaze into your company, take stock of your product plan, root out and correct all of its weak points, build core code libraries, and then move on. He was good enough and sufficiently in demand to command the right to behave this way, and he wouldn't have it any other way. My view was, it was an extended celebration of his liberation from the legal villainy of Nick Cassidy III: having narrowly escaped a cage, he was determined never to be locked up again.

Art's "engagements"—as he called them—earned him the respect and camaraderie of half the programmers and hardware engineers in the Valley. This, in spite of the fact that he was a public and ardent member of the Lavender Panthers, wore the badge on his lapel, went to the marches, and brought his boyfriend to all the places where his straight colleagues brought their girlfriends.

He'd come out to me less than a week after I arrived by the simple expedient of introducing the guy he was watching TV with in our living room as Lewis, his boyfriend. Lewis was a Chinese guy about our age, and his wardrobe—plain white tee, tight blue jeans, loafers—matched the new look Art had adopted since leaving Boston. Lewis had a neat, short haircut that matched Art's new haircut, too.

To call the Art I'd known in Cambridge a slob would be an insult to the natty, fashion-conscious modern slob. He'd favored old band T-shirts with fraying armpit seams, too-big jeans that were either always sliding off his skinny hips or pulled up halfway to his nipples. In the summer, his sneakers had holes in the toes. In the winter, his boots were road-salt-crusted crystalline eruptions. His red curls were too chaotic for a white-boy 'fro and were more of a *heap,* and he often went days without shaving.

There were members of the Newbury Street Irregulars who were bigger slobs than Art, but they *smelled.* Art washed, but otherwise, he looked like a homeless person (or a hacker). His transformation to a neatly dressed, clean-shaven fellow with a twenty-five-dollar haircut that he actually used some sort of hairspray on was remarkable. I'd assumed it was about his new life as a grown-up living far from home and doing a real job. It turned out that wasn't the reason at all.

"Oh," I said. "That makes a lot of sense." I shook Lewis's hand. He laughed. I checked Art. He was playing it cool, but I could tell he was nervous. I remembered Lucille and how she listened, and what it felt like to be heard. I thought about Art, and the things he'd never been able to tell me.

There'd been a woman in the Irregulars who there were rumors about, and there were a pair of guys one floor down in Art's building who held hands in the elevator, but as far as I knew up until that moment, I hadn't really ever been introduced to a homosexual person. I didn't know how I felt about it, but I *did* know how I *wanted* to feel about it.

So Art didn't just get to know all kinds of geeks from his whistle-stop tour of Silicon Valley's hottest new tech ventures. He was also plugged into this other network of people from the Lavender Panthers, and their boyfriends and girlfriends, and the people he knew from bars and clubs. He and Lewis lasted for a couple of months, and then there were a string of weekends where there was a new guy at the breakfast table, and then he settled down again for a while with Artemis, and then he hit a long dry spell.

I commiserated. I'd been having a dry spell for nearly the whole two years I'd been in California. The closest I came to romance was exchanging a letter with Lucille every couple of weeks—she was a fine pen pal, but that wasn't really a substitute for a living, breathing woman in my life.

Art threw himself into his volunteer work, and he was only half joking when he said he did it to meet a better class of boys than you got at a club. Sometimes, there'd be a committee meeting in our living room and I'd hear about the congressional committee hearing on the "gay plague" and the new wave of especially vicious attacks. It was pretty much the only time I heard about that stuff—no one I worked with ever brought it up, unless it was to make a terrible joke.

It was Murf, one of the guys from those meetings, who told me that Fidelity Computing was looking for an accountant for a special project. He had stayed after the meeting, and he and Art made a pot of coffee and sat down in front of Art's Apple clone, a Franklin Ace 1200 that he'd scored six months ahead of its official release. After opening the lid to show Murf the interior, Art fired it up and put it through its paces.

I hovered over his shoulder, watching. I'd had a couple of chances to play with the 1200, and I wanted one more than anything in the world except for a girlfriend.

"Marty," Art said, "Murf was telling me about a job I thought you might be good for."

The Ace 1200 would have a list price of $2,200. I pulled up a chair.

Fidelity Computing's business offices were attached to their warehouse, right next to their factory. It took up half of a business park in Colma, and I had to circle it twice to find a parking spot. I was five minutes late and flustered when I presented myself to the receptionist, a blond woman with a ten-years-out-of-date haircut and a modest cardigan over a sensible white shirt buttoned to the collar, ring on her finger.

"Hello," I said. "I'm Marty Hench. I—uh—I've got a meeting with the Reverend Sirs." That was what the executive assistant I'd spoken to on the phone had called them. It sounded weird when he said it. It sounded weirder when I said it.

The receptionist gave me a smile that only went as far as her lips. "Please have a seat," she said. There were only three chairs in the little reception area, vinyl office chairs with worn wooden armrests. There weren't any magazines, just glossy catalogs featuring the latest Fidelity Computing systems, accessories, consumables, and software. I browsed one, marveling at the parallel universe of computers in the strange, mauve color that denoted all Fidelity equipment, including the boxes, packaging, and, now that I was attuned to it, the accents and carpet in the small lobby. A side door opened and a young, efficient man in a kippah and wire-rim glasses called for me: "Mr. Hench?" I closed the catalog and returned it to the pile and stood. As I went to shake his hand, I realized that something had been nagging me about the catalog—there were no prices.

"I'm Shlomo," the man said. "We spoke on the phone. Thank you for coming down. The Reverend Sirs are ready to see you now."

He wore plain black slacks, hard black shiny shoes, and a white shirt with prayer-shawl tassels poking out of its tails. I followed him through a vast room filled with chest-high Steelcase cubicles finished in yellowing, chipped wood veneer, every scratch pitilessly lit by harsh overhead fluorescents. Most of the workers at the cubicles were women with headsets, speaking in hushed tones. The tops of their heads marked the interfaith delineators: a block of Orthodox headscarves, then a block of nuns' black-and-white scarves (I learned to call them "veils" later), then the Mormons' carefully coiffed, mostly blond dos.

"This way," Shlomo said, passing through another door and into executive row. The mauve carpets were newer, the nap all swept in one direction. The walls were lined with framed certificates of appreciation, letters from religious and public officials (apparently, the church and state were not separate within the walls of Fidelity Computing), photos of groups of progressively larger groups of people ranked before progressively larger offices—the company history.

We walked all the way to the end of the hall, past closed doors with nameplates, to a corner conference room with a glass wall down one side showing a partial view of a truck-loading dock behind half-closed vertical blinds. Seated at intervals around a large conference table were the Reverend Sirs themselves, each with his own yellow pad, pencil, and coffee cup.

Shlomo announced me: "Reverend Sirs, this is Marty Hench. Mr. Hench, these are Rabbi Yisrael Finkel, Bishop Leonard Clarke, and Father Marek Tarnowski." He backed out of the door, leaving me standing, unsure if I should circle the table shaking hands, or take a seat, or—

"Please, sit," Rabbi Finkel said. He was fiftyish, round-faced and bear-shaped with graying sidelocks and beard and a black suit and tie. His eyes were sharp behind horn-rimmed glasses. He gestured to a chair at the foot of the table.

I sat, then rose a little to undo the button of my sport coat. I hadn't worn it since my second job interview, when I realized it was making the interviewers uncomfortable. It certainly made me uncomfortable. I fished out the little steno pad and stick pen I'd brought with me.

"Thank you for coming, Mr. Hench." The rabbi had an orator's voice, that big chest of his serving as a resonating chamber like a double bass.

"Of course," I said. "Thanks for inviting me. It's a fascinating company you have here."

Bishop Clarke smiled at that. He was the best dressed of the three, in a well-cut business suit, his hair short, neat, side-parted. His smile was very white, and very wide. He was the youngest of the three—in his late thirties, I'd guess. "Thank you," he said. "We know we're very different from the other computer companies, and we like it that way. We like to think that we see something in computers—a potential—that other people have missed."

Father Tarnowski scowled. He was cadaverously tall and thin, with the usual dog collar and jacket, and a heavy gold class ring. His half-rim glasses flashed. He was the oldest, maybe sixty, and had a sour look that I took for habitual. "He doesn't want the press packet, Leonard," he said. "Let's get to the point." He had a broad Chicago accent like a tough-guy gangster in *The Untouchables.*

Bishop Clarke's smile blinked off and on for an instant and I was overcome with the sudden knowledge that these two men did not like each other *at all,* and that there was some kind of long-running argument simmering beneath the surface. "Thank you, Marek, of course. Mr. Hench's time is valuable." Father Tarnowski snorted softly at that and the bishop pretended he didn't hear it, but I saw Rabbi Finkel grimace at his yellow pad.

"What can I help you Reverend Sirs with today?" *Reverend Sirs* came more easily now, didn't feel ridiculous at all. The three of them gave the impression of being a quarter inch away from going for each other's throats, and the formality was a way to keep tensions at a distance.

"We need a certain kind of accountant," the rabbi said. He'd dated the top of his yellow pad and then circled the date. "A kind of accountant who understands the computer business. Who understands *computers,* on a technical level. It's hard to find an accountant like that, believe it or not, even in Silicon Valley." I didn't point out that Colma wasn't in Silicon Valley.

"Well," I said, carefully. "I think I fit that bill. I've only got an associate's degree in accounting, but I'm a kind of floating CFO for half a dozen companies and I've been doing night classes at UCSF Extension to get my bachelor's. I did a year at MIT and built my own computer a few years back. I program pretty well in BASIC and Pascal and I've got a little C, and I'm a pretty darned good debugger, if I do say so myself."

Bishop Clarke gave a small but audible sigh of relief. "You do indeed sound perfect, and I'm told that Shlomo spoke to your references and they were very enthusiastic about your diligence and . . . discretion."

I'd given Shlomo a list of four clients I'd done extensive work with, but I hadn't had "discretion" in mind when I selected them. It's true that doing a company's accounts made me privy to some sensitive information—like when two employees with the same job were getting paid very different salaries—but I got the feeling that wasn't the kind of "discretion" the bishop had in mind.

"I'm pretty good at minding my own business," I said, and

then, "even when I'm being paid to mind someone else's." I liked that line, and made a mental note about it. Maybe someday I'd put it on my letterhead. *Martin Hench: Confidential CPA.*

The bishop favored me with a chuckle. The rabbi nodded thoughtfully. The priest scowled.

"That's very good," the bishop said. "What we'd like to discuss today is of a very sensitive nature, and I'm sure you'll understand if we would like more than your good word to rely on." He lifted his yellow pad, revealing a single page, grainily photocopied, and slid it over the table to me. "That's our standard nondisclosure agreement," he said. He slid a pen along to go with it.

I didn't say anything. I'd signed a few NDAs, but only *after* I'd taken a contract. This was something different. I squinted at the page, which was a second- or third-generation copy and blurry in places. I started to read it. The bishop made a disgusted noise. I pretended I didn't hear him.

I crossed out a few clauses and carefully lettered in an amendment. I initialed the changes and slid the paper back across the table to the bishop, and found the smile was gone from his face. All three of them were now giving me stern looks, wrath-of-God looks, the kind of looks that would make a twenty-one-year-old kid like me very nervous indeed. I felt the nerves rise and firmly pushed them down.

"Mr. Hench," the bishop said, his tone low and serious, "is there some kind of problem?"

It pissed me off. I'd driven all the way to for-chrissakes *Colma* and these three weirdo God-botherers had ambushed me with their everything-and-the-kitchen-sink contract. I had plenty of work, and I didn't *need* theirs, especially not if this was the way they wanted to deal. This had suddenly become a negotiation, and my old man had always told me the best negotiating position was a willingness to get up from the table. I was going to win this negotiation, one way or another.

"No problem," I said.

"And yet you appear to have made alterations to our standard agreement."

"I did," I said. *That's not a problem for me,* I didn't say.

He gave me more of that stern eyeball-ray stuff. I let my negotiating leverage repel it. "Mr. Hench, our standard agreement can only be altered after review by our general counsel."

"That sounds like a prudent policy," I said, and met his stare.

He clucked his tongue. "I can get a fresh one," he said. "This one is no good."

I cocked my head. "I think it'd be better to get your general counsel, wouldn't it?"

The three of them glared at me. I found I was enjoying myself. What's more, I thought Rabbi Finkel might be suppressing a little smile, though the beard made it hard to tell.

"Let me see it," he said, holding his hand out.

Bishop Clarke gave a minute shake of his head. The rabbi half rose, reached across the table, and slid it over to himself, holding it at arm's length and adjusting his glasses. He picked up his pen and initialed next to my changes.

"Those should be fine," he said, and slid it back to me. "Sign, please."

"Yisrael," Bishop Clarke said, an edge in his voice, "changes to the standard agreements need to be reviewed—"

"By our general counsel," the rabbi finished, waving a dismissive gesture at him. "I know, I know. But these are fine. We should probably make the same changes to all our agreements. Meanwhile, we've all now had a demonstration that Mr. Hench is the kind of person who takes his promises seriously. Would you rather have someone who doesn't read and signs his life away, or someone who makes sure he knows what he's signing and agrees with it?"

Bishop Clarke's smile came back, strained at the corners.

"That's an excellent point, Rabbi. Thank you for helping me understand your reasoning." He collected the now-signed contract from me and tucked it back under his yellow pad.

"Now," he said, "we can get down to the reason we asked you here today."

about the author

Jonathan Worth / jonathanworth.com

CORY DOCTOROW is the author of more than two dozen books. He is a special consultant to the Electronic Frontier Foundation, an MIT Media Lab research associate, and a visiting professor of computer science at The Open University. His award-winning novel *Little Brother* and its sequel, *Homeland*, were *New York Times* bestsellers. His novella collection, *Radicalized*, was a CBC Best Fiction of 2019 selection. Born and raised in Canada, he lives in Los Angeles.

craphound.com
pluralistic.net
Twitter: @doctorow
Mastodon: @pluralistic@mamot.fr